COOLEST
AMERICAN
STORIES
2022

COOLEST AMERICAN STORIES 2022

**MARK WISH
& ELIZABETH COFFEY**

EDITORS

coolest stories press
new york

www.coolestamericanstories.com
@JustCoolStories

ISBN 978-1-7375739-0-6
ISBN 978-1-7375739-1-3 (ebook)

"The Summer My Sister Was Cleopatra Moon" by Frances Park. Copyright © 2021 by Frances Park. Material therein first published in *When My Sister Was Cleopatra Moon* by Miramax Books. Reprinted by permission of the author.

"All of This Is Water" by David Ebenbach. Material therein first published in *Glimmer Train*. Copyright © 2021 by David Ebenbach. Reprinted by permission of the author.

"Habitat" by Susan Tacent. Material therein first published in *Ontario Review*. Copyright © 2021 by Susan Tacent. Reprinted by permission of the author.

"The Tallest Mountain in the World" by Michael Hopkins. Copyright © 2021 by Michael Hopkins. Material therein first published in *Wisconsin People & Ideas*. Reprinted by permission of the author.

PRINTED IN THE UNITED STATES OF AMERICA
10 9 8 7 6 5 4 3 2 1

CONTENTS

WARNING

Our goals at *Coolest American Stories* are 1) to create a national love of the short story and 2) to decrease division in the United States by providing a common ground of enjoyment for *all* people, from *all* walks of life and backgrounds—by publishing the most interesting and compelling stories with the widest appeal. Interesting, compelling, and appealing storytelling, however, can at times prove disturbing to some, so please, by all means, do enjoy the stories that follow, but be prepared to be surprised, startled, and maybe, here and there, shocked.

INTRODUCTION

Roughly twenty years ago, in his introduction to *The Best American Short Stories of the Century,* John Updike opened with a sentence uncommonly short for him: "These stories have been four times selected." Slipping into prose that was a bit more lyrical, Updike then explained that his selections had needed to impress Katrina Kenison, as well as the guest editor of each year's volume of *The Best American Short Stories,* as well as each year's volume's series editor, as well as, of course, himself. He also, in this first paragraph of his introduction, discussed the odds against a short story being accepted into a well-respected magazine in the first place. *Ploughshares,* he mentioned, claimed they received 750 submissions a month, *The New Yorker* 500 a week. Given these statistics and Updike's belief that editing-by-vetting resulted in the rising to the top of the absolutely finest short fiction written, he concluded that first paragraph by letting his inimitable writing voice flow: "A fathomless ocean of rejection and exclusion surrounds this brave little flotilla, the best of the best."

Lovely as that last sentence sounded in my mind back then, I now believe it's fallacious. And please know I take issue with Mr. Updike with all due respect, and with gratitude for all he did to help me distinguish myself in NYC publishing. After all, his work informed my literary coming of age—*Rabbit, Run* was the first novel I bought that wasn't on a required reading list. (I bought and read it because, back then, everyone was buying and reading it.) Furthermore, he was generous enough to answer a letter of mine while I served as the founding fiction editor of CUNY's short-lived *New York Stories* by typewriting on a plain white 3 x 5 postcard to inform me he'd have Judith Jones send me an excerpt from *Bech at Bay*, the novel of his that was forthcoming in 1998. I can't deny that this refusal of his to snub me probably caused the lit world to notice me—the young lit-mag editor who'd landed fiction by Updike!—and perhaps led a short story of my own to appear in the *Pushcart Prize XX: Best of the Small Presses*.

Still, I think the assumption beneath his sentence about "the best of the best" is invalid. As does my wife Elizabeth, who, by the way, is the only other acquiring editor here at *Coolest American Stories*. What E and I disagree with is Updike's assumption that a story becomes "the best" by merely dodging rejection numerous times—particularly if it dodges rejection by a cadre of people who are well-educated and privileged, some of whom have rarely if ever ventured west of New Jersey. Our sense, to the contrary, is that the same firing line of acquiring editors a story must please in order to appear in an anthology like *Pushcart* or *Best American* is a firing line which, unfortunately, and often at the very start, shoots down some of the most interesting, compelling, and potentially appealing short stories around.

To wit: In order for a short story to have reached the eyes of Bill Henderson at *Pushcart* or Heidi Pitlor at *Best American* (both of whom I have met and get along with well), it must first have been submitted, accepted, and published elsewhere.

And generally this means submitted by someone who can afford the time and money to send it to dozens of venues, then, if that writer was lucky enough to have garnered an acceptance, published by a literary magazine. What's been problematic, if one's goal is to see *interesting* stories out in the world for public consumption, is that, for decades, the most prominent literary magazines have been funded by and associated with universities. And, well, given my brief time at both *New York Stories* and, before that, the original *California Quarterly* (associated with CUNY and the University of California, respectively), I know what can happen in the editorial offices of such magazines. There are considerations of funding—sometimes agenda-based government funding, not to mention funding from wealthy donors who are kowtowed to at every turn, and who certainly must never be offended. There are considerations of tenure: If your department chair decides that a story you published in your capacity as fiction editor is too this or too that, there might go your career in academia, which, for many aspiring writers, means their livelihood. There's the I'll-publish-you-if-you'll-publish-me "camaraderie" that goes on at conferences such as AWP, and the pariahdom one suffers if one doesn't partake. There are interns who are barely out of high school and who avoid rocking the literary boat even more than the editors who hired them. Indeed, there are more than a few reasons why the most riveting short stories have never appeared before the eyes of the upper echelon gatekeepers at *Ploughshares* (to use Updike's example), let alone in the offices of Heidi and Bill.

Add to this the increasing presence of the internet and social media in the past two decades, and no wonder the short story has—in the hearts of many book-loving readers nationwide—lost its fizz. And by presence I mean all the inescapable wrath, hatreds, accusations, bullying, postured taking-of-offense, and illogic that has characterized literary discourse where it happens most often of late—online. Let's face it: If you're a writer who's just starting out now, in 2022, and you've been tuned in to why various authors have been vilified and shamed and left to die beside the road toward publication, why would you risk your own career by writing a story that's extraordinarily *interesting*? Interesting, for fuck's sake, can mean controversial, and controversial, much as it might have launched careers in Updike's day, can now mean being more or less blacklisted. Interesting isn't for you then, which means for you, out goes storytelling loaded with conflict and surprise, or candor about sex, or the use of words an "influencer" might deem evil in a tweet. What's for you is less conflict, less down-and-dirty and therefore maybe disturbing humanity; what's for you is playing it safe. In fact, if you go the route taken by tens of thousands (hundreds of thousands? millions?) of your aspiring writer peers, what's for you is the creation of flash fiction or maybe even poetry. And if you write in either of these genres, there are oodles of online venues for you to publish in! No, you probably aren't courting an agent or signing a book deal, but still, you can tweet often about your success getting acceptances and you can score hundreds of likes by complaining about how you, similar to your most endearing online buddy, can't score a book contract either.

The problem, though, if you take a broad view that puts aside yourself and considers readers across America—including readers who aren't privileged and who instead hail from walks of life far and wide—is that there are millions of people out there who, darn it, wish they could simply *read an interest-*

ing story. E and I know this because we've worked in publishing for years: I, yes, primarily as a faceless freelance book doctor (though that doesn't mean I haven't heard scores of sob stories about which manuscripts garner "significant" deals and which don't); E, yes, as a "mere" VP in design at Random House (though that doesn't mean she hasn't attended plenty of book launch meetings). And one thing we've learned from the days and nights we've put in professionally since the mid-nineties is that, hey, there are countless people out there who like to read but would never part with any of their hard-earned dollars to read poetry—or to read fiction pieces that end only a page or two after they start.

Not to mention, we're quite sure, in that gut-felt way you probably are sure too, that millions of people across America are tired of arguing online. These people want instead to enjoy emotionally engaging narratives that satisfy them as would a full meal. To hold a book and turn page after page while guessing and finally seeing and feeling what happens next. They've had enough tweets, enough witty, angry blips of thought that express yet another self. And they do *not* believe a well-developed plot makes a story "lesser." Nor do they look down their noses at suspense, tension, and other "pedestrian" elements of storytelling that have caused it to survive since their forebears drew on the insides of caves. They don't have time to mull over the latest theory PhDs in literature are bickering about. They simply want a story told old-school style. Period.

So that's why we founded *Coolest.* And that's why we're excited to offer the thirteen short stories that follow. We've taken more pains than we'd anticipated to find them, and, as it turned out, to encourage the conception of some of them despite discouragement elsewhere—and to push their authors to revise to make them yet more substantive, startling, and heartfelt.

"What do you mean by 'cool' story?" is the first question of the FAQ on our website, and the answer that's been there since we set up shop in January 2021 is—to quote Jerry Seinfeld—"*interesting* writing." And lest you think E and I and Jerry are the only souls in the universe who believe short stories need to be interesting for their genre to survive, take note of what a couple friends of ours in publishing have said since we declared our philosophy on that frozen, Covid-infested day a year ago. Four months after we made that declaration, in his book *Languages of Truth*, Salman Rushdie echoed our sentiment by way of giving this advice to writers: "Unless what you know is really interesting, don't write about it." And a month or so later, as quoted in the *New York Times*, author of twenty-nine novels Francine Prose was also noticeably direct about the need to prevent the readers of fiction from falling asleep. "I'm very conscious of keeping the reader's interest," Prose said. "And I'm easily bored—I'm easily bored by books, I hate to say. And so I want there to be some sort of suspense or some sort of payoff."

So already a few major players in the literary establishment are, like us, not only accepting but also acting upon the notion that interesting is the optimal way for short stories to present themselves going forward. We believe it'll be the best way for short stories to go regardless, and because of this we pledge to continue to anthologize annually the most compelling stories we can find despite any flak we might take, online or elsewhere. If the narratives on the pages that follow cause you to blurt the word *Wow* or the sentence *That was a cool story*, we will have accomplished our goal, for this year at least. We and our new friends, the thirteen authors in *Coolest 2022*, many of whom have endured painful amounts of rejection and despair for having dared to write without fear, thank you for giving us a chance.

MARK WISH

COOLEST AMERICAN STORIES 2022

SHEPHERD'S HELL

LORI D. JOHNSON

Shepherd stepped inside the house and closed the door behind him gently. Like a novice hiker scaling a steep incline with several pounds of unnecessary gear strapped to his back, he trudged toward what, to most, would sound like an argument about to rage into a full-blown brawl, but in his family passed for everyday conversation. His was a headstrong bunch, always ready to lock horns. In years past he'd often volunteered as referee by thrusting himself into the middle of a fray. He'd felt duty bound back then to protect them, if only from themselves. But lately he'd been feeling a bit differently.

He focused his somber gaze on the stove in search of the savory aroma that had lured him into the kitchen, only to discover his loud-talking, spoon-waving sister, Cheryl, obscuring his view. Shepherd frowned. He loved his sister, but not enough to keep the thought *What a waste* from arising whenever his spectacled gaze rested on her. With her almond-shaped eyes, high cheekbones, and gorgeous skin, Cheryl might have secured a career in modeling had she not possessed the body of a 300-pound steroid-plumped hen—all breasts, butt, and thighs.

Shepherd opened his mouth to say something silly to put everyone at ease, but his sister's "Dammit, Mama!" beat him to the draw. She slammed her spoon against the countertop. "Why you always gotta be so doggone stubborn?"

"Chile, please," their mother said, slouched in a chair at the kitchen table, a cigarette poised elegantly between two fingers of her right hand. "Long as I got insurance, I ain't studyin' 'bout no damn will. And you need not be neither." Lips pursed tight, she sucked in a long draw of smoke, then snorted most of it out through her nose like a disgruntled bull. "Shit, somethin' happen to me, insurance got it covered and then some. Ain't that right, Shep?" Both women glared in Shepherd's direction as if waiting for him to usher them into a corner or at least issue a warning about unfair jabs.

Rather than waste his breath, Shepherd peeked around his sister until he spied the large pot on the stove's front burner. "What smells so good?" he asked.

"As if you didn't know," Cheryl said, raising the pot's lid for him to take a whiff, offering a crooked grin not far from him.

Steam from the simmering chili wafted onto his cheeks and forehead and well into his sinuses, the unpleasant stirring he felt under his ribs momentarily soothed. He grabbed a spoon from the sink, but before he could dip it into the pot, Cheryl smacked his hand.

"Uh-uh," she said. "Give me a minute and I'll fix you a bowl. Meantime, why don't you help me explain to your mama why she needs to start working on her will before it's too late?"

Shepherd grimaced, turned towards his mother, who, cigarette still in hand, was now wheezing and coughing like some old, sickly version of the big bad wolf.

"Really, Ma?" he said. "Where's your oxygen? Would it

hurt you, just this once, to put down a damn cigarette and go get your oxygen?"

The scrawny, grayhaired old woman snatched up her ashtray full of unfiltered, lipstick-tinted butts. "Far as I'm concerned, the both of y'all can go straight to hell. Always trying to tell me what I'm finna do in my own damn house. . . ." A thick cloud of acrid smoke shot in their direction as she ambled out of the room.

Shepherd rubbed his side, feeling the slow burn in his stomach his doctor had said had the makings of an ulcer. He scrubbed his hands in the sink, dropped into a chair at the table, doused a generous amount of hot sauce into the big bowl of spicy chili Cheryl placed before him.

"What I owe you for the furniture?" she asked.

Shepherd had purchased a new set of outdoor furniture to replace the ones stolen off their mother's front porch by the neighborhood crackhead, a haunted young man who'd sought and found refuge in their mother's basement and who also held the distinct honor of being Shepherd and Cheryl's younger brother, Ricky Junior.

"Don't worry 'bout it," Shepherd said, shaking his head. "I got it." He'd completed the thankless task of arranging, chaining, and padlocking the furniture into place only minutes before entering the house.

Cheryl sighed and eased her heft onto the chair across the table from Shepherd's. She dabbed her glistening forehead with a napkin and, upon catching her breath, said, "You talk to him yet?"

Shepherd swallowed hard. Squinted. "For what? All he's gonna do is deny it."

Cheryl shrugged. "Still, might not hurt to go down there and have a man-to-man chat with him."

Shepherd sighed. Talking to Ricky Junior was worse than talking to his mother. At least his mother would act like she was halfway listening, even if she wasn't. But Junior? That boy didn't know squit about squat, yet he *must* outtalk your ass and have the last word. After a decade of repeat arrests, incarcerations, and the reckless chasing of illicit highs, Junior had only recently re-entered their lives on a regular basis.

Shepherd's mind wandered as his sister rambled on about his need to speak with not only Junior but also her fifteen-year-old son Troy, who'd recently been suspended from school for mouthing off at the teachers, and, apparently less important to the principal, for fighting. As big a badass as Troy was, he was hardly the worst of Cheryl's five-member brood. At the moment, that particular rep belonged to her sixteen-year-old daughter Chantell, who was on lockdown in juvie, accused of snatching a knife from the kitchen of her forty-year-old sugar daddy and attempting to slice and dice his wife.

Seemed like every time Shepherd turned around, he was helping Cheryl with something. Money. Mama. Junior. Those five hellions she'd birthed into the world. Those worthless bums she kept letting knock her up when they weren't knocking her down. My God, when would it end? After helping her land a decent-paying office gig at FedEx, Shepherd had figured he'd finally be able to catch a break, but the pleas for assistance had only increased. Obviously, they had him pegged all wrong. A lowly accountant was all he was, not a man of means nor a miracle worker. Was this truly his lot in life?

Only in counsel with his pastor had Shepherd ever wondered aloud why his constant prayers for a tiny portion of peace seemed to no avail. Reverend Watchman assured Shepherd that anything a faithful petitioner took to the Good Lord in prayer would always receive one of three responses—yes, no, or wait. Shepherd had interpreted the Rev's response as further indication the answer he sought wouldn't be forthcoming anytime soon.

The Reverend's comment this past Sunday had raised additional alarm.

"Young man, I get a sense there's some kind of special calling on your life. Yes, mark my words. Something grand and spectacular is headed your way. Stay patient. It's coming. It'll both astound you and lift your spirit."

A calling? Oh, great. Shepherd's own father, the Reverend Walter Gatekeeper, had prophesied something similar for years. "Son, according to the Holy Spirit, you, my boy, have been called. Yes, sir, called to preach. Called to follow in your daddy's footsteps and possibly even one day take the reins from me as head pastor of this-here church."

To hell with callings, Shepherd thought now. Especially the grand and spectacular type. To him, a calling could only mean even more unwanted responsibility was headed his way.

Cheryl rose and plodded into the utility room off the kitchen where the family kept a second refrigerator and cabinets packed with the bulk of their food. Does anyone else live like this? Shepherd wondered as he sat through the jangle and click of the chains and locks employed to protect against in-house theft and unchecked gluttony.

His sister emerged minutes later cradling a plastic handbasket so full of items she looked like a grocery store shopper in search of an open checkout line. A "party" size bag of chips.

A two-liter sized soft drink. A large container of cold cuts. An assortment of packaged cookies, candy, and crackers.

And several cans of beer.

She plucked the two tallest cans of beer from the basket and placed them on the table in front of Shepherd. "Just put the chili in the fridge when you're done. The kids probably won't get back from the skating rink till sometime after midnight."

"Sure," Shepherd said. "Thanks." He wasted little time in cracking open a can, Cheryl already headed for the double-locked comfort of her bedroom where, unless interrupted, she'd eat, drink, play with her phone mindlessly, and watch bad reality TV shows until the wee hours of the morning.

Shepherd put away the food, washed the dirty dishes, wiped clean the counters and kitchen table before joining his mother on the sofa in the living room.

Beers in tow, he settled in the tight corner opposite the one where she'd reclined, her arms folded across her chest, her eyes partially closed and fixed in the general direction of the wide-screen TV, which flashed and blinked no less than six feet from them, the sound graciously muted.

A thick plastic tube trailed from his mother's nostrils to the portable tank that provided her with the extra oxygen she needed to stay alive. Noticeably absent were any signs of the nicotine that had helped bring about her ailments, two of which Shepherd was familiar with, emphysema and congestive heart failure. But he knew as well that when it came to his mother, a carton of cigarettes was never far away.

"You know Cheryl's right, don't you?" he said. He raised the open can of malt liquor to his mouth before placing both cans atop the magazine-strewn coffee table in front of him.

"Wouldn't be a bad idea for you to make a few decisions now about what you want to happen with the house and all of the stuff you've got in it. That way we'll all know exactly who's supposed to get what, and there won't be a whole lot of unnecessary confusion."

His mother glared and leaned toward the beer with an outstretched hand. "Man, you think I care? What-so-*ever* y'all choose to fight over after I'm dead and gone—that's on y'all."

His face cloaked in a scowl, he moved the open can toward his mother's beckoning palm, but stopped it short to ask, "Didn't the doctor say you weren't supposed to mix your meds with—"

"Hush up 'bout that damn doctor. What the hell he know? A little sip ain't never hurt nobody. And as far as that other mess is concerned, I done told y'all, I got insurance. Enough to see that I get a nice casket and a proper burial."

A thunderous crash and the sound of breaking glass brought both her and a wide-eyed Shepherd to their feet. After a quick exchange of glances and a silent acknowledgment that it was only Junior doing Lord-only-knows-what in the basement, Shepherd and she sank back into their respective positions on the sofa.

"I don't get it," Shepherd said, frowning as she guzzled from the tilted can. "Wasn't his last arrest for illegal gun possession? Why would you ever think it was a good idea to let him move back in?"

She passed the beer back to Shepherd's hand. "I sleep better knowing where he is," she said, her voice soft and devoid of its usual high-pitched edge. She resumed her pose of folded arms and partially closed eyes. "Maybe one day, if you're blessed to have children, you'll understand."

Shepherd shook his head and finished the contents of the can. To be blessed with children was one thing. To be cursed with one like Junior was yet another. Furthermore, he'd never understand how anyone owning the good sense God gave them could sleep peacefully knowing that, on any given night, that crackhead in the basement could lapse into a drug-induced stupor, grab one of his guns, and smoke every got-damn body in the house.

He picked up the TV's remote and surfed from one channel to the next in search of something that might hold his attention and ease the pain in his belly. He stopped on a celebrity cooking show, a cowboy movie, a twenty-four-hour news segment, a home makeover series, and a sports talk program before settling on a science channel documentary about the Christian origins of Satan. After watching intently for several minutes, he turned and looked at his mother. Curled up even tighter than he was in her corner of the sofa, she was, or so said the rhythmic pattern of her breathing, fast asleep.

It never ceased to amaze him how young, peaceful, and almost saintlike his mother—Eva Jean Gatekeeper—looked when sleep overcame her. Even though he was amused by the thought of her loud, mean, old ass being a church pastor's "first lady," he often wondered how her life and his own might have differed had she not divorced his father.

"Your daddy had too many damn rules, Chile. His rules. God's rules. Rules to govern everybody's behavior 'cept his own."

While his father, the Reverend Walter Gatekeeper, certainly had his share of faults, providing for the child he'd sired with Eva Jean had never been one of them. The house Shepherd's mother had lived in comfortably for the past forty years would never have been possible on her wages as a warehouse worker for Sonny's Pet Mart without her ex's monthly checks. Similarly, Shepherd's siblings, neither of whom shared the Reverend's DNA, had benefited from his generosity in the face of their own father's willful abandonment and neglect.

Shepherd refocused his gaze on the television. Another series of flips through the channels led him to a national park's efforts to save bighorn herds by killing off the more rapidly expanding mountain goat population. He fell asleep while listening to the program narrator's description of the differences between domesticated sheep, bighorns, and mountain goats, and at some point found himself trapped in the fitful clutches of a horror story that began with him waking up to the smell of something awful.

His mother, he realized when he woke up, was no longer asleep at the other end of the sofa. He spotted her standing at the small catch-all table near the front door, where she sported a wide grin as she sorted through a stack of large envelopes. Her beloved insurance papers, he concluded. He was about to turn away when he noticed something that prompted a doubletake. Horns. Not only did his mother have a small set of horns jutting from the top of her head, her rear-end was home to a happily wagging and very forked tail.

A loud bang and the clatter of a metal object striking a hard surface drew Shepherd's attention toward the kitchen, where he ambled to find a more intense form of the horrible odor, as well as the sight of Cheryl standing next to the stove stirring a pot similar to the one that contained the chili he'd eaten earlier. Thankfully hornless, Cheryl did have a small forked tail, and, unlike their mother, possessed the wide, woolly body of a mountain goat.

When he asked about the stench, she waved him over for

a look. What he saw when he peered inside the pot was the floating, severed head of a lamb, a lamb which he noticed bore a human face not dissimilar to his own—minus the glasses. He gagged and covered his mouth. His sister studied him curiously and said, "What? I thought you knew."

At which point the floor slid open beneath his feet and he experienced the sensation of falling, which woke him from the terror drenched in a cold sweat and feeling as if he'd just crash-landed onto the sofa. As his breathing and heart rate returned to normal, he thought, *Okay, Shep. Calm down. You're fine. So you had a nightmare? But wait. What's that smell?*

He jumped up and jerked his head toward the other end of the sofa, half-expecting to see his mother distinguished by a forked tail and horns. Instead, he found her snoring peacefully and looking like her deceptively angelic self. Though gone was the oxygen tank, and back were the cigarettes, including one that was slowly burning a hole into a cushion of the sofa.

"Jesus, Ma!" he hissed, moving the cigarette to the butt-filled ashtray that, while he'd slept, had made its way onto the coffee table.

"What?" his mother said. She sounded both groggy and pissed off.

"You almost set the couch on fire, that's what!"

He seized the twenty-ounce can that he thought he'd left unopened, his intent being to soak the burn hole with a generous splash of the beer. He discovered the can not only open but also half-empty.

Eva Jean glanced at the scorched hole in the sofa and rolled her eyes before shutting them. "Man, whatever," she said. "Ain't like I haven't been meaning to get this raggedy thing reupholstered for years now."

Shepherd threw up his arms and reclaimed his seat. He bowed his head before turning his eyes to the ceiling in a silent gesture of thanks. It was a good thing that, just last week, he'd thought to replace the old batteries in all of the home's smoke detectors. Then it struck him like the claw side of a hammer. The smoke detector that should have been affixed to the ceiling above the sofa was gone.

He rose and, with his hands clasped behind his back, set out on a slow, meandering walking tour of the other rooms on the main floor. He didn't need to traipse upstairs to know he'd likely find more of the same: All the spots where there had once been intact smoke detectors now had only the screws and plastic framings designed to secure them in place.

Why that thieving, sorry-ass, low-down, son of a bitch . . .

Trembling, Shepherd snatched open the door to the basement.

"Lord, protect me and give me strength," he muttered as he began down.

"Nigga, you'd best announce who you be," a raspy voice called out. "Unless your ass looking to catch some heat."

"Who in the hell you think?" Shepherd said, ratcheting up the bass in his voice. "Other than the one somebody you know stupid enough to venture down here?"

Junior laughed. "My, my, my, if it isn't Little Bo Peep. If you come looking to deliver a sermon, I'd advise you to save your breath, 'cause we both know *I* ain't trying to hear it."

Even though Shepherd knew the basement well, he paused when he reached the bottom of the stairs and waited for his eyes to adjust to the dim lighting. Soon the silhouette of his brother seated at an old card table took on full flesh and form. While Shepherd was relieved that no signs of horns or hooves were readily detectable, what he saw, spread like an expensive multicourse meal in front of his shirtless and mat-headed brother, brought him little comfort. Scales. Bongs. Blunts. Wrappers, lighters, matches. Syringes, spoons, needles. Small piles of greenish-gray leaves. Vials and plastic baggies full of a variety of white substances—pills and powder and rock. And lest it not be rudely uninvited, a half-empty bottle of Jack and a full shot glass.

If Shepherd hadn't known any better, he would've thought the fool was in the process of filming a Home Shopping Network segment intended for drunks, dopeheads, and dealers.

"You really are a piece of work, you know that?" Shepherd said. "First the porch furniture, and now the freaking *smoke detectors*? What's next? The copper wiring and the pipes?"

"Now how you just gonna assume it was me? Could be it was our nephew—that little badass Troy. To be honest, that's who I thought you was. I'll be damned if that nigga's little narrow behind ain't getting slicker and bolder by the day."

"Man, please," Shepherd said. "That's some trifling shit that's got your name written all over it."

"Yeah?" Junior said, scratching at the scraggly beard covering his chin and neck. "Well, allow me to make up for it by welcoming you to my lair, Big Brother. What's your pleasure? Ecstasy? Meth? Heroin? Oh, pardon me, I forgot. You one of them church boys. Only thing gets you high is the word of God, am I right?"

"You need to be careful. Nothing good liable to come from you mocking God like you doing."

Junior's eyes seemed to brighten with a red glow. "Nigga, I don't even know God and he sho' as hell don't know me! So don't go getting it twisted. It's yo black ass I'm mocking, if anything."

Shepherd took a couple of steps toward his brother but stopped when an odor ten times worse than the one he'd encountered upstairs assaulted his nostrils and swirled into his throat.

"Why in the hell does it smell like a fucking army latrine down here? You having plumbing problems with the toilet or something?"

"Ain't got no problems I know of. Could be I didn't flush, though. Go in there and check for me—less'n you scared there's a good chance you'll see something in the bowl that looks a lot like you." Junior unleashed his ugly laugh again.

Shepherd's stomach convulsed. The sour taste of bile leaked up into his mouth. "You, my brother, need help. I'd advise you to get some before it's too late."

"You's a fine one to talk. From the looks of things, Bo Peep, you done went and lost control of all your got damn sheep. Strutting 'round here like you God Almighty, when the truth is you just barely a decent Shepherd. When was the last time your ass took a good hard look at yourself in the mirror? Huh? Shit, could be you the biggest damn devil of us all."

"Don't take a devil to know all them drugs you steadily ingesting got your brains scrambled and your soul damn near burnt to a crisp. Keep it up and you're bound to end up like your ole deadbeat derelict of a daddy."

Shepherd regretted the latter comment the moment after the words rushed past his parched lips.

"*My* daddy? Nigga, let me tell you a thing or two 'bout *yo* daddy . . . the Reverend Walter *Muthafucking* Gatekeeper.

Want me to tell you what his pleasure was? 'Cause if anybody would know, it would be me."

"You don't know shit about my father," Shepherd said between clenched teeth.

"Oh, now that's where you're wrong. For instance, I know your daddy like them old Negro spirituals," Junior said, bowing his head and snapping his fingers before changing his voice to render a fairly decent imitation of Louis Armstrong:

"Yes, the Lord said, 'Go down Moses, way down in Egypt land. Tell old Pharaoh to let my people go…if not, I'll smite your firstborn dead . . . but, hey, man, if not, do what you can to let my people go.'"

He stopped singing and looked up at Shepherd. "Yeah, I know your daddy like those old Negro spirituals and dark-ass basements. I know your daddy like laying more than just his anointed hands on the limber bodies of ten-year-old boys."

Every nerve in Shepherd's body suddenly felt on fire. It took all of his willpower not to charge across the room and smash every bone in his brother's frail body.

Junior shook his head, broke into a grin. "I'm sorry, Shep. Truly I am. I know it must come as a terrible shock that all them years you thought that scripture-quoting, Bible-thumping nigga was coming to see you, it was really the likes of little ole me."

"Wow!" Shepherd said, chest heaving in his struggle to suppress the emotions threatening to split him wide. "Can't say I don't admire your creativity and the depths to which your lying ass is willing to sink."

"You think I'm lying?" Junior said. "Ask Mama. Didn't you ever wonder about that big fight they had—the one where she pulled a gun on the Right Rev and threatened to have him thrown up under the jail if he ever showed his face around here again? You ain't ever wonder what that was all about? Well, let me tell you—that nigga cold got himself busted. Caught in the muthafucking act, that's what. Go 'head, ask Mama. Hell, Cheryl know, too."

As much as Shepherd didn't want to believe, a small part of him, a part buried way down deep beneath tattered folds and torn layers, knew he'd just heard the God's honest truth.

The tears streaming down Junior's contorted face attested to as much.

"Look, Junior man, you're sick. Why don't you let me get you—"

"You know, Shep, I hate to be the one to tell you this, but you really are one miserable-looking muthafucker. But I bet I've got a little something here that could help you with that. Yeah, I've got something that will put a right quick end to all of your misery, pain, and then some."

Junior reached beneath the table and brought forth a gun, one equipped with what Shepherd assumed was a silencer attached to its muzzle.

"I was saving it for myself," Junior said, tapping and rubbing the gun's barrel against his temple. "But from the looks of things, Shep, ole boy, you need it a whole lot worse than me." He stretched his arm toward Shepherd, the gun now lying flat and turned sideways on his palm.

Shepherd's anger slid first into gut-wrenching fear, then into an angst far more bitter than the bile he could still taste on the sides of his tongue. *Did this fool have murder—suicide—or possibly both on his mind?* He contemplated the risk involved in rushing over, snatching the gun, and blasting a hole in Junior's thick skull. But as Shepherd stood there motionless with his mind racing on, an odd sense of peace, like a pulsating hedge, descended around him.

"Put the gun down, Junior," he said in the calm, weary voice of one long accustomed to shouldering heavy loads. "Before you hurt somebody."

"Ain't that the whole point?" Junior said, tears still falling like fat drops of rain from his bloodshot eyes.

Shepherd stared at his brother and nodded. He turned and started back toward the stairs, then began climbing them wondering with every creaking rung if a guy like him could hear the whiz of the bullets before they pierced his flesh.

But the only sound he heard on his slow, flat-footed, straight-backed ascent was Junior's mournful hum of "Go Down Moses."

Within seconds of his stiff-legged, zombie-like return to the living room and his seat on the sofa next to his slumbering mother, Shepherd noticed another lit cigarette on the sofa, this one burning a hole in the cushion, too.

"Hell," he said, and he reached over and picked it up. Rather than extinguish it in the ashtray with the other his mother had dropped, he held onto it, then turned and stared at the pair of burnt holes in the sofa's cushion. For a few intense seconds, a wild conglomerate of images from his crazy nightmare and the TV documentaries segued into scenes from his mind's replays of his basement encounter with his brother, then to the more awful and even darker ones conveying his father—the Reverend Walter Gatekeeper—huddled in some dank corner of the dimly lit basement with Junior, engaged in the unspeakable. A wisp of grey smoke curled from one of the cushion's charred holes and drifted toward Shepherd's face. He studied his mother's posture for a moment, flicked ash from the glowing end of the cigarette, then returned that end back into the smoldering hole it had made carefully, not crushing it out but instead allowing it to remain bright orange.

He grabbed and finished what remained of the beer. Then, hands trembling, he seized the empty cans and crushed them together. The noise drew a slight moan and stir from his mother, but nothing more. With the tiniest glance at the now reddish, smoldering gouge in the sofa that was growing deeper and wider, he rose and covered his mother with the multi-colored knit throw that had usually hung over the back of the sofa. While tucking the cover around her, he heard her mutter something in her sleep. The only two words he could clearly make out were *good* and *Shepherd*.

He stepped outside of the house and closed the front door behind him gently. He stood on the porch and filled his lungs with the sweet nighttime air. Upon exhaling, he felt lighter than he'd felt in years. So strong was the sensation he was convinced that if he closed his eyes and concentrated hard and long enough, he'd float, if not fly. A few curious and unsuspecting passersby might have wondered something similar had they seen him standing on the porch with his face tilted toward the stars and his outstretched arms raised high above his head. They would have had no way of knowing that, at that very moment, Shepherd had been deep in prayer.

His prayer? That the Lord would be merciful. And that the smoke would take his flock before the flames would.

Then, after leaving the porch, as his feet led him toward his car, he cast a final glance back at the house. "Forgive me, Lord," he said. "I just got tired, so very tired of waiting."

SPIES

D.Z. STONE

My husband slammed his fist on the kitchen counter. I looked over. I was arranging the tuna cans in a cabinet according to expiration date, as per his desire.

"You know why I'm drying those tea bags?" he asked. "If you had put the box of tea bags where it belonged instead of precariously perching it on top of a *canister* where it could easily fall into the *sink*, these tea bags never would have fallen into the running water when I was *cleaning* the sink."

"I see that," I said.

"You *know* I scour the sink every day!"

I'd had enough. It was time to be the strong woman I was. Or once was.

"So of course it's *my* fault," I said. "If the box of tea bags hadn't been on top of the canister—where you your*self* put them now and then—your elbow never would have knocked it under the running water while you were cleaning the sink for the third time today. So *I* should've known better."

He had that look on his face. The one I'd never seen before we'd gotten married.

"I accept your apology," he said.

"Who said I'm apologizing?" I asked.

He studied me up and down. Huffed off, into our bedroom, where you could bet he was already playing tic-tac-toe on one of his devices.

He always plays tic-tac-toe.

Without me.

I avoided him for ten minutes. By the clock. But then I wanted to change, so I did. Right there in front of him while he lay on our bed with his phone. I took everything off. Well, almost everything. But I thought about taking everything off while also thinking about putting on something leopard print. No need, I told myself, and I redressed into a scoop-neck top and a pink skirt. Bar clothes. Clothes he should have noticed, but he didn't even look up.

So out I went. Screw it, I thought. Strong, weak, angry, or sad, I'm going to goddamned Phil's.

I got in my car and started it. You can always go back, I thought, but you're doing this now, so do it. What's one drink? What's two?

Sure, three would mean you wouldn't be able to drive home when you want, but you can always stick to seltzer or cola.

I released the brake, took off. It felt good. The drive to Manhattan always did. I knew it would cost more than twenty to park three hours in the Hippodrome Garage, as opposed to $5.95 all day, the early bird special at the Park & Easy over on Eleventh. And boy, did my husband hate when I was frivolous. He being the kind of guy who doublechecks the tab in restaurants, adds and re-adds, then leaves *maybe* ten percent. Whenever he's not been looking, I've always tossed in the rest. I can never help it. My father had been a bar owner who, if ever he went out, overtipped. When I got older and he'd leave all that cash on a table, I'd lecture him on how his generosity was rooted in low self-esteem. He'd smile and say maybe so, but he always got the best table.

I made it to Manhattan without being pulled over for speeding. In Phil's place, which is in Soho, I made myself comfortable on a barstool and started chatting with Phil. I'd known Phil since I was fifteen and would sneak into his musty, dark punk-rock club using a Xerox of an older cousin's birth certificate to prove I was eighteen.

"You know?" Phil said as he set down my diet cola with a twist. "Today you look right at home here."

"Guess that comes from growing up in an apartment over a bar."

"I can see that."

"I'm serious, Phil."

"So am I."

He walked off to my right, washed a few glasses, stood with a wrist slung over the arched sink faucet while facing the window you couldn't see much out of except sunlight.

"Phil?" I asked, hopefully loudly enough. "Remember when bars couldn't open early on Sundays because of the blue laws? Well, after church, while other kids were out doing hula-hoops, I'd go downstairs and build castles with maraschino cherries and swizzle sticks."

"Don't knock it, doll. It's one reason you are like no other."

And just like that, Phil glanced away from me, to my left.

"Excuse me, anyone sitting here?" asked a guy standing there.

A suit. A man in a suit. A nice one.

"No," I said. "No one."

The guy sat on that barstool, the one directly to my left,

ordered Scotch on the rocks, reached into a well-tailored pocket and took out a fifty.

It really was a very nice suit.

Still, I kept on talking to Phil: "What a day, Phil. It all started with my friend Kate calling. She wanted her magnets."

"Magnets?"

"Yeah. I went to a magnetic therapy demo at her house. They sent me home with some trial magnets taped to my wrist, and now she wants them back."

"Who's she?"

"Kate."

"Kate's your friend?"

"Yes."

"I thought maybe she was the salesperson."

"Well, she might be that too. You know how those things go."

Phil nodded. When Phil nodded, you could be sure he knew. The guy beside me took in a mouthful of Scotch—or so I sensed out of the corner of my eye. I drained my diet cola. I was fine with things exactly as they were: me, Phil, and this guy, the three of us doing what people do in Phil's place when everything there's running smoothly.

Then, after an attempt to sip cola that wasn't there, I thought: Why did you go to hear someone talk about having magnets taped to your ass?

Phil headed my way, saw my glass, turned, and walked off.

I called at his back: "'Girls, for those of you who cramp terribly, you'll find magnets helpful if you slide one inside your sanitary napkin. All the heavy flowers I know swear by it.'"

He stopped and turned but said nothing. He refilled my glass with cola using the seltzer gun, meaning he must've been out of bottled RC.

"A rattling Kotex," the man in the suit said. "What woman *wouldn't* find that helpful?"

"But then," I continued, sort of to him but not really, "she asks if anyone has pain in their joints, and Kate, my *friend* Kate, raises my hand and says, 'This woman's wrists hurt from typing!'"

"Uh-huh," Phil said.

"So then the salesperson," I said, "who's really an earth science teacher, directs her assistant—a former school nurse—to magnetize me. She places magnets the size of half dollars on each wrist, securing them with surgical tape. Then the earth science teacher explains how magnetism is *imperative* to life on earth."

"She actually used the word *imperative*," Phil said.

"Oh, yessiree she did," I said. "And probably not even ten seconds later, she goes with an as-we-speak. '*As we speak*,' she says, 'the earth's magnetic field is shifting from the north to the south pole.' And, maybe even worse, she goes on to say, 'It's a scientific fact, girls—*a fact I know for a fact as an earth science teacher*—that the earth's magnetic field is weakening. And you girls should all now definitely be aware that the last time this happened, we lost the dinosaurs.'"

Phil smiled enough that I knew that, yeah, I should definitely go on, so I did:

"'So it's crucial that you start magnetizing now, not only to stay healthy but to *survive*,' this earth science teacher says. Then she asks me, 'Can you feel something?' And of course all I feel is irritated, so I raise a hand, flex my fingers and say, 'Holy

God, I think I can type again!' I mean, I didn't say that just because all these hopeful eyes were staring at me. I said it just to mess with her without her realizing I was. But then, swear to Christ, I *did* feel something—the circulation in my hands being cut off from the tape, except by then the earth science teacher is telling me to wear the magnets for three days for permanent relief. The point being that now Kate wants them back, and I can't freaking *find* them."

"Freaking *Kate*," the guy in the suit said.

Phil smiled. "Anna, you bad girl. You faked it with the magnets."

A pony-tailed waiter summoned Phil aside. Mr. Excellent Suit brushed a well-tailored knee against mine. I caught his reflection in the back-bar mirror.

He spoke to my image: "You could tape my wrists anytime."

I took another sip of my cola, averted my eyes.

I had no comeback.

I didn't like that.

He continued, "Anyone ever tell you you have a beautiful mind?"

I crunched a small piece of ice. "Yeah. All the time." I rolled my eyes.

He adjusted a cuff. He seemed a little thrown off, too, so I decided to let him in on a fresh anecdote:

"This morning, when I ran into my neighbor Mimi from down the street, she complained about getting a bill for hundreds of dollars for phone sex. So she calls the credit card company and says there must be a mistake, but the credit card lady insists that her husband must be having phone sex behind her back."

"Probably as good a place as any."

What? I thought. Who *is* this guy?

But I said nothing.

This guy, this guy in this suit—there was something about him.

And it had nothing to do with the suit.

So I went on: "But Mimi says if her husband needed phone sex, he could have phone sex, but that, hey, her husband's at the age where he's already going deaf—so, you know, what's he going to do with phone sex?"

Mr. Suit was using the mirror to watch me again.

"Perhaps," his image said to mine, "the thrill is getting the woman at the other end to shout."

Jesus, I thought. He kinged me.

And for the time being, at least, I gave up.

Not to mention I noticed he was wearing a wedding ring, too.

I mumbled, "What am I doing? I can't believe I just told you, a total stranger, a phone sex story. I'm really not like this."

"What are you really like?"

"I don't know. Like anyone, I mean."

"What do you do for a living?"

I pulled myself together.

"I'm a spy," I said.

"Whom do you work for?"

"Whom."

"Okay. Who."

"Your wife."

"You're delightful."

"And you are?"

"Charles."

"As in Atlas?"

"As in Wade."

I was looking directly at him now. I was looking directly into his eyes, which were looking directly into mine.

"Doesn't ring a bell?" he asked.

His eyes were okay. Not great, not Romeo eyes, but okay.

"No," I said. "Sorry."

"Interesting," he said. "If you're into reciprocation, I'm a network exec. I specialize in half-hours."

"I'll bet you do."

"Maybe you remember me from homeroom?"

"Right."

He pointed at his face in the mirror, as if this was still some kind of flirtation game that had worked for him in the past and now he wanted me, *me*, to play along.

"Right," I said again. "I recognize you from homeroom. Charlie Wade from homeroom. Twenty on the bar right here, right now—Phil holds the cash—says you use that line all the time." I opened my purse, my wallet. Started fingering the top edges of my cash and peeking at each bill hoping to God Charlie wouldn't see that I had mostly fives and ones.

"I *have* tried it," he said. "And, yes, in fact, I've tried it several times. But no one ever believes it."

"So it doesn't work."

"I didn't say that."

"So what works?"

"I don't know. I was hoping you would tell me that."

And right then, Sinclair O'Rourke, an old friend from college, strode in, making a sophisticated here-I-am entrance.

I waved at her barely as I muttered to Charlie about she and I having been friends since forever and that somehow I'd ended up being the jolly chubby one and she the Queen Bee.

Charlie surprised me by keeping his eyes on me instead of looking over.

I hopped off the barstool, pulled my purse strap up and around and onto my shoulder.

I was about to wave Sinclair over with an air of confidence when Charlie took hold of my hand and pressed his card into my palm.

Stealthily, behind my back, and a lot closer to my neck than he'd been, he said, "Call me."

. . .

For days, all I could do was think of Charlie. I knew it wasn't rational. After all, what was it based on? Repar*tee*? And I knew calling him was wrong. I was married. He was married.

"Speak up, doll," he said after I told him his spy was calling.

"So all you want from me is loud phone sex?"

"I suppose that could be a decent start."

"You know I'm married, right?"

"I saw the nice rock."

"To a respected sociologist."

"Is that right?"

We talked for over an hour about nothing and everything. My husband was out shopping for office organizers. Even worse, from IKEA. So I had an hour easily.

I asked Charlie, "Ever play a sport in college?"

"Ice hockey."

"Ice hockey. That's rough. Ever get hurt?"

"Once I was knocked unconscious. I didn't remember my girlfriend at the time."

"You remember her now?"

"Not presently," he said, and he asked if he could jot down my phone number and email address.

"Next thing you know," I said, "you'll want my fax."

"To be honest, Babe, I wouldn't mind faxing you."

"Did you just call me 'Babe'?"

"I did. Did you not like that?"

I thought it over. I wasn't sure. I did and I didn't, so I said, "It was okay."

"It was bad. A bad joke. Stupid. I shouldn't make like I know you."

"No. It was you being you."

"You think so?"

"I know so."

"Okay then, Babe," Charlie said. "Gotta go."

. . .

I got my first email from Charlie that afternoon. In it he said he found me intriguing. I wrote back that all men did, what could I say? He started sending daily emails addressing me as "Babe" in all-caps. He'd write something like, "Admit it, BABE, you want me," and I'd answer with something like, "Pretty sure of yourself, aren't you?" It was fun. A harmful correspondence that went on for months. Yes, he'd often ask to meet, but I'd always think of some excuse not to.

But then he sent an email that said nothing but, "You write beautifully."

Coincidentally, I received this on the same day my husband

later saw me on the computer and said, "What are you working on? *War and Peace?*"

I didn't tell my husband I was emailing Charles Wade Network Exec. I didn't tell him I'd been having fun lately emailing Charlie little bits of stories I was writing, some made up,
some true, some mostly true but with enough names changed
that I'd never be sued if anyone published them.

"Huh?" my husband said, and I shrugged and typed on.

It was as if he sensed I wasn't thinking all that hard about
him right then.

As if he knew that if I'd switch over to typing about him,
what would come of it wouldn't amount to much.

· · ·

The next morning, while my husband was at work, probably
lecturing about one of the terms he'd invented, maybe *social
symbiosis*, Charlie broke out of his recent mold and called
rather than emailed.

"So, round table for lunch?" was the first thing he said.

I went with a point of reference: "Lana Turner and John
Garfield."

"That was a rectangle, and I want to ring you more than
twice."

"Charlie, you're being too bad of a boy. We're just meeting
for lunch."

"You know what, Babe?"

"What."

"When you let me tie your wrists, you won't need to fake
anything."

"Shut up."

"Okay. But if I do shut up, it's a date?"

"Are you even capable of shutting up?"

"You'd be surprised."

I glanced around my husband's and my second bedroom, where my desk is.

I looked as closely as I could at everything sitting on my desk.

"Sure," I said. "Next Tuesday at the Algonquin at noon."

And before I could change my mind, Charlie hung up.

· · ·

I decided to forego my usual baggy pants and top and bought a new black two-piece suit—no blouse, very 1995 New York—a leopard-print scarf tied nattily around my neck, and a brand new pair of thigh-high stockings. Tuesday morning, as I went through my underwear drawer, my husband wondered out loud about the thigh highs. I told him they were on doctor's orders, that because of "the circulation of the air," I needed them to keep my legs feeling young. I also wore a new red-and-black lace bra and crotchless panty set, which I'd stashed in the torn lining of an old winter coat as soon as I'd come home from Victoria's Secret. I put those on now while my husband scoured the tub.

I'd bought the matching bra and panties because I was certain Charlie would want me to coordinate. Whenever he'd called, it had been the first thing he'd ask.

"What color bra and underwear?"

"Charlie, I really don't know."

"Check."

"Hang on."

"You got it."

"Green bra and salmon panties."

"Cognitive dissonance, Babe."

But to be honest, in the week or so before the Tuesday we were set to meet at the Algonquin, it hadn't been only one way between Charlie and me. Sometimes I'd be the one to call. *And* the one to inquire.

"Charlie, what are you wearing?"

"Jeans."

"Jeans to work?"

"Dress-down Friday."

"Zipper or buttons?"

"Zipper."

"I could never get those buttons open."

Charlie paused dramatically.

Then continued pausing.

Then:

"Babe? You can always fumble with me."

"Are we having phone sex, Charlie? Is this phone sex?"

"I promise you, Babe, when we have phone sex, you'll be the first to know."

I was relieved. But disappointed. One way or the other I decided to roll with things by being the one to dole out a dramatic pause myself.

One that pushed the limits of drama to a hilt.

I ended that by saying, "I don't know if I can see myself having phone sex."

"Well, if you'd like, you can grab your cordless and head upstairs. I'll wait."

"Charlie, you're the worst."

"In some ways that makes me the best."

"I bet you call housewives in Ohio."

"No. Just one. Alternate Wednesdays at 3:45."

Sometimes, during those days just before the Tuesday we were scheduled to meet at the Algonquin, I thought I would've been perfectly content if Charlie were to call every few weekdays or so, tell me how pretty I was, tell me how smart.

But no.

That had never proved to be quite enough. I'd also been loving the emails. The *real* words, typed with the real fingers he used when he did whatever he did to other women.

The *correspondence.*

As in:

Sometimes, Babe, I think you're just using me as a pen pal.

Don't be ridiculous.

Just being honest. Just telling it like it is.

And I'd think: Was Charlie right?

Was I just another email-female, another of the millions of married women whose husbands really weren't interested in a word they had to say?

No, I'd tell myself. Charlie was more than just talk.

Because when he'd asked me to the Algonquin, I'd gotten all revved up. And then I hadn't been able to stop thinking about doing things with him—on the floor, near the door, on, over, and under the bed. I had never felt that way about a man.

And it wasn't like he'd been the first deep voice ever to whisper sweet nothings. Hell, only a year ago a good-looking news guy I'd worked with when I'd been young had told me he wanted me, needed to have me, thought about me every once in a while.

"But Charlie," I'd said on the phone the night before our

date at the Algonquin. "I knew what this guy with the slim WASP wife wanted. To have his good wife while I'd be his Polack trollop, romping in my babushka, feeding him kielbasa link by link."

To which Charlie replied, "Babe? You and me can do costumes. You name the game, I'm in."

. . .

"You look wonderful."

That's how Charlie greeted me in the lounge of the Algonquin.

He found me sitting in an overstuffed chair where I'd carefully positioned myself ten minutes earlier. Did he notice that, with my legs crossed, my skirt was a generous two inches above my knees? Not to sound conceited, but when I was young and strutted around in miniskirts, men and boys both would notice. To the point that I'd say things like, "You wish."

Charlie held out a hand. I took hold and tried to inch my way out of the chair like a lady—but I was stuck. I'd sunken into the down cushion. Charlie smiled, gave me a steady tug, had me up in no time.

"Hungry?" he asked.

"A little."

The maitre d' led us to a table. We sat. Under the table, Charlie's foot touched mine. I ignored this. He looked at the menu, then at me.

"What do you feel like?" he asked.

Sautéed veal with capers or seared tuna with wasabi? I thought.

I couldn't make up my mind.

"Charlie, I can't decide."

"When we're going to make love?"

"No, Charlie," I said.

"Wait—*what?*"

"That can't happen."

"Why not?"

"You didn't let me finish."

"Go ahead. Finish."

"That can't happen until our fifth date."

. . .

How do you know when it's the right time to have sex with a man?

I told Charlie that, on the radio, Dr. Judy had once said that if either party has to ask, this means at least one of you is uncertain and both of you should wait.

"Dr. Judy? You're quoting Dr. Judy?"

"Yes. And she said one should also consider the consequences."

I bit on a breadstick and thought about Richard, the gorgeous, angst-ridden English major I had sex with on my dorm bed in college when I was barely twenty.

"I care a lot about you," Richard had whispered as he undid my bra with one hand.

Cares a lot about me? I'd thought then. Should I *thank* him?

Guys had said they loved my legs, my eyes, my hair, and my lips—but *cared about me?*

I studied Charlie as he ate his raw beef appetizer. Was he who I was sure he was, the kind of guy to pursue you, have sex with you once, and then drop you?

"Admit it, Charlie," I said. "You just want to make mad passionate love."

He patted my knee. "That's one way of putting it. Anyways, what's wrong with that?"

Anyway*zzz*, I thought, and the waiter came over and held a giant grinder over my head.

"Yes . . . uh . . . thank you," I said.

Charlie had me by the hem. He smiled. "I think she's had enough."

The waiter nodded, glided away like he had better things to do. No way was I going to let Charlie know that a hand up my skirt was throwing me off, so I got hold and told him about my friend Manda's recent visit. I couldn't believe it'd been thirteen years since I'd last seen her. She'd recently split with her husband after he'd found out about her affair.

"The affair broke them up?" Charlie asked.

"Nah. It wasn't so much the intensity of the affair. They're English. The problem was, the affair was with a colleague of her husband's, who he—the husband—wasn't so hot on. When the husband found out, he didn't ask her why or if she was unhappy; all he said was, 'Good God . . . how could you shag a man you bloody well knew I disrespected professionally speaking?'"

Charlie laughed.

I didn't tell Charlie that my old friend Manda had also asked me outright, "What's been happening with you?" And that I'd said, "Nothing," but that then, as I'd talked on with her about my husband and me, all I could think of was *Charlie*.

"So how's your writing going, Babe?" Charlie was asking me now, here, at the Algonquin.

"Writing?"

"Yeah. You told me, a while ago, in an email I think, that you were trying to get into writing more seriously. I assume that you're the kind of person who, when you want to do something, you hop-to."

"I'm writing about you," I said, and I winked.

Charlie set down his fork.

"So tell me, what do you *really* want to be when you grow up?"

I downed a good portion of my wine. "Your lover."

"And when will that be?"

"Today."

"Now?"

I nodded as I sipped.

"You sure?"

I sipped and managed to smile.

As I set down my glass, I said, "Sure as I'll ever be."

Charlie pursed his lips. Cleared his throat. Sat up a little straighter.

We finished the meal quickly, but in silence.

And in that silence, our sexy rapport felt gone.

. . .

While Charlie registered, I waited in the lobby and thought about Joan, a married waitress who worked in my father's bar and had an ongoing affair with Stu, a tanned, personable landscaper. On Tuesdays and Thursdays, when lunch was over, Joan would rush upstairs to our family's apartment to freshen up and change. In front of the bathroom mirror, she'd pout, apply lipstick, douse herself with Tabu, and then hum as she'd run her hands up her sides. Finally, she'd pucker her lips, grab her coat and bag, and head down the stairs to meet Stu, who'd be waiting around the corner in his big idling Thunderbird.

Joan never hummed around her husband, a city hall bureaucrat who spent his spare time trimming his hedges and pruning his trees.

"Babe, you with me?" Charlie asked, snapping my attention back toward his everyday eyes.

"Yes, Charlie," I said. "I'm with you."

On the elevator up to the hotel room, he asked, "You sure this is what you want?"

"Charlie, I ever tell you about the first time I committed adultery?"

"Not yet."

"I was barely eight years old, about to confess my sins, when Father Hagen stopped me cold and asked, 'Have you been eating oranges?' 'Yes,' I admitted, 'before I came to confession.' Then his voice got real stern as he said, '*Don't ever do that again.*' I couldn't believe it—me, the girl who won all the medals for knowing her Catechism, had done something so wrong that a priest would yell at her."

The elevator came to a stop. Ding. Eighteenth floor.

I continued talking, undaunted, Charlie-style, as we walked to the room:

"But when he asked me if I'd been eating oranges, all I could think was that I had *sinned*. But I didn't know exactly *why*. It wasn't as if I'd put strange oranges before God and honored them, or made a sacrilegious image out of any orange before I'd eaten it. And I never called one a *goddamn* orange; it was always a Sunkist, and everyone in my family, including me, always called them that. So what had I done? I hadn't killed for any orange, stolen from one; I'd born no false witness against or coveted any oranges. So all I could figure back then, when I was eight, was it must be sin the nuns always glossed over: *adultery*. So now, along with foregoing meat on Fridays and giving up chocolate during Lent, I think about oranges whenever I'm about to have sex."

"Room 1812, Babe. This is it."

"Like The-War-of," I said.

"I'm sorry?"

"Never mind."

"Okay."

He slid in the key card and opened the door.

Then: "Okay, Babe. This is gonna be good."

I peeked inside. The room was smaller than I'd thought, even for Manhattan, and there it was: the big bed.

I went in first. Charlie took off his jacket and tossed it on a chair. I hung it up. Something to do. I had this sudden need to keep busy.

"Charlie, you need to take better care of your clothes."

"Let's take care of *your* clothes."

He pulled me over and down onto the bed. He grinned a grin so evil I figured it had to be fake.

"Charlie, are we going to make out with all our clothes on like in high school? I was pretty good at that."

"I bet you were."

He undid my jacket and pushed up my skirt.

"Babe, you didn't—"

"I did."

"Freaking *matching*."

"Freaking right."

"Babe, I love you."

"Charlie, you love my underthings."

He kissed me, hands all over, and, just as he was about to kiss his way past my navel, I said, "Gee, Charlie. I bought those things just for you . . . and you took them off without even looking at them."

"Whaddya mean? I kept the thigh highs on."

And I had to admit, to myself, in my mind, that I liked how the thigh highs felt between us. The trio of us, Charlie, the thigh highs, and me. The thigh highs not really stopping the sensation of him lying on top of me but then again not allowing his skin to touch mine directly.

Still, he got up from the bed and undid his tie. Tossed it on a pillow, his shirt on a chair, his pants on the ridiculously expensive desk probably very few people wrote on. He stopped at his underwear. Jockeys. Brand new. I thought of his wife, tired, slugging down a supermarket aisle, checking her list, picking up a Fruit of the Loom three-pack and plopping it on top of the Arm & Hammer detergent she always bought because anything else would give him a rash. I thought of him, Charlie, the real Charlie on any given day, feeling his own kind of tired, fighting his way east on the Long Island Expressway, going home, eating dinner, watching TV, then finally tossing his new three-pack of jockeys on top of the hamper.

His wife would remind him that it didn't take much effort to keep the toilet lid down.

They'd read in bed.

Charlie would be "all worn out."

Good night.

And now here he was, past the decent if rote foreplay that had sent my mind off, sliding his body on top of mine.

Missionary? I thought.

"I'm sorry," I said.

"Babe, I know you're nervous. Relax."

I took a deep breath.

He said, "You can touch. I won't break."

All I could think was that his body didn't feel anything like my husband's. Then: What if he—my husband—wanted sex later? Two men in one day? What in hell was I doing? I was really committing adultery. I couldn't believe it. Me. Mrs. or Ms. *Adultery*.

Charlie pressed himself down. I barely moved. I wondered if he wondered if I could possibly be the same woman who'd revealed her number one sexual fantasy to him over the phone only three days earlier.

"Okay," I'd finally told him then. "Aidan Quinn. My face to the wall. He gets me from behind. You get the picture?"

"Anyone watching?"

"Just a few people peeking because they'd happened upon us."

But that, of course, had always all been in my head. And this was a real hotel room. I looked up at the ceiling. A small crack. And just when I was about to tell Charlie to stop, he really went to town, and, still inside me, finished himself off.

Then he lay down beside me.

The crack in the ceiling wasn't as small as I'd thought. Part of the middle of it had been painted over, which of course meant it led to more of itself. It stretched across the whole goddamned ceiling.

"Tell me, Babe."

"Tell you what?"

"What's it like with your husband?"

"What's it like with my husband? What's it like with my *husband*. I don't know. He did once call me Tiger. As in, 'Wow, you were really a tiger last night.'"

"You've never moaned, have you."

"My husband and I never speak during sex."

He sounded certain: "You'll moan for me."

I wasn't so sure about that. Not that I didn't want to—I just never had. And I wasn't sure I wanted to see Charlie again. I pulled the bedsheet over my face, glad that it reached an inch above my eyes.

"Babe, a man ever whisper naughty things to you while you did it?"

Of course not, I thought, but I couldn't say that.

All I could do was blush.

"No one ever *has*, have they?"

I could hear Charlie grin.

"Come on, Babe, you can tell me. You can tell me anything."

Charlie pulled the sheet down from my face, took my hands and held them over my eyes with one of his hands. Just one of his hands.

"You're spying on me," he said.

"I am?"

"Yes. You and me both. Spies forever."

"We are?"

"You started it, remember? I'm just catching up with you. From now on, you and me—I mean, as long as it feels good—can be spies."

And suddenly it occurred to me: I was naked. Except for my disheveled thigh highs, completely naked. How was I going to get out of the bed and make it into the bathroom without him noticing what jiggled? I didn't have a robe—not even a towel. Would he think me odd if I grabbed the bedspread and ran?

He brushed a hand along the side of my face.

Splayed two of my fingers wide so I could see more of him. His eyes weren't that bad, really. They weren't stunning, but they appeared to be kind.

He said, "Whatchya thinkin' about?"

"You," I said. "Charlie, it's awfully bright in here."

He smiled. "The better to see you, my dear."

"Jesus, you're like a regular goddamn comedian. Okay, you know what, Schecky?"

"What."

"Here's what I want you to do. I want you to keep your eyes closed while I get up, grab my clothes, and go into the bathroom to get dressed."

"Babe, I hate to break this to you, but I've already seen you naked."

"Charlie, what about my husband and your wife?"

"You think they'd like this room?"

"My husband? He'd throw a fit. Four hundred dollars to use a bed for not even an hour?"

He sat up and ran a finger across my lips. "Worth every penny."

"Oh, Charlie . . . I must look a mess."

"A beautiful one."

How, I wondered, is this guy always able to say the right thing? He's just too good at this. I sat up and, holding the sheet against my chest, faced away from him. Then I yanked down the sheet and, as soon as he glanced at his phone on the twin nightstand on his side of the bed, slid out from under the sheet and off the mattress and grabbed my clothes and made a dash for the bathroom, stubbing my big toe on the threshold on the way in.

I didn't yelp, though. I sat on the toilet seat cover and rubbed the pain out of the toe, the longest one next to the big one, the crookedest, ugliest one that always hurt like a bitch when I stubbed it. I closed the door except for the width of a blade of grass. I wanted it closed all the way but couldn't reach it unless I'd stand, and I didn't want to stand—the toe hurt that much.

Then, through that skinny opening, I heard Charlie on the phone. He was talking to a contractor about work being done on his kitchen. He was telling the contractor how unhappy he was with the grouting job they'd done on the backsplash, and he was pissed.

So he's done with me, I thought. On to other projects.

I listened more and it became clear he was speaking for himself about the backsplash, not for his wife. Then it became clear that he had no wife. He'd made up the wife, I realized. He'd made her up for *me*? He'd made her up for me so I wouldn't feel I was more of a cheater than he was?

I stood up despite the toe and looked in the mirror. What had happened to my exquisitely applied makeup? And was it my imagination, or had my nose gotten bigger? I zeroed in for closer inspection and the door flung wide open—and Charlie came in, stood directly behind me, rested his hands on my shoulders.

"Anna, I think there's something I need to make sure we have straight."

"That you're not really married and just told me you were so you could fuck me?"

"No," he said, addressing my reflection in the mirror.

"So you could impress me?"

"No."

"So you could keep me at a distance?"

"Wow, you really have an imagination."

"Okay, then what is it?"

"I think I really need for you to know that you were my first big crush."

"What?"

"Just what I said."

"But wait. Me? How could *I* be? What are you talking about, Charlie?"

"I had a huge crush on you, but I didn't stand a chance. All the cool guys liked you, so how was I going to even get you to glance at me?"

"Charlie, what are—"

"You had this spark. Still do."

"What do you mean?"

"In high school. You really don't remember?"

"Stop doing this to me!"

"I'm not doing anything!"

"You're making shit up!"

"I'm not! I sat behind you in homeroom! Directly behind you!"

He was smiling, but he also looked serious, damned serious.

"Why are you saying this?" I asked.

"Because I need for us to both be more up front about it."

He *is* serious, I thought.

"But why are you telling me about this only *now*?" I asked.

"I tried to tell you—just after we first met. You know, that afternoon at that bar in Soho. But you seemed more interested in having an affair with a network exec."

"So wait. You're not a network exec?"

"I am. But I'm not really Charles Wade. I anglicized my name. My name used to be Karol Wadak. Karol with a K."

His eyes, still in the mirror and zeroed in on mine, appeared not only earnest, they again appeared kind. They also appeared familiar.

And I remembered: "One day in homeroom, a Karol Wadak did ask me to the prom."

"And you said no."

My jaw dropped. In the mirror, I suddenly looked older. My face was one big after-sex smear. Half my life was probably behind me, and I was far from perfect and definitely dissatisfied; and I couldn't handle that and despised Charlie for letting me stay so clueless for so long.

"I have to go," I said.

I grabbed my clothes and rushed out of the bathroom, dressed as quickly as I could, then left. On the elevator, I ignored the woman who was staring at the thigh high that had slid down and scrunched around my ankle. As I strode through the lobby, no one at the registration counter or the concierge's desk seemed to care, as if, for them, my disappearance would be business as usual.

I didn't mean to go through the revolving door twice. But that was when I was realizing—while also trying to deny—that I'd left my wedding ring on the nightstand on my side of the bed.

Okay, I thought as I went around the second time. Collect yourself. Assert yourself. Be polite but assert yourself.

But as I rushed through the lobby toward the elevator

bank, a young woman at the registration counter called, "Ma'am?"

Plus she had that look in her eyes: *Where do you think you're going?*

"I just," I said. I pointed at my naked ring finger. The look on her face didn't quit. I stepped closer to her so I could say very quietly, almost whisper, "I just left an important piece of jewelry up there, if you know what I mean."

It took a few seconds for her eyes to light up.

Then, with a nod, she said, "Oh."

And it seemed like an hour before an elevator came down. After one did and it emptied out, I took it up. As I did, I thought, 1812 like the war.

Facing the door to 1812, I took a deep breath, exhaled, and knocked.

Knocked again.

And again.

Charlie-Wade-aka-Karol-Wadak was gone.

So I rode a crowded elevator car down to the front desk, where the young woman was gone also. A young man was there, clean-shaven, some obviously high-end product in his hair. I told him straight out that I'd left my wedding ring in 1812. At first he acted as if he'd heard this line a thousand times. Then, though, after I said, "*Look* at me—do *I* look like a con artist?" he allowed me to return to 1812 with a bellhop. The bellhop knocked softly, then harder and harder to no avail. He opened the door with a passkey and, after I ran to the nightstand and saw that my ring was gone also, shrugged empathetically enough.

But there, on the nightstand, was a note on a sheet of Algonquin Hotel stationery.

Two words in Charlie's handwriting, or what I guessed was his handwriting, were scrawled across the middle of it.

They weren't easy to read, but I could manage them:

Call me.

The bellhop, keeping enough distance to assure my privacy with the note, said, "So. Is everything okay?"

I pictured my husband at home, exerting himself down into the kitchen sink. I pictured myself interrupting him to say that, because I'd lost weight, my wedding ring had slipped off, that I hadn't been able to find it for the life of me. I pictured him getting ticked off, *really* ticked off, then finally calming down after he'd phoned an insurance agent and talked things through. I pictured him taking me out to drive around incessantly until we found the lowest price on a new ring.

Then I began imagining Charlie again: Charlie and I pawning the old ring, Charlie and I spending the cash on nice hotel rooms, Charlie and I being ourselves on all the big, comfortable beds.

"You know?" I said to the bellhop. "It's going to be. I'm gonna be fine. I'm good."

GOOD ACTORS

MEGAN RITCHIE

There were five significant incidents, of which this was the first: In two days' time, she was going to have sex with someone else. Also, it would be televised.

She told him this in the morning while they were still half asleep. But don't worry, she said, stretching from her pillow to kiss his cheek. It's acting. There'll be a thing strapping his thing down. And cameras everywhere. Very unromantic. Very unsexy.

Morning light leached the color from their bedroom, which was also the kitchen, which was also the living room. It was cluttered with half-dead plants stolen from parties in the Hills, and dishes undone. The face of a long-forgotten star looked down at him from a movie poster, toted from his childhood bedroom in Michigan.

You're quiet, Drew, she said. What is it? Are you jealous of him?

Maybe, he said.

He did his best to think it through.

Kind of, he said. No, I don't think that's it. Is he attractive?

Not to me. But it's not like you need to be attracted to someone to have sex with them.

Yeah, he said. You're right.

I know, she said, and she slid one of her hips up onto one of his.

It occurred to him again that their apartment was stacked between hundreds of others, a pinpoint in Silver Lake. It occurred to him his head was dampening his pillow. He studied the textured white ceiling and thought of things he was keeping from Lany.

He thought of things he was keeping from himself.

And he thought, lastly, of Mateo.

. . .

And it wasn't that he was jealous. He hadn't been lying when he'd said that. Instead, he had been thinking of the night he'd met Lany, at some godforsaken—bar? club?—in DTLA, the place's air dank and smelling of the dorms he'd lived in back at Michigan: sweat, weed. The place had been teeming with college students, one of whom Mateo had already slipped away with to some dark corner. Mateo—lovely Mateo, who'd told him he'd had talent after seeing him in just one show of *A Midsummer Night's Dream* in the dingy university theatre, who'd encouraged him to come out West (*It's all happening there, man; I just know it'll happen for you, too*), who'd then allowed the infrequent rent payments, who would go on to cover Drew's drinks after every failed audition. Drew now watched Mateo's body twining with another's. He watched with interest from the edges of his eyes. The girl, and she really was only a girl, was saying something into Mateo's neck, and Mateo was laughing, a real laugh—Drew knew the difference—with his eyes squinted shut, his eyelashes tight against his cheeks, the small scar from another drunken night stretching pink. A sting of desire, and Drew looked away, embarrassed and hurt and feeling old and out of place, though he was only twenty-four. Mateo was his only connection here, the only connection he cared to have. He could not lose him.

And then he saw a dark-haired woman his own age watching, too. She was bored—anyone glancing at her could tell. She stood in a tight circle with a man and a woman who were talking over her. She stirred her drink with a pinky, sharp nails, downed all of it. And then she appeared to feel Drew's eyes on her, because her gaze drifted past Mateo and met Drew's. Blue eyes. Hollywood blue. She smiled. Her teeth shone.

In the morning at her apartment, the apartment he would move into a year later, he saw that her eyes were brown, not blue in the least, not even the tiniest bit hazel—her contacts had been colored. And he learned that she, too, was acting.

Something like fondness stirred. Only fondness, but it felt like a start.

. . .

Is everything okay? she said, her hand propping up her head. He was looking again at the ceiling. A small insect ran across a corner of it. Her body was now the one radiating heat. He felt humid, his body a greenhouse, his skin the glass. He shifted away from her.

Drew?

The tightness in his chest expanded, a balloon.

Tell me about the part, he said.

Oh, she said. She smiled broadly, her bicuspids showing.

It's for a procedural. I'm the victim of a crime. I hook up with the detective.

He said nothing, just kept himself collected, which was easier than it might be for some—after all, he was an actor, too.

I know it's not very interesting, she said, rolling from her side onto her back. But there's a chance they'll make me a recurring love interest. *If* I do well enough.

All he could think to say was, Hmm.

What is it? she asked.

He said nothing.

You *are* jealous of him, aren't you? she said. I *knew* it.

Outside were the off-gases and the sounds of the commute, the horns blaring, a fork-on-glass screech of tires. In the apartment above, the neighbors were waking too, footsteps moving diagonally. A blender went on, whined, went off.

I'm not, he said. I promise.

Are you jealous that I have a role?

That's not it either. I just need to think.

About what?

Nothing, he said, although it obviously wasn't nothing.

But he couldn't quite articulate it yet.

I'm fine, really, he said.

Are you saying that in the passive-aggressive way, or the real way?

The real way. I think I just need to go to work.

Don't be ridiculous. It's barely eleven.

I want to run some errands before.

She sat up. When will you be back?

Late. It's a double shift, he said, and he rose to dress.

Alright. I have a hair appointment, so I won't be around anyway.

He put on his watch. He tucked his phone and wallet into his pockets.

Sure you're not upset? she asked.

He found the keys to the bar.

Yes, he said.

See you later, she said. I guess.

He waited for eye contact, which they both managed to make.

And with that having been done, he left.

. . .

He walked to Mulligan's instead of driving. No one was on the sidewalk. Nobody would be at the bar yet, either. Nobody would be there for hours. It was a Saturday, the day it was most obvious that Angelenos craved to be late risers. He let himself into the bar and locked the door behind him.

His phone vibrated. His mother was calling. She had the uncanny ability to sense something wrong, even from across the country. He let it ring. She'd never gotten over the disappointment of having a son who was an actor. Or, worse yet—was failing to be an actor. Even in high school, when he'd first discovered how much he enjoyed being someone else, full of someone else's wants and needs, she'd refused to go to any of his plays. Their hometown, a one-traffic-light hamlet on the thumb of Michigan, was too small, she'd said. There would be gossip. There would be rumors. She didn't want any part of it.

And then, when he first moved out to LA, she'd eyed the shambles that had been his and Mateo's apartment.

Can't you do something a little more . . . manly? she'd said, as soon as Mateo had left for downtown. Something a little more respectable? Was that econ degree really for nothing?

I only did it for *you*, he wanted to say, but he didn't. So yes, he knew, it had been for nothing.

She forgave him, slightly, only when she met Lany. Lany had a talent with parents, for knowing the right face to put on. She was an LA native, which made her a convincing actress, growing up in a place where every block was a set, every passerby a potential director, or producer, or agent. She did more than believe in a part, even if that part was only potential daughter-in-law—she *was* the part. It was that which had drawn Drew to her in the first place.

Now Drew looked for things to do. Too early still to prep the garnishes, so he dragged over the floor mats and unlocked the coolers and taps. The counters and sink were already gleaming. He went to the storeroom to restock the glasses, and there he realized: Much as there was no one in the storeroom or the bar with him, he was never alone, not in Los Angeles, not in his apartment. There was always an audience, if only in his mind.

He set down the glasses and thought again of Mateo, whose accounting firm had transferred him back to the Midwest, to Chicago. (At least that was what Mateo had *said*.) So Mateo had gone back to his hometown friends—Drew saw the photos of him and his high school girlfriend together again on Instagram, felt a prick of hurt, because here Drew was, stranded out in Los Angeles, where he had only Lany.

He hadn't spoken to Mateo in months, he realized as he considered leaving the storeroom.

Should he call?

No. He would not call.

Instead he would let the hours pass and watch the day allow its pallor to seep into the reality of night, and the bar populate with the faces of men and women, and be filled with slow regret.

· · ·

The second thing, less dramatic than the first but somehow more discomforting: He woke up next to someone else.

At least he thought so. He had come home late and fallen asleep fast beside the dark shape of her, and here she lay now, a blonde stranger. Then she turned onto her back and faced him, and she was Lany again, her hair yellow instead of near-black. She was always dyeing her hair different colors for auditions—that aspect wasn't unusual. In the different magazines she'd read when she was young, she'd once told him, this was what all the A-list celebrities reported: They'd taken risk after risk to demonstrate their dedication to the character. Dyeing their hair to match their character's, wearing strange clothes. Piercing body parts, getting tattoos—anything to make the part less a performance, more an incarnation.

It's who we are, Lany'd said. We're chameleons.

And *she* was.

No matter how many times she'd dyed her hair, she was always the same Lany at the end of a day.

That was not true of him, he suspected.

But maybe he was just being tough on himself.

Maybe he was fine.

Maybe his path to acting success would prove to be different from hers.

Is this, he said now, for your . . . role?

She stirred.

What? she said, not bothering to open her eyes.

For it. Your part.

Oh.

She turned onto her side to face him more wholly. Let her eyes flicker open.

They asked me to, yeah. I'm supposed to be a dumb blonde. Blonde bombshell. Something sexist like that. She yawned.

Hmm, he said.

Don't tell me this bothers you, too.

No, it doesn't.

Then I still don't get it, she said. I know there's something wrong. You can tell me whatever it is, you know.

I can't, he said. I have an audition.

The same way you had to run errands?

Yes, he said. Exactly.

The truth (because clearly she knew this was a lie): The last time he'd gone into a waiting room crowded with men who all looked like him, he'd decided it really would be the last. The small slight men, the cropped blond hair, even the brown eyes: a funhouse of himself.

One actor across from him, in his cheap plastic chair, had leaned forward and smiled at him. He'd opened his mouth, as if to ask a question, but Drew had looked away. And Drew had then gotten up and left. The audition had been in Beverly Hills, and he'd then left his car (its dented headlight a perma-

nent wink) parked in the spot he'd lucked into and walked
Santa Monica Boulevard all the way to WeHo, passing the
Abbey, then Micky's, then finally slowing down just outside of
Hamburger Mary's. He and Mateo had gone there, only once,
when they'd first moved out here (*It's like an initiation*, Mateo'd
said; *where else can you do this shit?* But then after: *No, I don't
think we need to do* that *again*). Now, in the daylight on this last
day he would audition, a drag brunch had been happening, all
the doors and windows open, tourists leaning forward at their
tables, mimosas forgotten, a drag queen singing something,
rapt. He'd known the feeling that day: both embodiment and
not. A sense of distance from oneself.

And then the queen had opened her eyes, letting them
land on him. She'd smiled, the purple tint of her eyeshadow
discoing under the fluorescents.

Come on in, Honey! she'd said, and then the tourists had
all turned to *him*, their mouths pulled into wide and expectant
grins, like he was their newest performer.

We've got plenty of room for *you!*

. . .

The third thing:

After work four days into Lany's gig as the blonde, he slid
his tongue into her mouth and felt cool plastic. He pulled
back, startled.

Braces, she mouthed. She bared her teeth, clicked a finger-
nail against the transparent covering.

Tell me this wasn't for what I think, he said.

It was not.

Then what's it for?

Improvement.

What needs improving?

I have an underbite, she said. She ran her tongue over her gums, winced a little. They were standing near the stove, and he pulled back to look at her.

You're changing everything, he said, feeling cool about it.

I can always change back.

You're right, he said. You can.

Then he let himself ponder, really let himself, more than he usually did.

I think I've figured it out, by the way, he said.

Figured what out?

What was bothering me. And you were right. I am jealous.

She grinned. I knew it—I knew you were—

I don't think you do.

What does that mean?

Never mind, he said. What I mean to say is, I'm not jealous of *him*. I'm jealous of your acting.

The corners of her mouth fell. My acting?

It's so easy for you, he said, to change shape. You just dye your hair, or put in contacts, and you're another person. You're whoever the audience wants you to be.

The audience? She wrinkled her nose. I'm not a better actor than you, if that's what you're saying.

That's exactly what I'm saying, he said. Yes. Yes, you are.

· · ·

Then there was what had happened a year ago, before her blonde hair and her braces:

Not long after Drew first slept with her, in fact. Maybe

only a few days. Drew at a bar, the one on Sunset he and Mateo frequented the nights Drew didn't get a callback, the one they'd Uber to from their apartment.

Could you meet me, was what Drew texted to start that night.

Sure, Mateo texted back, and then he was there, slipping into the seat beside him, his brown eyes hesitant, or not really hesitant—rather it was Drew who was hesitant, Drew who was drunk.

Are you good, man? Mateo asked. Everything alright?

Have you ever, Drew started, and then he stopped. He looked down at his drink. It was clear. The ice cubes had all melted away. Have you ever felt a way about someone—that you shouldn't?

What do you mean? Mateo said. He was just taking off his suit jacket now, still dressed from work. His watch glinted under the dim lights. What kind of way?

You know, Drew said, and he glanced up, toward the ceiling.

He half-raised an arm, dropped it.

You know, he said again, looking outward, at the far wall that kept everyone in the room.

Okay, Mateo said, nodding. Yeah, sure. Are you talking about that girl from the other night? The one with the—

No, no. Not her.

Who, then?

Mateo had a mole exactly where his jaw met his neck. Drew was staring at it. He hadn't noticed it before.

Drew?

Yes?

Who?

A friend.

Do I know her?

It's not—he closed his eyes, so he wouldn't have to look at Mateo's—not a her.

Not a her, mouthed Mateo, as if practicing a line, and he looked off to the side, then said it out loud and clearly: Not a her.

Correct, Drew said.

Mateo said nothing. Then he leaned forward. Man, Mateo said. Can I ask—

His lashes shuttered. Why, Drew wondered, did men always have longer eyelashes than women? Mateo's practically touched his eyebrows, which were dark and angled.

Then Mateo asked what he apparently needed to ask: Is it me?

Drew stared.

Drew?

Could you ask that again? Drew said. One more time?

Mateo cleared his throat, sat up straighter, faced Drew to say, Is it me?

Drew's pulse had stilled. It seemed that the pulse of the bar had also stilled. There was just Mateo, sitting across from him, who was opening his mouth to say something, and then closing it again.

You knew, Drew said. You *knew*.

He looked down at his glass. Up again.

He asked, And you never—

I think it would be best if I left, Mateo said.

Yes, Drew said, nodding. But I'll come with you.

No, Mateo said. I should go on my own, I think.

And for a long while then, or maybe a short while—Drew would never be sure—the two of them, men, friends, whatever they were, assessed each other squarely.

We're cool, Mateo then said as he stood up. Just so you know. I'm not, like, mad or anything.

Why would you be mad? Drew wanted to say, except he didn't say it. He only watched as Mateo pulled on his jacket and pressed past the crowded tables and pushed open the glass door.

He watched the silhouette diminish until he couldn't see what he was looking at.

And then Drew called Lany.

Then Mateo moving out of their apartment, supposedly transferred to the Midwest office. His room empty, the door closed always so that Drew might pretend he was still there. Drew deciding that Mateo was wrong, that Mateo had read too much into their friendship on that drunken night, and that Lany, Lany, yes, Lany—*that* was who he wanted.

Then Drew moving in with her.

Then a year passing. Then something in Drew starting to realize that maybe she, Lany, the talented and sometimes very candid Lany, was maybe only who he wanted to be.

• • •

And now:

He's been getting drunk at the bar. His and Mateo's. It's the first time he's been back in a year, and the place is now an upscale place, this bar on Sunset (no escape from Hollywood tropes *here*) definitely out of his budget, which means definitely out of Lany's, too. No chance of running into her or her friends. Not now, while he tries one last time to fit into his role, to prove Mateo wrong.

He orders two G&Ts and then another two, not feeling the first. He watches the bartender, the only one on this quiet night, pour the drinks. The bartender is wearing a black shirt that seems uncomfortably tight. Drew watches the shirt try to cling to muscles as the able hand lifts the tap. Christopher, his nametag reads.

Here you go, Christopher says, sliding the drinks across. Meeting someone?

Trying to.

Drew turns away and surveys the room. It's done up like some old English estate: green velvet couches, brick wallpaper, and, over the large gas fireplace, a stag's head, obviously fake, because nobody eats animals in this city. He hates it, this thing that's yet another thing wearing a guise, so he looks at the people instead. There are not many, except for a brunette two seats over. He leans toward her, past a balding patron who rolls his eyes. Are you a model? he asks. The woman tilts her head down at him and frowns.

I've heard that one before, she says. No.

The eye-rolling patron pushes back his chair, getting up with a grunt.

What do you do then? Drew asks.

I'm an accountant, she says, her eyes fixing themselves on the stag's head, then on her watch. An accountant waiting on her date.

On cue, the door swings open and the woman's attention swivels away. Drew sits back and slumps. Another, he says softly to Christopher. He's pathetic and he knows it and he figures Christopher knows it, too.

Christopher obliges and fills a glass with clear liquid.

Christ, he says to Drew. That was terrible to watch.

Drew glares. I'd like to see you do better.

How about that one, in the corner?

Drew looks over. Says, She's got to be, like, nineteen.

Don't say that. You'll get me in trouble. And you're not much older than that.

Twenty-seven, Drew says. I'm twenty-seven.

Oh. Christopher studies Drew's face closely. For the first time, Drew thinks. You're my age then, Christopher says. Then: What about them? On the couches?

A cluster of women are tapping away on their phones. Their faces are angular and unfriendly.

Try again, Drew says.

Think you're out of luck, Christopher says. That's all the women there are.

The balding patron summons Christopher over. Drew watches the finesse used in the pouring of this drink.

Then Christopher reappears in front of him. Try us on a Thursday, he says as if he never left.

It can't wait, Drew says. He holds up his glass. Refill?

Christopher complies, hands over the drink carefully, Drew feeling the warmth of the strange fingertips, and this devastates him.

Why can't it wait? Christopher asks.

It's hard to explain, Drew says. I'm trying to prove something.

What, exactly?

I—

And then, again, the hesitation, the inability to articulate precisely. Also the realization that his words were beginning to slur. So Drew chooses a fiction, which is not entirely a fiction, but is simpler than the truth, which is that he's beginning to question in earnest the role he's chosen to play.

My girlfriend is going to sleep with someone else, he says.

A sharp intake of breath. *Going to?* Christopher says, eyes rounded. His eyebrows make small accent marks on his face. How do you know she's *going* to? You see her phone or something?

Yes, Drew says, nodding. That's exactly what happened. They're meeting up tomorrow.

God, that's awful, Christopher says. Jesus Christ, *really* awful. One second.

He disappears behind the wall of bottles.

And then he's there, directly beside Drew, sitting far closer than the brunette was.

I'm so sorry, man, he says.

Up close, Drew can see how full his lips are, how small and plump, a pink O.

Look, Christopher says, it's probably none of my business. But I feel for you, I really do. Had the same thing happen to me with an ex.

Really, Drew says, trying very hard to look at Christopher's eyes only.

Yeah. Really.

Christopher shifts closer, and Drew can feel his breath, salty and warm, barely reaching his skin.

I found him swiping on some dating app. Been cheating on me for *months*.

Damn, Drew says, at a loss for more words.

So I get it, Christopher says, settling back somewhat. And I'm here for you if you want.

What do you mean? Drew is about to ask, even as he feels the finger start to trace circles around his knee, even as he allows it to happen.

PANTERA REX

S. A. COSBY

Trey hated driving his car out here to the country. The car in question was a 1980 Pontiac Bonneville painted a high-gloss money green and outfitted with 24" rims and smoked-out windows. He gave the car a bath twice a week and didn't allow anyone to smoke cigarettes or blunts in it. His girl said he rubbed on the car more than he rubbed on her. Yet here he was, dodging mudholes in the dark, as he drove down a long winding dirty road going deeper and deeper into a darkness as black and impenetrable as a banker's heart. Even with his high beams on, it seemed like his headlights could only threaten the darkness, not penetrate it.

A thump rumbled up from the trunk and echoed through the big car.

"Guess he awake," Chino said.

"Save us the trouble waking him up when we get there," Trey said.

"Shit, if I was him, I'd want to stay unconscious," Chino said. The car crested a curve and rolled into a wide clearing surrounded by twisted crepe myrtles and towering Leyland cypresses. Trey's headlights illuminated a huge tricked-out Caddielike Escalade with rims almost as big as his. The Escalade was parked at an obtuse angle in front of a weathered barn.

Trey put the Pontiac in park and killed the engine. It was then he could hear the soft wet sobs coming from the trunk. A series of moist mewling cries that made his skin crawl.

"Well, let's get him out," Trey said. They climbed out of the Pontiac and went to the trunk. Chino pulled a nine from his waist band as Trey popped the trunk.

"Please, man, don't do this!" the man in the trunk screamed. "I got kids, man." His wide eyes were rimmed in red and snot trailed from his nostrils and over his chin. The mucus mixed with the blood dripping out of his split bottom lip.

"Yo man, get out the trunk," Trey said. "I ain't getting a hernia pulling on your big ass."

The man didn't move.

"Get out or I'm have to shoot you in the knee, then he gonna really be mad cuz you bleeding all over his interior," Chino said.

"Okay, okay," the man said.

"And don't run. Cuz when I catch you, I'm gonna be really pissed. And trust me, son, I *will* catch you," Trey said.

The man climbed out of the trunk, fell to the ground, and landed on all fours.

"Come on man, don't do this," he pleaded.

Trey didn't respond. He just bent over and grabbed the man by one arm, and Chino gripped him by the other. They half-walked, half-dragged him around to the front of the Pontiac before letting him fall onto the dirt again.

Trey leaned against the hood of his car. Chino stood with his gun dangling near his left thigh. The man continued to weep, and Trey thought that if the guy kept it up, he would shoot him to put him out of their misery. Just then the driver's side door of the Escalade opened. A short, slim man dressed in a skintight leather suit exited the vehicle. Trey thought D-Train looked like he was cosplaying Eddie Murphy from his *Raw* concert film. How he could stand being wrapped in all that cowhide on a hot sultry night in June was beyond Trey's powers of comprehension. Maybe it protected him from the mosquitoes that were buzzing around his head like fighter jets. Crickets were chirping all around them, too. In the distance, someone's dog was barking with everything he had, and a chorus of frogs chimed with their musical selections. It was like battle of the bands' animal edition.

"Hey, Leonard. How you doing homie?" D-Train asked.

"Leonard?" Chino asked. "I thought your name was Domino."

"That ain't his real name," Trey said. "You think his mama named him Domino?"

Chino shrugged. "Some famous chick named her daughter Apple," he said.

"What the fuck does that have to do with Leonard?" Trey asked.

"I mean I'm just saying some people name their kids weird shit."

"Hey, can you two shut the fuck up? I need to talk to Leonard here," D-Train said.

Trey and Chino glanced at each other but didn't say a word.

"Alright then," D-Train said. "Now that we got your name situation straight, I got some questions I want to ask you . . . *Leonard*. Who hit my stash house? You know, the stash house you were supposed to be running? The stash house that had ten kilos of horse in the back."

"I . . . I don't know, man. I swear on my kids."

"Hey, Leonard, fuck yo kids. They ugly as you are. Look like they mama was a fucking pit bull. Don't swear on them little monsters."

Trey looked down at his feet. He knew they were probably going to kill Leonard, but talking about a man's kids was just mean.

"I'm telling you, D, I don't know who did it."

"Ah Leonard, you lying. You know how I know you lying."

Before D-Train could enlighten them as to his shrewd powers of deduction, a sound ripped through the stygian night. Trey felt his balls crawl up somewhere near his neck. His mouth was suddenly so dry he could've spit gravel. Trey noticed the crickets and frogs had cut their performances short. The sound even made Leonard stop his blubbering.

"Um . . . what the fuck was that?" Chino asked.

D-Train smiled.

"That is what is gonna get the truth from Leonard here," he said.

Trey watched as his diminutive boss walked over to the dilapidated barn and threw open the doors.

"Dios Mio!" Chino exclaimed. Trey scrambled backwards, slipped, caught his balance, then opened the driver's side door and crouched behind it. Chino did the same with the one on the passenger side. As Leonard scooted backwards on his butt, he let out a high-pitched wail that hurt Trey's ears.

"You gonna talk now, motherfucker?" D-train said.

"Yo what the fuck is that, man?" Trey said.

D-train laughed.

"What the fuck it looks like, man?" he said.

Trey stared over D-Train's head and peered into the barn. His eyes had adjusted to the dark but he almost wished they hadn't. Stalking back and forth in the barn with what appeared to be an incredibly inadequate chain around its neck and attached to the floor was an honest-to-goodness, big as hell, antelope-killing king of the goddamn jungle fucking lion. The tawny beast flicked its tail from side to side as it walked back and forth just inside the barn door. Trey could see its massive musculature move with sinewy power under its fur. The lion shook his enormous mane like the lead singer of a hair band.

The lion roared, and Trey realized that was what had inspired his atavistic response. Some memory deep in his DNA from some terrified ancestor thousands of years ago had recognized the sound of an apex predator.

"It looks like you got a goddamn lion in a fucking barn," Trey said.

"Damn right. Now stop hiding behind that door like a punk and help me introduce Leonard to Rex."

"Who?" Chino said.

"The lion," Trey said. "He named it Rex. It means King."

"Um. I ain't going near that motherfucker," Chino said. His voice quivered like the last leaf at the end of autumn.

"Negro, if you don't get your ass over here, I'm a push you in there with him," D-Train said.

"Where in the fuck did you even get a goddam lion?" Trey asked.

D-Train frowned at him. "Yo man, don't worry about that. Just get over here."

"I mean, how much do a lion even cost?" Trey asked.

"Look how big his paws are," Chino said. "They like fucking dinner plates."

"Ya'll two is pissing me the fuck off," D-Train said. "Now get your asses over here."

Trey didn't move. He could hear the lion breathing like a slow-moving locomotive. A deep sonorous panting that loosened his bowels. "I don't' think I'm gonna be able to help you with that, son," he said.

D-Train groaned. "Ya'll embarrassing me, man. Coming off like a couple of pussies. Like I'm getting real fucking pissed here."

"It says here a lion can kill a wildebeest with one swipe," Chino said. The glow from his cell phone gave his face an eerie green hue.

"It was Luther Barnes," Leonard said. "He gave me five grand to leave the back door unlocked." His voice was a harsh whisper. Trey figured his mouth was dry as kindling, too.

D-Train laughed. "Uh huh. See, I knew your ass would talk. Now you fucked. My boy here is reaallllll hungry. Trey, Chino, I ain't gonna tell ya'll again. Get your asses over here."

"What kind of chain is that?" Chino said. "It says here a lion has the equivalent strength of a dozen full grown men."

D-Train stomped over to the passenger side of Trey's car and snatched Chino's phone out of his hand and heaved it into the crepe myrtles. Trey heard it land with a clack and a thud.

D-Train returned to his position in front of the barn. The lion had sprawled across the floor and was licking its paws. Trey could see they were coated in dust and dirt.

"I don't give a fuck how strong a lion is," D-Train said. "I don't give a fuck how much they eat. I don't give a fuck if this

lion come from a wildlife preserve in Florida run by a motherfucker with a meth problem. Now I'm gonna give the two of
you till the count of three to get over here or"—D-train
pulled a small nickel plated .22 from his pocket—"I'm gonna
shoot Leonard, then the two of you, and then I'm gonna feed
all of you to Rex."

Trey stood up but stayed behind the door.

"One."

Chino came out of his crouch.

"Two."

Trey raised his hands.

"Okay, okay, we coming. Shit," he said.

"That's what the fuck I'm talking about. Stop being a
bunch of pussies and handle your motherfucking business.
And I tell you something else—"

Trey heard a new sound. One that was more familiar than
a roar but filled him with more dread. It was the sound of
metal hitting wood.

"D-Train," Trey whispered. "Don't. Fucking. Move."

"Oh Jesus . . . Jesus, Jesus," Leonard moaned.

D-train stood stock-still as Rex stepped out of the barn
dragging his broken chain behind him.

"Shoothimshoothimshoothim," D-Train mumbled like an
amateur ventriloquist.

"Chino," Trey whispered. "Wait until he moves from behind D."

"Shootthismotherfucker," D murmured.

Trey could hear Chino's gun clattering against the car
door. Trey didn't dare reach for his piece in the glove com-
partment. Not yet anyway. The lion locked eyes with him, its
irises as green as the paint on his Pontiac. Trey wasn't sure but

he thought he could see a dark wet patch expanding at D-Train's crotch like an amoeba.

Suddenly Rex flicked his tail and ran back into the barn.

D-Train spun on his heel and aimed his .22.

"Now I got to kill this motherfucker. Paid fifty thousand for his ass, now I gotta kill him."

"D, just get in the goddamn car," Trey said. "You aint gonna do nothing with that pea shooter but tick him off."

"Nah, this just like that dog I had that bit me. You gotta show them who's boss."

"You shot a dog for biting you?" Chino asked.

"D, for real man, get in the fucking car," Trey said.

D-Train turned and faced him.

"You know what, Trey? I'm getting real sick of—"

Rex exploded out of the darkness and clamped his jaws around D-Train's head. Grunting and snorting, he dragged the well-dressed gangster deep into the barn.

Trey jumped in the driver's seat, Chino already in the passenger seat. Leonard, showing remarkable agility for a man of his size, sprung up from the ground and sailed through Chino's open door and into the back seat. Trey started the Bonneville and flicked on the headlights. He was greeted by the sight of Rex's bloody muzzle level with his hood ornament. Trey slammed the car into reverse, spinning mud and dirt onto his wheel wells and not caring at all. He threw the car into drive and sped down the dirt lane.

Forty minutes later, they were back in Richmond on Broad Street, stopped under a traffic light.

"Get out, Leonard," Trey said. "Consider this your lucky day."

Leonard didn't respond but slipped out of the car on Chino's side and took off down the sidewalk like today might still be his last.

"Do you . . . think we should call somebody?" Chino asked.

"Like who?" Trey asked. "Mutual of Omaha wild kingdom? Who gonna believe us anyway?"

"Yeah. I guess you right."

They were both silent for a few moments as the traffic light took its own sweet time.

"I'm hungry. You wanna hit Waffle House?" Trey asked.

"What?" Chino said. "Man, we just saw a guy get eaten by a goddamn jungle cat. I don't think I'm ever gonna be able to eat meat again. Let alone a Texas cheese melt."

"I know. But we was chasing Domino, I mean Leonard, all damn day, and I ain't ate nothing since yesterday. You down or what?"

Chino was quiet for a few seconds before shrugging.

"I mean . . . I guess I could go for some covered and smothered," he said.

"Alright then," Trey said.

The light turned green, and Trey hit the gas. The engine of the old Pontiac growled as they took off down the street.

THE SUMMER MY SISTER WAS CLEOPATRA MOON

FRANCES PARK

Cleo was back, her yellow convertible Mustang lined up with the buses. I remember running down the school steps so fast I almost fell. When she saw me, she went wild with her signature honk—*beep, beep, beeeep!*—calling up something I can barely feel today. My big sister at the wheel. My heart racing.

"Cleo, you're home!"

She hugged me like I was a beloved rag doll. She wouldn't let go for a long time. I needed that hug, it almost got me crying. What stopped me was the shocking sight of her bosom spilling out of a red-and-white striped tube top. In those days I lived in Cleo's hand-me-downs, mostly her oldest faded jeans and threadbare T-shirts, but the thought of me in that tube top next year was going too far. I would never have deep cleavage or wear Wet 'n' Wild Hot Pink Lip Gloss so deservedly. And my hair was black straw no matter how I cut it. It would never move like the ocean when I walked. Our mother often pointed out that Cleo inherited her beauty from our grandmother, but Cleo brushed this off. I don't think she wanted to be linked in any way, shape, or form to some Korean peasant squatting in the fields. Could I blame her?

Cleo played with the tuner on the radio, her wrist jingling

with silver bangles. "I can't get over how *cute* you're getting, li'l one," she lied through her teeth. "I'm *so* jealous." When she found her song, she lip-synched and her faux diamond-studded sunglasses caught the sun in a dazzling display of how the whole world can miraculously turn. The Mustang's top was down, and the sky was blue. Cleo shifted into gear.

"Hang on, school's out for summer!"

And with one rebellious thrust we zoomed past Glover Intermediate and bus 14. I secretly flipped off the creeps on the bus, namely Mitch Mann, Dave Kelly, and Frog Fitzgerald. Next year they'd get me, at another school, on another bus—probably spend their whole stupid summer thinking up a new name to call me—but now I was with Cleo. Idol of my life and the hereafter. In this world, in this Mustang, they were nothing to me.

. . .

I blinked and we were on the Beltway, weaving between and beyond trucks. Our destination, Taco Town, two exits up. If Taco Town were a million miles away, we could keep on driving. Watch the sun set and the moon rise in our eyes. If the exit ramp curved on forever, we could go round and round and round, carnival style. I could do it, live on the edge of a spectacular, never-ending dream: Cleo and me running for our lives. It would beat real life as long as it would last. It would beat reading *American Teen Magazine* if I never woke up. When we got to Taco Town, we pulled into the drive-through.

The summer before, Cleo had a boyfriend named Leonard

who worked here on weekends. He was older than Cleo with a stringy blond ponytail, though his beard was reddish-brown. She dumped him, but she still hungered for Leonard's love day and night.

"He really loved me, Marcy. He would shoot old ladies if I told him to. *Two Beef 'n' Bean Burritos and two large Tabs!*" she hollered into the mike.

"He had a neat van," I said.

A cruel smirk came over her face, one I easily recognized. She was reliving the night she broke Leonard's heart, the night she cruised through the drive-through with her hands all over Chuck Boucher. They'd been to a pool party and chugged tequila under the deck. How many times had I heard the story?

We took our food and parked in our old spot, which faced a run-down route of strip malls and whizzing traffic. It was bleak for Washington, DC suburbia. Potholes, USA. Namely, Glover, Virginia. And there we savagely ate that afternoon in 1976. Nothing ever tasted so good, my heart told me as we wolfed down pillows of grease, the traffic music to my ears. In a blinding sun my eyes squinted into mere slits as Cleo lit up a menthol cigarette like a movie star.

"Are you home for the summer?" I asked. "The whole summer?"

My loneliness always hit her right in the gut. She crumpled up the bag with conviction. "I'm not going anywhere, li'l one. You want to go to the mall, we go to the mall. You want to go to the pool, we go to the pool. Get the picture? It's you and me from now on. The rest of the world can go up in flames."

"You mean until September," I lamented.

"No, I mean from now on. I'm thinking about dropping out of Jamestown, aka Dumbo U."

My heart stopped. Cleo and me, Cleo and me, Cleo and me. Just like the old days!

"But Mom and Dad will kill you!"

"I don't care! I can't face all those petunias in the dorm again! Pigs!"

I knew all about them. I had read each and every one of her letters from college so many times I knew them by heart. There was Libby, who went around telling everyone Cleo was a syphilitic slut. And Patty, who claimed she saw Cleo making out with a girl in some townie bar. And Maureen, who spread a rumor on frat row that Cleo shaved her breasts. An article in *American Teen*—"Make Friends with Jealous Foes"—said to take the calm, rational approach. *Take a deep breath. Talk it out.* But Cleo could drive girls to murder. Their angry eyes were on her everywhere we went. In malls, at the movies. Everywhere!

Three guys walked by us, going nuts over Cleo like hungry baboons.

Va va voom!

Give papa a kiss!

Sweet mama!

Cleo flashed them a smile that could make her famous. To me she *was* famous, and I was content to live in her glamorous fog.

"Cleo, every guy on the face of the earth wants you," I moaned, knowing that was what she wanted to hear. The world moaning her name.

She basked in her glory with a marvelous sigh and a flip of

her sunglasses. That's when I saw what I'd be staring at all summer. Her eyes! They were painted black with dramatic wings at the tips.

"Cleo?"

"Call me Cleopatra," she winked.

. . .

We went by Cleo and Marcy, but those were not our birth names.

We'd adopted them at some point and thrown the others away as if to hide the evidence, even from ourselves. The occasional sight of Misook on my report card struck a nerve, and for an ugly moment I'd be reminded of who I was. The only "Oriental" girl on this side of the planet. Besides Cleo, of course. But she didn't count. Who on earth would make fun of her? She walked with her head up high, crowned by her own confidence.

And now she had those eyes! They came out of a tiny Max Factor bottle I had seen advertised in *American Teen*. It was labeled Waterproof Eyeliner, and they weren't kidding. Cleo slept and showered and swam in those eyes—they never came off. After a while I got used to them, although my parents never would.

"You are not Cleopatra under this roof!" my father argued. He was a Harvard man, born to debate. But not with his daughters. "You are Kisook Moon. Do you understand? Do you hear me?"

"Don't call me that," she said, covering her ears. "I am Cleopatra Moon, I am Cleopatra Moon, I am Cleopatra Moon!"

My father had endured many hardships in his life, but none could affect him like the disobedient voice of his first child, a voice seldom heard because he usually looked the other way. On the rare occasions they fought, he would lock himself in his room and review a lifetime of suffering—poverty, war, his parents, whom I hated horribly. Cleo always went to him knowing his sorrow wasn't to be taken lightly. She'd knock on his door, and it wouldn't be long before I'd hear them engaged in one of their long philosophical talks, which my father desperately needed. In the end, Cleo always got her way. The eyes stayed.

With my mother, the clattering of pots and pans said it all. She and Cleo had a history of bickering over glitter nail polish, skimpy outfits, barefoot boyfriends, but these days she wasn't saying much. Her own history of fleeing her North Korean homeland as a child left her feeling helpless as an adult. Deciding which bunch of scallions to pick at the A&P could put her in a panic. Once she'd picked, she'd still fret, sometimes turning the cart back around.

My parents had come to America in 1954 so that my father could go to graduate school and study public administration. It was to be a temporary stay, but my father's ambitions were thwarted by the overthrow of Korean president Syngman Rhee. The political climate was too dangerous for a former aide who had his eye on the presidency himself one day. So my father began a life here as a transportation economist at the World Bank in the nation's capital while also starting a family in the Virginia suburbs. It wasn't the life of his dreams, but it was noble work, and he adjusted very well with his impeccable English. Most Americans assumed he came here by way of

Oxford. My mother didn't ask any questions and, although she had many housewife acquaintances, never mastered the language. Chipmunk was *munkchip*, fold the clothes was *hold the clothes*, and when the girl next door asked to borrow a pitcher, my mother came back to the door holding a baseball bat. She was adorable through no effort of her own. All the neighbors loved Mama Moon.

. . .

A week into that summer break, Cleo got a job as a cashier at The Rec Room. The sign for help had read, *Chick Needed, Talk With Ted The Head.* The Rec Room sold albums, eight-track tapes, guitar picks, incense, and what they advertised as *big bad bongs.* Meanwhile, I spent my days going to summer school and now and then tutoring a dyslexic set of twin brothers named Tim and Tom.

At night Cleo and I hung out at the public pool.

"Not a word to them about me not going back to school," she warned me, turning down her transistor radio. She wore a wild Hawaiian print bikini that could fit into a thimble. "Promise me, not a peep. I'll have to break it to them gently. What's a degree from a state college like Dumbo U going to do for me anyway?"

She looked at me like I'd have an answer. I did, from the pages of *American Teen.*

"You need a college degree," I said, even though I'd die a million deaths if she left. "You need it to get a good job, Cleo," I said.

She batted her painted eyes. "*Cleopatra.*"

"Cleopatra," I said.

"I'm not cut out for college. I'm not a genius like you. Einstein with pierced ears."

"No, I'm not."

"Yes, you are! You'll go to some Ivy League school and become something greater than the whole bourgeois universe put together."

"No-I-no," I stammered.

"Right now, right this second, under this ho-hum hick sky, you may be li'l Marcy Moon, but someday I'll look up and say, 'There's my superstar sister, beaming over us mere mortals.'"

"No, I'm nobody, I'm—"

"You're who?" she frowned.

I almost did the unthinkable, reveal my nickname at school. Miss Moonface. Down the hallway, on the bus, in the cafeteria. *Miss Moonface, Miss Moonface, Miss Moonface.*

"I'm nobody special," I said.

"Bull! You've got God-given smarts! Why do you think you're already taking Algebra II and teaching Mit and Mot that Z ain't A? Not everybody can write a paper in French on *Waiting for Godot* while watching 'Welcome Back, Kotter' and reading teenybopper rag mags."

"But I study a lot, Cleo."

"*Cleopatra*," she sang impatiently.

"Cleopatra," I said.

"Well, I study, too, and I flunked Chem Lab. Blew away my dreams of being a mad scientist!"

. . .

Cleo made fun of the two years of back issues of *American Teen* on my bed, but I learned about love from Dear Romeo & Juliet, fashion from Suit Yourself, and life from Socrates Speaks. Ever since my one and only friend and song-writing partner Meg Campbell had moved to Texas last March, *American Teen* was my sole source of companionship—until Cleo came back, of course. But by then Meg had hooked me on Meg and me writing what we coined The Song of the Century. Someday. But now that she was gone and The M&Ms were broken up, all I had were our B songs to remember her by:

Someday, one day
I shall leave this place forever
and find my hopes and dreams.
Someday, one day.
I want to laugh,
I want to cry.
I want to live.
I want to die.
So that I can be free.
So that I can be ME.

All lyrics aside, word of Cleo in her bikini got out, and in no time she had so many boyfriends at the pool I couldn't count them. They would go with her to her Mustang and make out with her like mad and do who knows what—how could I tell, all the way from the snack bar? And the whole time, she was on the lookout for Leonard, who used to do backflip dives here high as a kite.

"When's he going to show up?" she wondered, adjusting her bikini bra. "Surely he's heard I'm back."

A track of small red bites on her neck silenced me. I think I will always equate the smell of chlorine on a warm summer night with the first time I smelled sex.

She flopped around in her pool chair like a lovesick fish. "I miss him, Marcy. No one comes close to loving me as much as Leonard did."

"He'd cut off his ponytail, burn his guitar, and shoot old ladies if you told him to," I said.

"He'd die for me, li'l one. Up and die. But I guess I really hurt him, didn't I? The thought of me with Chuck Boucher did a number on him, didn't it?"

"It broke him in two," I assured her.

· · ·

Porcelain dolls and delicate flowers—symbols of Eastern grace and beauty. But Cleo was no fragile object. She was statuesque, built to command the sun and the stars and the atmosphere on earth. Her hair was mink and she wore it like a coat. People were stunned when they saw her, as though she had just walked out of a painting and into Dart Drug. Males were often moved to utter something, anything, even some Neanderthal grunt, as if, otherwise, they'd lose their chance forever. I remember an older guy with beer breath approaching us at the salad bar at Ponderosa Steak House and saying to her, *Miss, I'm a happily married man with four kids, but I just wanted you to know you're a breathtaking woman.*

I never dreamed of that power myself. It was not within my realm of dreaming. If God gave me smarts, He gave her looks for two. Cleo was always saying my turn was next, but I knew it would never happen, not in this lifetime. There was only one Cleo.

．　．　．

A special summer edition of *American Teen* hit the newsstand. It was a double issue, jam-packed with gossip, fashion, and celebrity interviews. The first annual Dream On essay contest was also announced. The topic? *Whatever you dream on.* The grand-prize winner would have her essay and photograph published in next year's Valentine's Day issue. I pictured my face in there, surrounded by a lacy heart. I read the announcement over and over. *Calling all American Teens! Send your most heartfelt essay with a recent photo.*

To write the winning essay—could I do it? I wanted more than anything to be part of that magazine. Even the notion of it hurt worse than any growing pain. But did I have a dream? What did I dream on?

．　．　．

From a poster taped up in the window of The Rec Room, Cleo discovered that Leonard was now playing guitar in a band called EZ Times in a Georgetown bar. She got in the habit of dropping me off at home and cruising down there with some guy she just met at the pool. Her plan? To drive Leonard mad with jealousy. I would wait up for her, dreaming on.

"Marcy?"

Cleo cracked open my bedroom door. It was especially

late. I'd woken up in a bed of magazines and now she was talking. Beer on her breath gave her away, even from where she sat, at the foot of the bed, just past the magazines. In the moonlight from my window, all I could see were those eyes. Cleopatra eyes.

"He still ignores me. He sees me on the dance floor with other guys and he just ignores me, like I'm smoke in the air."

"Maybe he didn't see you dancing."

"*Everybody* sees me."

"Maybe he's afraid of getting hurt again. Maybe he's afraid to love you again."

"He once told me if I ever left him, he'd come crawling back to me on his hands and knees on a bed of nails," she said bitterly.

"Hey, Cleo, want to take a quiz in *American Teen*? It's called 'How to Tell When He Really Loves You.' Let me get it," I said, going for the light.

"No!" she gasped. "Don't turn it on!"

But it was too late. It was on and before she switched it back off, I got a blinding glimpse of her in another light. Hair a knotted mess, lips swollen from too much French kissing and drinking and a host of other activities I'd never learn from Dear Romeo & Juliet.

Now she was whispering, "Shhh . . ."

My father's footfalls headed downstairs. Slow and heavy, as if he were in chains. We froze, listening for clues in the dark—how many times had we done this? His bouts of insomnia kept us awake, too. But that night he let out a monstrous groan, then broke down as if there was no one else in the house. Cleo sobered up just like that, ran to the bathroom she and I shared, combed her hair, and splashed her face with

water until she'd washed away her drowsiness, her drunken-
ness, her love for Leonard. She rushed down the steps while I
sat at the top of the staircase. In a minute, my mother joined
me. She was a ghost, clutching my hand. Moving as one, we
inched down a few stairs until we were close enough to spy.

"Dad, what's wrong?"

His voice could crack a wall. "Nothing. Go to bed now."

Cleo eyed a blue airmail letter in his hands—we grew up
believing PAR AVION spelled bad news.

"What do they want now?" she asked him. "Besides your
bank account."

"Don't judge them," he said. "For most of their lives they
were poor. In spirit, they're still needy."

"*Greedy*, Dad, not needy. *Greedy!*"

"I said don't judge! Do you know how it feels to go to bed
hungry every night? Do you know how it feels to wonder
whether you will eat or starve the next day?"

"Nope," she said without apology.

"Try to understand them, Cleo. To my parents, more
money means more security."

"Dad, don't kid yourself. This isn't about money." Cleo's
voice was maturing out of nowhere. "It's just that they were
born without the heart and soul you're famous for. They'll
never appreciate all you do for them. They've never congratu-
lated you when you've gotten a promotion, have they? They've
never even sent you a birthday card! All they want is more,
more, more. More money, more gifts, more sacrificial rites
from you."

"You expect me to let them starve?"

"No! Of course not! Give them all you want! Give them
your bank account! Just don't give them your heart and soul,

because they'll never give it back. *We're* your family, you know. Mom and me and Marcy. We're the ones who count."

Cleo hugged my father so hard he caved in to waves of torment. They came from so deep within him they nearly knocked me over, especially at this hour. My mother squeezed my hand, her pain traveling from her heart into mine like a splinter. Still, our pain was so small compared to my father's. He cried in Cleo's arms for a long time.

. . .

I worshipped Cleo more than God in the days that followed, for her aura in the outside world, and for her bonds within the walls of our house. It was only natural that she became the focus of my Dream On essay. Not that I ever dreamed of being Cleo—I was just her li'l hobo sister—but I did dream of being by her side in her yellow Mustang, suspended in time. Cleo and me, shifting into gear. By now, though, she was following Leonard from bar to bar. She was strung out on the memory of his love. I don't know how I got the nerve, but one day I looked up Leonard Lewandowski in the telephone book and called him.

"She's fucked up," he said dryly. "Tell her to stay the hell away from me."

"No, she's not! She's not fucked up!" My own swearing shocked me. "She's not!"

"Then why's she following me around?"

"You had a romance with her."

"A *romance*? Give me a break! We went out a few times! Partied!"

"But you said you loved her."

"If I did, I didn't mean it. Look, I'm sorry, kid. But your sister's got problems."

"No, she doesn't."

"Get her off my ass," he said before hanging up.

And I did try. I read Cleo advice from Dear Romeo & Juliet. She yawned. I begged her to at least wave to Owen, the guy down the street who spent every weekend washing his car no doubt hoping for just one private moment under the stars with her. Once he'd even washed and waxed her Mustang until it outshone the sun. She'd rolled her eyes.

Tell her I called Leonard? Over my dead body! Part of what was Cleo was what she wanted us to see.

· · ·

It was on a hot, muggy night—the air conditioner was broken, windows were open, portable fans were blowing—that I saw more than what I wanted to. Cleo was out, as usual. My parents were across the street at the Sullivans. An anniversary party, I believe. I was on my bed working on my essay and listening to some of Cleo's albums on loan from The Rec Room—Weather Report, Fleetwood Mac, Steely Dan's *Pretzel Logic*, my favorite. Just rocking and sweating the night away.

I thought it was a burglar, but it was just Cleo, home early. She stood in my doorway dressed in jeans, black stiletto sandals, and a sapphire blue sequin halter. A blind man could tell she was good-looking and stone-cold drunk. She staggered into my bedroom, stood over me with the apparent wrath of God, and uttered, "You stupid little shit."

My mind went blank.

"How could you do such a stupid little shit thing?"

"Do what, Cleo?"

"Don't play dumb with me! I know you called Leonard! Why? Why'd you do it?"

"I just wanted him to love you again," I blurted. "Please don't be mad at me, Cleo."

"*Cleopatra!*" she snapped murderously.

"Cleopatra. Sorry."

"Where did you ever get the stupid little shit idea to do such a stupid little shit thing?" She squinted contemptuously at me. Then at my mountain of magazines. "From those?"

"No," I said.

"Good, because I've got news for you. You can dream for a lifetime—dream on, dream on, dream on, li'l one—because you're *not* going to win any damn Dream On contest! They'll take one look at your picture and toss your essay in the trash!"

"That's not true!"

Cleo began flipping through magazine after magazine. "Do you see your face in here? Because I don't!" Now she was tearing out pages, one after the other, balling them up, and letting the fan blow them in a fury across my room. "All I see in here are blue-eyed blondes!"

"That's not true!" I cried.

"Face it, Marcy! You're not an American Teen! And you never will be! Just look in the mirror!"

She dragged me to the mirror like I was some sorry rag doll. Whatever she was saying hadn't hit me yet. All I saw was the stark difference between us. Cleo gorgeously wasted in sequins. Me so pitifully plain in an old smock top. How could we be sisters?

"Don't dream on about being with me," she said. She stumbled but stayed in place, "Look at me, I'm a fucking mess!"

Dizziness got the best of her and she sank to my bed. Her painted eyelids were magnificently winged tonight, and they fluttered up and down with confession:

"Leonard never loved me, okay? The guy never even *liked* me. And you know why? Because I look more like some Mama-san in the rice paddies than good old Aunt Bee, that's why. I'm not good enough for Leonard. Oh, I'm good enough to screw till he's blue in the face, but not good enough to meet his fucking white-bread family. I swear to God, if I ever see his gross-out face again, I'll strangle him with his own ponytail! Do you understand what I'm talking about? Do you?"

This was not Cleo talking. Not the Cleo I knew. My Cleo never knew the chill of inferiority delivering itself up and down the spine. The cruel valentines and lonely lunches. The Miss Moonface down the hallway, on the bus. *Miss Moonface, Miss Moonface, Miss Moonface.* Not Cleo, who carried herself like the queen of jeans.

"Do you have any idea what I'm talking about?" she whined before passing out.

"No," I lied.

．　．　．

In the morning—the aftermath—Cleo lay in my bed like volcanic ashes. It was over. She was asleep when I inched in, having already been to summer school and back. When she opened her eyes, it almost got me crying. Somehow her eye-liner had smeared off during the sweaty night, and I remembered who she was. My big sister at the wheel.

"What am I doing here?" she asked groggily.

"You got drunk last night, Cleo. You passed out on my bed. I called The Rec Room to tell them you were sick. They said, 'Far out.'"

"Wow." She rubbed her forehead. "The whole night's a blur."

She tried to get up, but her hangover won out and she sank back into my pillow with a smile.

"So, what do you feel like doing today, li'l one?"

By afternoon, her hangover was gone, and those Cleopatra eyes were back on. All that was left was a headache, easily remedied by a cruise in her Mustang. The top was down, and the white-streaked blue sky matched her tie-dyed tank top. She shifted into gear.

"Hang on!"

We zipped onto the Beltway, radio on, guys going wacko.

Slow down, foxy lady!

You're a thousand on a scale of one to ten!

You ain't built like a brick wall!

Why couldn't it always be this way? Eternal adoration on a never-ending highway? Cleo and me always playing hooky from life?

"Are we going to Taco Town?" I shouted.

"Taco Town?" she scoffed. "I don't want any memories of that messed-up dude!"

Cleo pulled off an exit and into a shopping center. Her Mustang came to a screeching halt in front of The Fotobooth.

The Fotobooth?

"What are we doing here?" I asked.

Her sunglasses slid down her nose and razzle-dazzled me into her spell.

"Have you lost your mind, li'l one? It's time to get your picture taken for the contest!"

After a few shots of myself, Cleo joined me in the booth. We must have spent an hour in there monkeying around. That hour captured a funny strip of our lives: There's me at fourteen, sticking out my tongue. And there's Cleo at nineteen, pouting her Wet 'n' Wild lips. Now she's got her chin on my head like some skull-crushing monster. We're both cross-eyed and crammed so close together it's hard to tell who's who.

BOSS

JOHN JEFFIRE

Was it really deceit if they had agreed that such things could and probably would happen? No, not really. They'd known the possibilities and even, in some ways, planned how they might handle the worst of what could happen. But even if what they'd gone on to do hadn't been deceit, it still somehow felt like deceit when it actually happened. And see it had been Corry—his wife's name was Corry—who'd started it by having these deep conversations about how things would be. How their relationship would work after they were married. They weren't even engaged at the time, but he, Gary, listened and, for the most part, agreed with her ideas. Even if he wasn't totally comfortable with them and hadn't fully thought about them for himself. After all, they were just ideas. Ideas were to think about, not to argue about or really commit to, right?

"You know, I can see, I don't know, maybe being away on business for a week, and, I don't know, some kind of cute guy comes up to me at the bar at the end of a long day," she said, looking off as if seeing herself at the bar next to a cute guy who was smiling at her. "And he buys me a drink, and one thing leads to another and we hit it off, and we end up upstairs in one of our rooms. . . ."

Gary would listen as Corry explained things, and it excited

him. He always thought the cute guy would have curly black hair and be named something like Tony or Marco. It wasn't cheating, she would explain, because at the time she'd be in some far-off city, so she wouldn't be denying Gary anything. He didn't think it odd for her to bring up such ideas. Ideas were what Corry did. It was the 1980s. People talked about things like this.

"And the same would go for you," she would continue, brushing back her feathered hair. "You could be at home when I'm away, and the same thing could happen for you. Or maybe you're away at some car convention or something and *I'm* at home. And I wouldn't be upset because I wouldn't know about it. As long as when we came back together we were with each other and committed to only each other. That's the key. That's the whole idea. That we're totally committed to each other when we're together."

This talking of theirs was before they married. They'd met in high school and gone out a bit junior and senior year, separated afterward, and then gotten back together in their early twenties when they were starting their careers. There was nothing remarkable about them other than they were very popular without doing or being anything remarkable. They were good-looking. Corry had long, thin legs and a thin, funky body—she was a fox—and Gary had straight, thick hair and a potential to grow a thick beard, a potential she and he both took pride in. They came from monied families (Gary's father owned a series of car dealerships, some as far away as Florida and Arizona, and Corry's father was a dentist), and they smiled often, and they laughed at jokes and were invited to countless social events. Gary owned almost a hundred different ties. Corry had done well in school and dressed sharply, her Farrah Fawcett hair blown in all directions, and she danced like she could be on one of those TV shows with Deney Terrio. Gary and Corry had a visible gleam of physical attraction to each other, which perhaps made others feel they were somehow special and worth knowing or at least worthy of inviting to parties or out for drinks.

When he was alone before they were married, Gary thought about Corry's vision of their relationship. It seemed easy, almost natural, to not get hung up on things, to let freedom win out over jealousy and the many other kinds of negative emotions. He even saw himself with other women. He'd always had a thing for Marina Painter, the customer service rep at his father's dealership, where he'd worked since he was in high school and was now full-time after finally finishing two years at the community college. Even in high school, when he did shuttle service and changed oil, he loved Marina's toothy smile and huge brown eyes. She was in her mid-twenties raising two kids of her own when Gary was in high school. She was a fox with curves even more pronounced than Corry's. She'd wink when she'd see Gary to call him on a run to shuttle a customer. Yes, the rule about playing around when the other person was out of town could be a good one.

"Yeah, Cor, yeah, it's like that song by that band my older brothers like. I can't think of the name of it. But I remember the words. 'If you can't be with the one you love' . . ."

"'Love the one you're with,'" Corry said. "Crosby, Stills, and Nash. Yeah, that's it, Gair. Exactly, exactly what I was saying. You get it then. Great band, too."

A year after being married, Gary and Corry were living in a condo off the freeway overlooking Lake St. Clair. He had moved on to sales at his father's main dealership, and Corry was a research assistant and techie at one of the city's big TV stations. She had finished a four-year degree in communications and was writing copy and managing the traffic of ads that appeared on commercial breaks. She liked her job. They lived well and made good money, and soon they were going on weekend vacations to places like Jamaica and the Virgin Islands, where they would stay at all-inclusive hotels that were advertised on TV featuring young, fit people who liked to dress up and hit nightclubs and lay on the beach and be waited on. They fucked in their room and on the balcony and on the beach, and no one could stop them. Life was good. But at this time Gary and Corry also began to develop a few bad habits. Like blow. Lots of it. They had the money. They had no children to consider or let down if they got out of control. It was fun. Their sex was better when they were lit up, all their senses firing. Why not have fun? Corry was the first to try. At work, the sound technicians all the way to evening anchor Phil Toms tooted nose candy, the thing to do to keep alert and jacked up when the stress and fatigue hit. At first, Gary was leery of getting too involved—it was cocaine, not Red Bud or Acapulco Gold—but he went to some of the parties with the TV crew, and even Phil Toms himself was there snorting, so it seemed harmless enough. It kept Corry laughing and happy. Gary liked the rush and feeling of endless power and energy it gave him. Cocaine wasn't so bad. It was still the eighties.

But it didn't take long before the TV parties were off the hook. Phil Toms was center of everything, everyone falling all over themselves to get him a drink, get him a this, get him a that. They treated him like he was Axl Rose or Bon Jovi. He was on all the commercials for the *Six O'Clock Action News*, turning suddenly in his swivel chair and looking right in the camera, squinting like Clint Eastwood. He was everywhere on the TV. Nobody in Detroit was bigger than Phil Toms.

"Why, hello there, Boss. So you're the lucky young man who swept my Corry off her feet. You're lucky, Boss. Corry here is my right hand. And sometimes my left."

Corry laughed at Phil Toms, who was holding a scotch. He was smaller in person than he looked behind the desk at six, but his dyed hair was blown back and sprayed into perfection, and his voice had authority in it, which made him seem bigger. Corry laced an arm through his and placed her other hand on the chest of his silk suit.

"Oh, you're too kind, Mr. Toms."

"Nonsense. And what'd I tell you, sweetheart? It's Phil to you."

"Well, I'm glad she's working out so good," Gary said, establishing a dominant presence, he thought. "She really likes working, working for you."

"Don't you worry about anything, Boss. Corry here has nothing to worry about as long as Phil Toms is behind that desk. Not a goddamn thing."

Phil Toms pointed right at Gary. Corry laid her head against Toms's arm, and he put that arm around her and gave her a hug. Gary looked away, caught himself in a mirror on a wall. His hair was good, his lime green shirt with the butterfly collar sharp. When he looked back, Corry was gazing up at Phil Toms as he took a belt of his scotch, but Toms's hair was nowhere near as good as Gary's.

Soon, though, the coke began to get the best of them. Even without children, snorting bags of it and going on getaway trips to snort more drained the old bank account. This started to become clear when Gary bought a new JVC stereo system and received a notice from the bank the following week that his check had bounced. When he went to the bank to correct the mistake, the cashier showed him a list of charges that had been made against the account: mortgage for the condo, no problem there; plane tickets to St. Croix, sure, he knew about that; but then nearly two thousand dollars at Lord & Taylor and *over four thousand to a shoe boutique in New York*? How could shoes cost that much? And of course there were the cash withdrawals he'd made to buy cocaine. They were broke. No, they weren't broke. They were actually in the hole—deep.

Which led to Gary's problems with Roger. Roger, the Artful Roger, Roger the Dodger, Jolly Roger—he dealt throughout the city, but to classy clients, up-and-comers, people like Gary and Corry. A few days after finding out about his bank account, Gary was supposed to pay off $1,500 to Roger for snow, but there wasn't even lint in his pockets. He was in a bind. He couldn't ask either of his older brothers, even if he didn't mention dope. They ran family dealerships out of state and would lecture him about being so stupid and irresponsible and sure as shit turn him in to their father. In this way, they were less his brothers than dutiful workers in the family business. And he could never ask his father. Chuck Reindel was The Duke of The Deal. He had raised Gary and his brothers like employees. He'd needed to start at the bottom in the car business and earn his way up, so, like anyone else who worked for him, Gary would receive no breaks and no special privileges. Gary had learned this particular idea young. Once, as a boy, he'd gotten into a fight with a neighbor who was a year older and much stronger. The neighbor had beaten Gary fair and square, sending Gary home with a bruised, swollen face slickened by tears. After Chuck Reindel heard his son's side of things, they marched out the front door and down to the neighbor's house, and Chuck Reindel, The Duke of The Deal, told his son to finish the fight with the boy without crying or he'd give him something to really cry about. The neighbor boy's dad, surprised by the circumstance but confident in his older, stronger boy's chances, agreed to the rematch. So they fought again. Again, Gary lost miserably, blood flowing eagerly from his nose and his mouth, but as much as he wanted to cry, he didn't. Lesson learned.

"*Never* come crying to me again," his father said, his finger aimed between Gary's eyes.

He never did.

Still, there came a second time Chuck Reindel laid down the law, as it were. Things were slow at the garage that day, so Gary wandered over to see what Marina Painter was up to. She was at her desk, and when she saw Gary, she flashed that diamond smile, and they talked and laughed, and Gary was enjoying himself when he was called over the intercom to report to the oil pits. Before he entered that area, he found Chuck standing in his way, apparently waiting for him, hands on hips.

"Where the fuck you been?"

Gary froze. He hadn't been anywhere, he thought. He couldn't have been gone for more than ten minutes.

Chuck slapped Gary across the face. Right there, where anyone around could see.

"I got your attention now? Now answer the question, where the fuck were you?"

"Nowhere. I was—"

Chuck slapped him again. Gary wondered if Marina was

looking on from her desk or if any of the veteran pit monkeys were watching.

"If you want to chase middle-age pussy on your time, be my guest. On my time, though, you work. I pay you to work, not fuck off. You understand?"

"Yeah."

"Yeah?"

A third time, the hand came hard.

Gary touched his reddened cheek, wincing the pain from his head.

"Yes. Yes, Dad, I understand you."

So family was of no help. And Gary felt he could not tell Corry. Everyone at her work was partying hard, and Phil Toms, creepy Phil Toms, was up to something that was obviously impressing her. A bigshot like Toms could buy all the blow he wanted. Hell, groupies were probably bringing it to him, hoping for a plug in the six slot. How could Gary compete with that? He'd have to cut back, maybe switch back to pot like they used in high school. He wasn't sure. It was complicated. But the main thing was he had to get clear with Roger before he did anything.

Gary started with the tale of Corry, her spending and partying, hoping maybe the guy angle would work with Roger. It didn't.

"Okay, Scary Gary, hold up, hold up before you go any further," Roger said at the Gold Digger Lounge one evening. Gary had phoned Corry earlier in the day to let her know he was working late, and she was okay with that because she was working on a special project with Phil Toms anyway and would be late herself. "Let's be straight here: You got woman problems, I got woman problems, we all got problems at the old sperm bank, but your woman problems really ain't my business and don't mean jack to me. Capeesho? And let me say this: Corry is a foxy mama, bet she bangs like a mink, congrats my man, but she really isn't the issue here. Now, with that said, the Dodger's been thinking this over. You and me are friends, I get that, but I'm also a businessman, Gary. I cut you lotsa breaks, compadre, filling your goody bags with a little extra. And what you need to understand is that I've got people to pay, too. I'm in some hot water here myself. Normally, I take a more direct route with people who don't pay, but, hey, no need to go into that, let's work this out with our brains. I've got a few ideas to run by you, so maybe we can come to some kind of alternative plan for repayment."

Gary was all ears. He was stuck. He owed the money. He had to listen. Roger sat before him, sipping on a Chivas Regal and looking off at the girls grinding the pole onstage. Roger looked a lot like one of the many plainclothes cops that Chuck Reindel hooked up with good deals on minivans. He lit a cigarette and continued.

"So, your dad, he owns car stores, whattaya call them, dealerships, dealerships all over butt-fuck everywhere. And some of them dealerships, they're in Florida, right?"

Gary nodded.

"Well, follow the Dodger here for a minute. I gotta lotta product that comes out of, guess where, Florida. Yeah, the Sunshine State. Palm trees and bikinis and a whole lotta high-grade goodies. And, follow me, if I could find another nice safe way to move that product north, well, after you pay me back what you now owe me, that's gotta come first, I could set you up good for the future. Shit, you'd make double, hell, triple what you make selling shitmobiles for Daddy. Capee-sho?"

They talked. The idea was simple. Sometimes Gary's dad needed models that weren't available on his lots in Michigan. Say he needed a tan Sierra or a blue Orion and all he had was white and red, but down in Florida they had exactly what he needed—simple, he'd send his extras to Florida on a big-ass ten-car carrier and load up what he needed for the return trip. The same with auctions. Chuck Reindel sold all kinds of used cars, too, and Florida vehicles made him a killing. Old people went there and died and left behind cars nobody wanted—next of kin was happy to get something for the vehicles, and they were in good shape, low mileage, no rust, no damage from salt like you had up north. In Gary's side business, you'd get the right driver, you have them pull over for a bit, take a nice long piss at a prearranged truck stop, and Roger's people would load up one of the used vehicles headed north with the product. And straight-shooter Chuck Reindel, hell, he was known all across the country. He was tight with the cops, always quick with a killer deal for the boys in blue. His face was on billboards. With "Reindel Automotive" and "The Duke of The Deal" painted on the doors of car haulers all across America, no one would bother his shipments. Could Gary handle this?

"Yeah. Yeah, Roger. Sure."

"Easy deal, right?"

Gary smiled. He lit a cigarette himself. He was now a player, a shaker *and* a mover, a literal wheeler-dealer, a guy with a little somethin'-somethin' of his own on the side. If his father was indeed The Duke of The Deal, then he was, what—what was just under Duke? Bishop? Senator? General?

He didn't know, but whatever it was, he was now it. He couldn't tell Corry about it—yet—until things were in motion and the debts were paid off and more money and coke were flowing in. The only issue was that he needed to find the right driver for the gig. Like Roger told him, somebody young, new, not so bright, who could follow orders and was loyal, and in need of some extra cash.

And that's were Marina came in. Sunny, hot, smiling Marina with the exotic curves and short skirts and chunky black leather high heels.

"Hey, Marina, how goes it?"

"Just fine, handsome." Her smile lit Gary up. As always, she was working away at the service desk, answering the phone, setting up work orders for the mechanics. Her red blouse was tight, and her tits were packed in so well he could see the line thingy between the fleshy mounds. How different would his life be if he were married to Marina instead of Corry? She would be great in bed, he knew that. A mink. You couldn't have that kind of body and not be good in bed. And she had kids. A real woman. Sure, Corry was hot, but Marina was right there with her, even shapelier, more alluring in that regard, and she smiled at Gary every time she saw him. She knew Gary was the goddamned owner's son. She would treat him right.

"Hey, a favor to ask here, Marina. But, I need to keep this on the down low."

Marina's eyes glinted, and Gary liked how he'd made them do that.

"You can count on me, partner."

Partner, he thought. She actually used the word *partner*.

"Good. Good. I needed to know that. So, I'm looking to

expand into some other, uh, business dealing opportunities, you know, branch out, grow outward a bit? The whole car thing, it's good, but I got bigger fish to catch. Anyway, I'm gonna need someone to . . . I'm looking for someone, someone who, you know, someone who might need some extra cash. One of the drivers, someone you think could use a little extra. A good man who can be trusted with some responsibilities in a new business. Someone who won't ask questions and can keep quiet. Nothing too complicated, just a good chance to fatten the wallet."

Marina's eyes were locked in on Gary's. "Darn, can I apply, Sugar?"

For a moment, he saw himself all over Marina, kissing her neck, her head tossed back in passion. His mind flashed to a TV commercial featuring himself and Marina in the Bahamas in one of the hotel rooms he and Corry had shared.

"Gary?"

"Yeah?"

"You were saying?"

"Oh, sorry. Little lost in thought. Complicated stuff—big stuff. So like I was saying, I need a guy who can be trusted and can use some extra help with his finances. A good guy, a guy who can be trusted."

"Hmmm, let's see. Let me look at the roll of drivers. Boy, the Duke must be so proud of his son, starting up his own business."

Gary lifted a finger to his lips and glanced furtively side to side. He had to cut this off right at the elbows.

"No, no, no. Remember, this is between me and you. The Duke, he can't know anything about this. I, I want to surprise him, you know, by doing this on my own. He can't know until, uh, I got everything up and running. It'll be a huge surprise."

"Oh, that's sweet, Gary. I'm sure he'll be real proud. Mum's the word here. And, you know what, I think I've got the perfect guy."

"Who?"

"Javier."

"Javier who?"

"Ramirez?"

Javier Ramirez was just slightly younger than Gary but looked older, his brow permanently knitted, quick to say "sir," nodding rapidly to show you he grasped what you were saying. He was short and blocky and spoke broken, heavily accented English. Despite his youth, he was married and supporting three young children, probably living in some two-room hole with little to no heat or air-conditioning in East Detroit. Gary could not ever remember seeing him smile.

The first meeting with Javier was rock solid.

"Everything clear, Boss?" Gary asked after he explained Javier's tasks.

"Yes, si, yes sir, understand, all good." Javier would alert Gary when he was an hour or so from the dealership, then Gary would greet him at the unloading bay, sign off on all the paperwork, hand Javier an envelope containing $150 in cash, then unload the product himself. At first, it was hidden in wheel well panels and in spare tires, neatly wrapped in taped plastic bags, which Gary would then deliver to Roger in the Gold Digger parking lot. In time, though, the runs were so problem-free that security softened and the product was placed in glove compartments and under front seats. There was so much of it that whenever Gary untaped a plastic bag and took a traveling coffee mug's worth for himself, no one ever noticed. The money was almost too easy, the business too simple, the pay-off almost way too incredible.

And life was almost too good also. What Gary wanted, Gary bought. A Harley, a pistol collection, jet skis, a cottage up north, a MasterCraft speedboat with powerslot transmission, you name it. What Corry wanted, Gary bought for her. They sold the condo and moved into a gated community in Grosse Pointe Farms near where Chuck Reindel The Duke of The Deal lived. Gary drove a Corvette, Corry a Porsche. Corry was now on-screen, doing short special interest bits, in one segment interviewing an old man who had his bank account cleaned out by a guy who promised to invest the money in a cereal-making factory in Poland. She interviewed the guy, and, at one point, he started crying. Boom. She looked real concerned, nodding, frowning, but not to the point of looking ugly. No, she looked sharp. She was wearing these business suits that made her appear one promotion away from sitting right there at the desk with Phil Toms. She could be more than the weather girl. She could be the one saying "Good night, Motor City" at the end of every night's news she was so hot. Gary wondered if maybe sometime they could get into the station after hours, after she was done helping Phil Toms with whatever they did, and *he* could be the one whose stash she could enjoy, not Phil Toms's, and they could do it right there on the news desk.

What would Phil Toms think of that?

Gary never found out. The problems started with the call from Javier. He'd called from this new thing, a cellphone, which reminded Gary of an old army walkie-talkie thing you saw in old movies. Chuck Reindel The Duke of The Deal had made sure all his drivers had one. No need to stop at a pay phone if something went wrong, and the range was better than a CB radio. No need to wait on a cop to stop and see what the problem was. No, you could just whip out the cellphone.

"Mister Ga-ry, sir, they crazy. Crazy-*loco*. They take car. They . . ."

Gary could barely make out what Javier was saying. The cellphone thing—it obviously had some bugs in it that needed some working on.

"Javier, hey, Javier, hold up, my man. Who is 'they'?"

"Wha?"

"You say 'they' crazy. Who are you talking about?"

"The mens, sir, and the lady. Three peoples. They crazy. They take car. Jag-war. Crazy. Crazy-*loco*. They have guns. All guns. Sir, they crazy peoples."

The Jaguar. Of all the fucking cars on that run. Gary was now vice president of Acquisitions at Reindel Motors. He had his own office and one of the cellphone things, too, and he'd made Marina his own personal secretary, and he took Corry out whenever she wasn't working on some extra project with Phil Toms—she had her own money and schedule now, so she didn't need much of his attention. Gary had taken Marina out after work for a drink a few times, introduced her to the nose candy. She was hot. Really hot. And he had a bad-ass mustache now. One Friday when he'd known Marina's loser ex-husband had been saddled with their kids, he'd invited her out. They'd hit the Freezer Theater, Todd's, and Tremors to dance and party. You could dice up lines right on the tables at any of those places and nobody did anything. Lord, Marina loved to dance, and once she hit the powder she didn't slow down. He'd spent that whole weekend with her, stopping in at home for an hour or so to keep Corry from getting suspicious, then heading back to Marina's. It was Corry's love-the-one-you're-with idea come alive, pretty much how she'd described it, so it was fine—the whole idea had been hers to begin with. And Marina had those big brown eyes and those curves, curves that, when the lacy underwired bra and everything else came off . . .

"Mister Ga-ry, sir, I call to you father, yes? This crazy."

"No-no-no, my man. You hear me? Javier, listen to me. You must not call my father. I got this."

The Jag. The Jag was gone. It was the prize of this run, '85 XJS, V12 engine, fully refurbished, they'd have a dozen collectors bidding on it. But now, shit. Somebody had freaking taken it. Who in hell were these three people?

"I call police then. These people, they guns. They make me take the car off hauler. They want that car, just that one car. Crazy people. They . . ."

"Calm down, my man, calm down. When, when exactly did this happen? How long ago?"

"How long? Just now. The three, they just drive away, maybe five minute."

Gary had to think. He was in charge here. *The* man. VP of Acquisitions. He sat in his office holding the cellphone up high enough with both hands. In a way, right at this moment, he was more important than his father. This was his rodeo. His horses. His Cowboys and Indians. Right now in this office, he was more important than Phil Toms or Chuck Reindel or Roger the Cokehead Dodger. He was Gary Charles Reindel, VP of Acquisitions at the largest dealership in Detroit, and he had a hot, hot secretary.

"Mister Ga-ry, sir?"

"Yeah, yeah. Stay with me, Javier. You stay right where you are. Don't move."

"But sir . . ."

"Javier, shut your piehole and stay right where you are and don't move, understand me? Capeesho?"

He was in control. People did what he said. He was the VP of Acquisitions, not some brainless flunky. He was a big guy. The guy to come to with any and all big ideas. But the Jag. Who in the hell would take the Jag? It had to be connected to the product he was bringing home. He didn't want the cops involved, even though over half the force bought their vehicles at Reindel Automotive. No, the Jag might have had goods in it, which actually wouldn't be a big deal because everything could be blamed on Javier. But the car. The car was a gem. A payday. He had to get the car back or else deal with his dad. He had to call Roger.

So he did, on his cellphone. He told Roger the whole story, ending with "that's all I know."

"Holy shit. Situation Red, amigo. A real shit show." Roger spoke calmly, almost as if he'd been expecting the call.

"What? Whattaya mean, Roger, 'shit show'?"

"*Shit* show, compadre. Snafu. Situation all fucked up. Problem in the supply line."

"Supply line?"

"Yeah, a supply line being a line of supplies. I get my product from people who get it from people who get it from people. The chain of life, my friend, a big circle, snake eats its tail. But I think I already have this all figured out. This is going to take some quick movement."

"Movement? What kind of movement?"

"Movement, Gary, as in we're gonna have to get you down to the Sunshine State to make some things happen."

"Me? Go to Florida?"

"Affirmative that. We've got at least three cowboys who are messing up the system, and I'd bet my last Benjamin I know who these three are, and they're down in gator country. So, we need a local rep to head on down to drain the swamp so to speak. A go-to guy, a studster, a real hombre."

"Yeah?" Gary said, not sure what Roger was saying.

"You get what I'm saying?"

"Yeah. But *me*? Why does it have to be me that goes? I mean, what exactly am I supposed to do?"

"Gary, Gary, Gary, lemme break this down for you, bro. You're out a Jaguar, man, and I'm out several hundred pounds of booger sugar. It's bad for all of us, sure, but mostly it's bad for you. Your daddy's expecting that car, and I'm expecting my dancin' dust. You don't wanna let down the old parental unit, and you sure as shit don't want him finding out about your little side business. Your driver screwed the pooch on this one, and you put him in charge, Gary. It's on you to make this right."

"But . . . the driver didn't do nothing, Roger. He got robbed. What was he supposed to do? And, and what am I supposed to do now? I don't know these people in Florida."

"See, that's the beauty of this. You're perfect. You don't have history with anyone. You're in deep, my friend, and it's time you get to know everyone involved. And you really don't know anyone or anything. You see, you have a special qualification that can help solve this whole problem."

"Okay, but . . ."

"No, there's no 'but,' Gary. You need to get your keister down to Tampa and get this resolved. I already got the planning part of it all worked out down to the dirtiest detail. You tell daddy there's a hitch with a purchase and that you'll take care of it personally. Don't even mention Tampa. Now, just to make sure, you do work for a registered dealer, right?"

"Of course. My dad's as registered as it gets."

"And you yourself are a licensed buyer, right?"

"Yeah. I'm the vice president of Acquisitions."

"Great, Gary, great. Perfect. The three losers who live in the boonies down there, last I talked to them, mentioned that they have the need for a licensed buyer's credentials. Do you see why this means they almost for sure can tell us where your Jag is?"

"Of course," Gary said, even though he didn't see completely.

"I'll need to double-check, but I think they're the key to solving the whole shebang here, and by that I mean your pop's missing Jag and my missing product that, now that I think about it, went pretty much almost for sure hand-in-hand with the Jag. The point being that you work some simple magic and we're all fartin' through silk, all of us, you, me, your pops, and even these three losers included. We got this, bro. Cake. I'll clue you in on where you need to be and who you need to deal with. Hell, I'll even buy your plane ticket and set up your car rental. Can't ask for more than that. And that's it. That's how we'll play it. And one big thing, my friend. You gotta keep your big fucking mouth shut, Capeesho? Anyone asks, you're just taking care of a little business outta town, be home soon, hugs and kisses."

Gary nodded against his cellphone. Smiled. Piece of cake.

The flight was the easy part. Tampa-St. Pete, pick up the rental, head to the prearranged meeting point off I-75. To put his mind even more at rest, Gary had packed his Colt Gold Cup .45 in his check-through—if these Florida crackers wanted to get cute, he'd use it to send a clear message. He'd also packed a can of Corry's professional-strength hair spray, the stuff that held up under the heat of the TV lights for hours. It was good. It was five times as strong as the kind housewives bought at drugstores, which meant, in Gary's mind, that if these three musketeers were the type to sit around bonfires at night, it could cause an explosion five times bigger than they'd ever seen. He'd be ready.

He smoked and drank the entire flight, made small talk with the stewardesses, then hit the car rental. Roger had a Ford Escort waiting for him, but no way he was driving that. The VP of Acquisitions at Reindel would not be caught dead in an Escort. He noticed a sweet-ass gold Datsun 280ZX and switched the reservation. He loaded his travel bag into the trunk and was out onto I-75 in no time. The heat, though, was bad. He could feel the weight on his scalp. Within fifteen minutes he found the meeting point where he would hook up with the three losers, a nearly deserted rest stop. He waited. Whoever these three kooks were, they'd get straightened out quick after they took a peek at the Colt.

The meet-up time came and went. He kept the windows rolled up and blasted the AC, burned a few more cigarettes, kept trying to find a local hard rock radio station that didn't suck. He could use some Van Halen or Foreigner or Loverboy or—

"Hey, you fucking *awake*? I said open your damn window."

The red, lean face of a gray-haired man filled the driver's side window. Missing teeth, and the ones he still had were brown with a blackish sludge long the lower gumline. And, shit, like some kind of cowboy, this guy had a holster and a .44 Ruger Super Redhawk—apparently here, down south, there were some real hucklebucks. Gary reached to find his own gun but, damn, he'd left it in his bag in the trunk. Okay, cool, he thought, and he checked his hair in the rearview mirror, then took his time lowering the window.

"Yeah?"

"Your name Gary?"

"Yeah. Yours?"

"Fuck, man. Shit, what the fuck you doing driving that car? You supposed to be in a navy Escort."

Gary's face lit up "It's a Datsun 28—"

"I don't fuckin' care what the fuck it is. Jesus fucking Christ, it sticks out like a pecker on a priest. Listen, we got no more time to talk. We're moving. Follow me."

The man was thin but hard, his sinewy arms veined and tatted up, his tank top and jeans stained and torn, his boots untied. He hustled over to a pickup truck and hopped in, honked once, and ground forward. Gary backed up, then gunned forward right behind him. As soon as he was in place, someone in a rust-colored Road Runner was at his rear bumper. The three-vehicle caravan moved out onto the highway.

They wove in and out of traffic for a good fifty miles, then exited using an off-ramp that had been barricaded off for construction. Gary had no idea where they were going. Everything was green and tropical, the homes along the side of the road weird but a kind of gentle pink. Soon the pickup turned off down a side road, then another, and another until finally there were no more homes, only swampy shit on either side. Gary lost the only decent radio station he could find. It had been at least twenty minutes since he'd seen any kind of building or house. He should have brought some cassettes.

With no use of directionals or warning, they turned off the paved two-lane road onto a dirt side road, which bent and twisted as it tried to follow a brown river. They turned several more times, and Gary swore they were in the jungle, with the trees growing right up alongside the road, which then became a more or less one-lane path. Some kind of strung moss hung down off the branches. Gary wanted his gun. He was sweating even though the AC was blasting. He was pissed at Roger. Why wasn't Roger down here? Why was it Gary? He was the vice president of fucking Acquisitions, not a dope dealer like Roger.

The pickup stopped, and Gary stopped. The Road Runner was no longer in Gary's rearview mirror.

The guy in the pickup didn't do squat, just sat, letting his engine idle.

Gary wanted to shout, What's going on, brother? but thought better of it.

This won't take long, he thought.

Guy's a loser *and* a chickenshit.

Then, even with his AC on, he heard someone shout, "*Welcome home.*"

But he couldn't see where the voice had come from.

"*Up here, shitbird.*"

Above him, a man who looked like an equally unshowered, sunburned version of the pickup truck driver was grinning down from a big tree. He was sitting essentially above the dirt path on what looked like part of a rocking chair that was somehow attached to the tree, which had several metal cables strung to it. He was holding a M14 rifle and a walkie-talkie. These boys were a trip.

The pickup driver got out and unhitched a moss-covered gate that Gary hadn't seen, then pointed into the jungle. He hopped back into his truck and pulled off the path and through the opening and into the jungle before disappearing. Gary wasn't going to take the Z any farther but the Road Runner, now behind him again, laid on the horn. Looking into the rearview mirror, Gary instinctively checked his hair, which was holding its own, then saw that the driver of the Road Runner was the same guy who'd been doing lookout up in the tree. Well, the Z was a rental, not Gary's property, so he crept forward and into the thinned wall of branches the pickup had pushed aside to disappear. He revved his engine, showing these hucklebucks he meant business, and kept on heading right in.

At the end of the trail was a clearing and a house. The house was filthy and beautiful at the same time. At some point, it had probably been clean and kept, but now the jungle had nearly consumed it. The chatter and screeches of birds and animals filled the damp air. The front door was off one of its hinges. Vehicles, cars and trucks and motorcycles, and parts of vehicles, cars and trucks and motorcycles, were everywhere, some overgrown with jungle, some laying out in cleared spaces around the house. Inside, where these hucklebucks led him, the marble and wooden floors were covered in dirt and bits of leaves and tree bark and debris. There was a fireplace but no furniture, and a number of the windows had no glass. Who would live in this dump? The two males were brothers, Dale and Kurtis—"with a K"—Wolf, self-proclaimed Vietnam vets who at most had a set of teeth between them. They smelled like sweat, fuel, and something dead, both of them openly armed with pistols in holsters. The third, Char, was their sister, and quite a bit younger—she was holstered up, too.

After the introductions played themselves out, they all three led Gary from the house to take him out back, where some kind of animal was roasting in a pit. It was growing dark, and Gary again wanted his pistol and again pictured it in the trunk of the Z, and, given the presence of the fire in the pit, he wished he'd packed the can of hairspray, too.

"So, my friend, it's time to get down to it," Kurtis said. "You know why you're here, right? Roger Dodger 'splained it all, right?"

Dale was handing out Budweisers while Gary lied smoothly enough by saying, "Basically." Char looked at Gary and he couldn't help but look back. She wore cutoff jean shorts, a tank top with a large hole in the stomach, and army boots (possibly a pair of one of her brothers), and her long blond hair had no order to it yet was still somehow shaped ideally. She was lean and hard, leaner and harder than Corry had been in high school, and a tattoo of a panther walked down the inside of her left forearm, its claws dug into her skin with red ink showing the blood. Unlike her brothers, she had all her teeth, which were straight and white. She drank her beer and turned the animal on the spit, the blackish smoke rising up into the heavy air. Her legs were deeply tanned, her eyes a glowing whitish blue.

"Anyway I've got my buyer's papers," Gary said to Kurtis. "That's all I was told."

"Then put two and two together, shitbird," Kurtis said.

"You ain't gotta talk mean to old Barbie here," laughed Dale. The brothers both burst out laughing while Char looked on sullenly. Gary could feel the heavy heat on his hair.

"Name's Gary, Boss, not Barbie. And I ain't buying anything until you tell me what's going on. And I need to see that Jag pretty damn quick."

The brothers looked at each other. Then Kurtis cackled, mahogany saliva splattering from his mouth.

"Well, lookit here, it has a backbone!"

They laughed harder. Gary widened his stance and placed his hands on his hips. Char turned the spit and continued to look at Gary. He tried to ignore her but his eyes kept returning.

"Okay, fuck it, I'm out, boys. You two geniuses can explain to Roger what happened. I'm headed back to Detroit."

Gary turned his back to the firepit and began for the house, but before he knew it, a boney hand was pinching his shoulder.

"Wa-wait up. You ain't going nowheres, Mr. Fancy Pants."

Kurtis spun Gary around. He was strong, apparently more sinewy than Gary had considered him, and his eyes were animal wild.

"You seem to have forgot about the Jaguar, didn't you, Mr. Britches? It's fine. Real nice car, in fact. Will fetch you a fat bag a cash up north. And you can have it back, on our honor, we'll give it back soon as we get what we need—no reason for all us here to see whose pecker pisses the farthest up a tree trunk, we can all play nice if that's what you want."

Gary's forehead was wet with sweat. If only he had his .45 or Corry's hairspray. He was the goddamned vice president of Acquisitions for Reindel Motors. His wife was hot. She worked with Phil Toms. His side woman was even hotter. Char was still looking at him. He needed to regroup.

"So, okay, what do you guys need?"

"Now that's better," Kurtis said. "I'll 'splain things. C'mon, Mr. Gary, siddown, siddown, don't get them panties in a bunch. Here, Char, cut him off a hunk a that there tenderloin and get our new friend another beer."

Dale grabbed Gary by the arm and led him over to one of the homemade wooden benches around the pit. Dale was as strong as Kurtis. Javier was right—these people were crazy. They were ex-soldiers, they lived out in the boonies, they smelled, they survived like cockroaches. Why had he agreed to come down here? He needed his gun. He needed to be back in his office, to put his hands on Marina's legs and slide one up her skirt to her ass when she brought him his coffee, to order various drivers around. He needed to be in his air-conditioned basement kicking his jams on his JVC surround-sound, his feet in his maroon shag carpet, toasting himself with Hennessy in the mirrored walls.

"Now, listen up here, sonny—I mean Gary. This here's the lay a the land. You're the certified buyer for an authorized dealer. We ain't. But as part of an overall group of people connected to the same general innerprize your boss Roger is, we believe we are owed a favor, well, in our eyes, several favors. And we need something we seen in the local auction inventory, and we plan on cashing in on one of them favors."

Gary loosened. They needed him. He started to run his hand through his hair, had enough coolness to stop. He looked over at Char. Her eyes were freaky and he made himself look away.

"Yeah, so? What do you need?"

Char brought him a large, stringy chunk of meat on a knife and a fresh beer. The meat was dripping, and Gary couldn't decide if it looked and smelled good or was the thing that was turning his stomach.

"We need us a dozer," Kurtis said. He was eating off a bone hacked away from the animal on the spit. Juice ran off his mouth and melted into his beard.

"You see," Dale continued, "we gonna be 'spanding. Now this is more than you need to know, amigo, 'cause it's our business, not yours or any other person's. But I ain't got nothin' to hide. 'Cept maybe that Jag, but that's just till we get what we need."

"Expanding? How?" Gary was actually hungry. Behind the outline of the swamp's treetops, where the sun was long gone, the sky glowed a kind of reddish navy. He looked at the hunk of meat again. Was it a pig? A German shepherd mix? He couldn't tell, and he didn't want to ask. But the smell of the roasting meat was now everywhere, and everything he saw through the black smoke waved and shimmered and refused to let him focus. The smell was probably soaking into his butterfly collar shirt. He bit the meat. Chewed. Then bit off some more.

"Look out there," Kurtis said, pointing out into the jungle. "What you see?"

"Nothing," said Gary.

"Shit, he don't see nothing," shot Dale.

"Nothing is right," Kurtis said. "It's good you see nothing. The more everybody sees nothing, the better."

Gary had no idea what they were talking about. They were simpletons who could shove the whole stinking swamp up their sweaty, stinking asses for all he cared. He wanted his car and to get the hell home.

"Get to a point," he said. "If it's nothing, then why am I here?"

"I'll tell you why," Kurtis said. "We need to get us a vehicle."

"Cat D7E with a Rome plow, 'bout same as in Nam," Dale said. "Powerful thing, easy to hide, but clear out a goddamn acre of scrub lickety-split."

"A plow?" Gary said, irritated. "So go buy a plow yourselves. You don't need to buy it at an auction. Just find some poor-ass farmer who needs to sell. You don't need a certified buyer for that."

"Maybe not for the plow," Kurtis said, "but that ain't what we want you to buy for us. We found the right rig for the job we gotta do—a dozer. See, we got too many eyes on us lately. Maybe more since you decided to roll here in that dickweed piece of Japanese shit. Anything we do, somebody looking. We can get you and the dozer here real quiet so's nobody knows, but we need you to buy the dozer in the first place."

"Tear up a nice long, straight swatch a that '*nuthin*'" out there," Dale said, gazing off. "Make us a nice, beautiful, kick-ass runway."

"Quiet, Dale," Kurtis said. "Excuse my younger brother, he gets 'cited. Could take out a Cong at 500 meters right between the eyes, and drives like Cale Yarborough. But he got loose lips."

"Can drive a damn plane, too, if I wanna. And a heel-icopter."

"Enough, brother," Kurtis said. "Okay?"

Gary sat without saying anything, hoping they'd argue their way into giving him an out. He finished off the meat Char had given him and chugged his beer.

"Sis, our friend here needs some more chow," Kurtis said. "So, like Dale said, we're gonna be 'spandin' the business here and cuttin' out some more middlemen. Can fetch our own product. Just need the right tools. You smell what we cookin'?"

Gary smelled the meat everywhere. It was good enough for human consumption, and he wanted more. Char took his knife and brought him back a chunk with a bone attached. The sky was black. The fire illuminated their faces. Animals were yacking and chirping here and there in the jungle.

"All I get is you need me to buy you a bulldozer," Gary said. "Piece of cake. Auction is tomorrow. I'll need bid money and directions how the hell to get out of here to the auction site. Then I get the Jag and go home. Capeesho?"

"That's the plan," smiled Dale. "Everything else is taken care of."

After dinner, or what these people treated as if it were dinner, they all went indoors and Kurtis told Dale that he was off to the lookout post. Dale broke out some of the blow he was peddling, which he doled out in healthy lines for Char and Gary. It was powerful stuff. Gary felt his heart rate quicken, and he could sense Char's heat from across the cracked concrete kitchen counter where they stood under a chandelier with half the lightbulbs out. She added to the menu by bringing out a baggie that apparently she or Dale or Kurtis had labeled SWAMP WEED, marijuana that Gary figured they'd grown on the property. A radio was on the counter, and they found a station that didn't totally suck. There was no air conditioning, but Gary's hair, considering how often she kept glancing at it, was holding strong.

"You're stayin' in the back room, Boss," Dale said. "Ain't got no water inside, but we got a well and a bucket out back if you wanna wash your ass. Other'n that, we'll get you on the road bright an' early. Char, take him to his room."

Gary was hazy from the evening's revelry. Char moved like a cat, fast yet seemingly in slow motion. The weird mix of chemicals in Gary had left him with little if any will. He followed her down the hall, his entire body pulsing with coke, Swamp Weed, bottled Bud, and the thought of Char's legs and arms and lips. He was a hundred feet tall and he could walk through the walls of the house if he wanted. Everything inside him hummed. Char let off an odor like the trees and the air and the vines in the swampy jungle. She opened the door and then grabbed his hand to lead him in. She closed the door behind them and then, with one remarkably deft move, grabbed Gary's ass. It was on. There was only a mattress on the floor without any sheets, but that's where they fell. Char was a hungry beast, gnawing at his lips, tearing at him and his clothing. Gary couldn't decide if her breath was rancid or entrancing—he bit back at her, tasting the meat they'd eaten for dinner. She was Corry when he and Corry had done lines. She was Marina and every other woman he'd ever done it with.

He pulled his face away from hers to say, "What about—"

She sucked at his mouth, smothering him, taking away his voice. He struggled to free himself and turn his head so he could speak.

"—your brothers?"

Her assault continued without answer. For a brief second, Gary imagined Kurtis and Dale barging in with pistols drawn. He wanted his .45 but with each split second he wanted Char more. She had not taken off her boots. He could not get inside her fast enough.

He was not sure how long they were together, only that everything they'd done was like a storm that knocked things over and drenched everyone and refused to let up. At daybreak, Dale was in the room, kicking the side of the mattress, telling Gary to get his lazy ass up. Char had disappeared. Gary wished he had Corry's hairspray—he'd be doing everyone a favor if he blew the place up.

Outside, his head throbbing, he followed both brothers, who gave him a truck with a huge-ass trailer that could haul the bulldozer back to their place. Then Dale, after handing him a map with the route blazed in black marker, led him out to the highway. Gary was a sweaty, filthy, skanky mess. He grabbed his bag from the back of the Z and tossed it into the cab of the truck, and Dale, without seeming to care at all about the bag, got in his pickup and led Gary to the highway, then saluted Gary after Gary had glanced at the map and stepped on the gas to go ahead on his own.

En route to the auction, Gary stopped off at a motel to shower and change his clothes. He had his gun. He had Corry's hairspray. He was ready.

At the auction, he picked up the inventory sheet and found the vehicle. It was a stout little tank, over 60,000 pounds. The bidding wasn't even close—he was using someone else's money, cash, so the buying was done quickly. In fact, he had some cash left to return to Frick and Frack, so he held back two grand for himself for a buyer's fee and expenses, which he

placed in the inner pocket of his sport coat. He signed everything with the auctioneer and was the proud owner of a dozer.
He picked up the bill of sale, and the house crew hooked the
rig to the back of the truck, and he was off to meet Dale in
the parking lot of a Kmart.

"Nice work, my friend," was all Dale said there. "Now let's
git that baby home."

For one pleasant moment, Dale was a big toothless grin.
Gary smiled. They had to respect him now. He had done
what they couldn't do. He handed Dale the remainder of the
bid money but he kept the bill of sale in his pocket with his
take. Once in his truck, he pulled the Gold Cup .45 from his
bag and settled it into the back waistband of his pants, inside
his sport jacket. He had seen many bad asses do this on
TV—tuck a gun into the back of their pants. He and Dale
followed a new labyrinthine course back to their base, so he'd
never be able to retrace the way to the house. He needed to
get home. He would update Corry on everything he did and
he'd find a way to be alone with Marina. He would drive up
in the Jag and show it to The Duke of The Deal, show him
what he'd done and tell him how he'd wheeled-and-dealed
and battled it out with lowlifes to bring home the prize. Yes,
he needed to get home.

For now, though, he and Dale drove through the country-
side, grinding over the dirt roads, but nothing looked familiar
until they found the opening in the brush that led to the
house.

"*Welcome home, lover boy*" was what Gary heard from above
this time.

Kurtis was again looking down from his perch. Gary now
noticed that a ladder had been nailed to the side of the tree.

Dale unhitched the gate and drove in, and Gary followed along the leaf-walled path that led to the house.

"Okay, my friend," Dale said. "We gonna celebrate a little. Let me bust you out some product. Pure as it gets. Thunder snow. Char, you got something cooking out there? We gonna celebrate. Hoo-wee, got us a goddamned plow *and* a dozer. Makes me wanna start workin' right away."

Char walked through the open back door. She brought in cooked meat that looked like steak on an actual plate, and it was not a paper plate. Gary looked at her and winked, hoping for something furtive in return, maybe a quick smirk letting him know that he'd been the king of kings last night, but she set the platter on the concrete counter without looking up.

"Way ahead of you."

Those, he realized, were the first words she'd spoken around him. He wasn't sure whether she'd said them to him or to Dale, but her voice was low and swampy, and her eyes bore straight through him. He wanted to be back on top of her, tearing off the rest of the torn tank top she was wearing but didn't seem to notice was there.

"Love the celebration, Dale," he said. "But our business isn't over."

Dale looked at Gary. Helped himself to a piece of meat with his hands.

"Sure, it is. We needed us a bush-beater, and now we got one."

"Yeah, but I don't have the Jag."

"You'll get the Jag."

"When? I haven't even seen it."

"I told you we had it stashed somewheres else."

Gary felt his Gold Cup .45 tucked nose-down into the back of his pants.

"Then you need to go get it, Boss," he said. "You don't get a bill of sale to the plow until I get the Jag."

Dale laughed. Before Gary's mind could register all of what was going on, Dale dropped his chunk of meat on the floor and had his pistol out and pointed at him.

"Bill a sale? You serious, city boy? What the fuck I care 'bout no bill a sale? None a these vehicles out there got no paperwork. You can take that bill and wipe your ass with it."

Gary looked at Dale, whom he considered a fool. How could anyone say that? Of course they needed a bill of sale—how could they prove they owned the dozer without one? It was the whole point of him coming down to Florida. And the gun—what had he said to have this hillbilly dipshit pull a gun on him?

"Get off it, Dale," he said. "Of course you need a bill of sale. And a title and registration."

"Dumbfuck city boy. Don't need no title or registration for no dozer."

"Well, okay, maybe you don't. Hey, I generally deal in cars, not bulldozers. Come on, just put down the gun."

"Fuck you, bitch. You think you holdin' any cards here? *Huh*? We done with you. We don't need you no more. Don't nobody even know you out here."

Dale's eyes looked double their normal size, like his eyelids could no longer cover them. Sweat broke on Gary's forehead. His arms and legs stung.

"But—"

"Ain't no *but* here, boy. You a stupid fuck is all there is.

Lemme axe you a question. You know how many assholes like you out there in them trees? Huh? Just bones left. Where you think we get all these cars from? You gone, man. You think you're still here, but you gone."

Gone? What in hell was this inbred talking about? He and Gary were both right here, in this shitty house. It was time for the Gold Cup .45 to make its appearance. Gary moved the sides of his jacket to place his hands on his hips, to both ready himself and to make the reach to the pistol easier.

"Char."

She was behind Gary and had his gun before he'd even considered turning to face her.

"We seen that gun," Dale said. "And you kin fuck Char all you want—hell, who don't—but she's a sister to us, you little shit weasel. You really think you come down here and gonna fuck with us? Huh? You think we stupid, right? Huh? You so fuckin' smart. There a couple dozen a you out there."

Dale pointed his pistol out into the jungle. Gary wanted to turn around to look at Char, to see her silvery blue eyes, to detect some affection or recognition, but Dale's lunatic mood had him frozen other than a throbbing ache in his gut.

"What, what are you saying?"

"What the fuck you think I said? *Huh?* You smarter than me. What you think I said?"

"Look, Dale, all I want is the Jag. Get me to the Jag and I'm out of here."

"Jag. You ain't gonna be needin' no Jag."

"Dale, c'mon, what are you doing? Why, why are you saying this? I think you're making a mistake."

"News flash, son. You the one made the mistake."

Gary looked as searingly as he could at Dale. Dale had to be joking. Dale, he thought, would lower the gun and break out into his toothless hucklebuck laugh, then hand Gary the keys to the Jag, and off Gary would go, back to Detroit, loaded down with pretty much only some barely believable stories to tell. Out of the corner of his eye he saw Char circle around to his side, pointing his Colt at him, her eyes burning through him no problem.

"Listen, here's the paperwork for the plow," he said to Dale, and he reached for the inside pocket of his sports coat, but Char stopped his hand by aiming his Gold Cup .45 at it. "I'll write you out a new bill saying you bought it from me," he continued. "I got all kinds of official receipts in my bag. Heck, I won't even charge you for buying the vehicle."

"Now what you say?" Dale cackled. "*Charge* me? Here, give Char that bill a sale and that cash you got in change."

With his .45 still in Char's hand and still on him, Gary reached into his pocket. Without facing his face, Char took the bill and the cash. The ache in his gut lifted—maybe they were now willing to listen to some reason, some good old Detroit used car reason.

"Okay, now count what's in that there bid money," Gary said. "You remember how much you give him to start with, right?"

Char nodded.

"Go ahead and count it out."

Char looked over at Gary for a scant split-second. She thumbed through the money quickly, her lips moving silently as she counted.

"Two thousand light."

"Two thousand light?"

"That was my buyer's fee," Gary said. "You can't expect . . ."

"You fuckin' think anybody was gonna pay you something?" Dale said. "Roger right, you a greedy-ass little pig. Now I know you twice as dumb as you look."

Gary's eyes tried to plead with Char. Her eyes didn't meet his but bit his face. The previous night did not exist for her. He was on this island alone. This island where all he could do was realize why Roger had told these brothers that he'd been greedy: because he'd been skimming a pound or two here and there from the bags stored under the front seat in the truck Javier drove.

"Look, you got your dozer," he said to Dale. "I'll give you back the buyer's fee. Shit, I'll even throw in the Jag."

Dale couldn't contain himself. "The Jag! Hell, you think the Jag *around* anymore? You *retarded*, man. Ain't no Jag. What you think you bought that dozer with?"

No Jag, Gary thought. *No Jag?* How could there be no Jag? It was the whole point of coming down. He felt like he was seeing himself in some kind of show on TV after the six o'clock news.

"But . . . you can't kill me. They can trace me."

"Who gonna trace what? How that, smart guy? Ain't nobody at the auction gonna say they sold us no Cat. You done bought it. Everybody at the auction seen you and only you. City boy show up all alone and buy hisself a dozer and then leave. All official, in your name, you drove off with it in some truck can't nobody trace and won't nobody ever see again. Didn't nobody there see me, or Kurtis, or Char—didn't nobody there see anyone but you."

Gary could feel nothing. Not in his hands or his feet or his crotch or his hair.

Then all he could feel was himself saying, "What's that mean?"

"What that means," Dale said, "is ain't nobody in a lifetime around here know where you at. You drifted in, you drifted out. And ain't nobody near enough to this house you're in, or this acreage you're on, to hear nothing or know nothing about you being here."

Gary was holding his hands out now, open, begging. He needed a card to play, any card, even if it was just an unmatched deuce.

"Roger knows," he said.

"Who the fuck you think wanted you down here, shitbird?" Dale cackled. "*You a pain in Roger's ass!* Don't pay your bills to him, take cuts on the sly from what you ain't done shit to git, a greedy-ass pansy from day one till your last. He already got hisself three other mules who'll work for half a what he promised your stupidshit face. And who don't *skim.* Who *buy* their blow from him, like anyone who respect a man with balls the size a his. Anyhow you know too much and you too dumb to know it. You see, we got us the perfect circle here. We take the bodies out to the woods, the critters eat the bodies, we eat the critters, it all goes round and round. Shit, sometimes we don't even got to wait on the critters—heh, hope you enjoyed your barbecue. Meantime, we send product up north, we get paid, and now we got a dozer so we gonna have our own airstrip, we gonna cut out more middlemen and make even more cash than we do. Time and again, though, we in the circle run into a bump like you. But then, see, then you and them other bumps get to be part of the circle, so it's all good."

Dale flicked the nose of the gun out toward the back of the house with new resolve. Circle. Gary felt so outside of himself that he couldn't quite put it together. What kind of circle was this guy talking about? With critters, and eating, and middlemen?

"Let's go, Boss," Dale said. "Enough talk. We can take a walk or we can do this right here. I'd rather take the walk—less messy."

Javier was right, Gary thought. These people were crazy. Crazy-*loco*. Because Gary had done exactly what Roger had told him to do. But here Dale was, extending his arm, the one aiming the pistol at Gary, so Gary held up his arms in surrender. As they headed through the mudroom for the back door, he caught himself in a cracked mirror on the wall and saw that his hair was fading. He wished he had that can of hairspray. As soon as he'd roll into Detroit with the Jag he'd pick up Marina and hit a club, and as soon as they'd bone at her place he'd show his father the Jag and act as if bringing it to his father had been no big deal. But for now, he would take this walk, take a little more time to talk sense into this brain-dead Dale. Maybe, after Marina but before he'd see his dad, he'd swing the Jag home to show it to Corry also, and maybe she'd get a kick out of it and they'd do it before she headed off to work. For now, though, this Dale guy would certainly listen to Gary, then cut a deal. After all, Gary could always call his father, Chuck Reindel, The Duke of The Deal, who, being the millionaire he was, could buy Dale and Kurtis and Char a *fleet* of bulldozers and more land than they needed if they wanted that, too. Not to mention Corry could now broadcast any story she wanted to tell, especially stories about law-breaking losers who thought they were bigger than their grimy britches, and she could do so *live*, on the air of a network affiliate—and, really, really, if anyone ever really thought about it, who would ever want to mess with that?

"Keep moving, Boss," Dale said, and Gary felt the unforgiving tip of the gun press against the back of his scalp. "Keep it going, we're almost there."

ALL OF THIS IS WATER

DAVID EBENBACH

I guess it makes a creepy kind of sense that I was in a traffic jam—an inexplicable Sunday traffic jam—when I got the news. My little car was surrounded by SUVs and minivans, me sitting there on Massachusetts Avenue, squeezing the steering wheel and worrying about being late to pick my brother up at Union Station and thinking why does something like this *always* have to happen, when it came over the radio in soft tones: two days earlier, September 12, 2008, the writer David Foster Wallace. Suicide.

It hit me like a smack in the head. I snapped my eyes to the radio on the dashboard, like I was going to see an explanation there, or maybe somehow my brother's face reacting to the news, and though I was only looking down for a moment, it was long enough that I missed the chance to tap my brakes in time; I bumped the Jeep in front of me. Not hard, but definitely a bump. And the guy, in a banker's button-down Oxford shirt on a Sunday morning, got out of the Jeep fast. He was surrounded by traffic but he ignored it. Came around to the back. More cautiously, I got out, too. Into the heat, the press of metal.

"I'm really sorry," I said, a sort of trembling in my chest. "I was a half-second late with the brakes."

The guy was bent over, examining his bumper closely. It looked untouched to me, particularly for a Jeep, but my car was a mess of scratches, so I may not have had the sensitivity. Everything on all sides was humidity and vehicular grind. I could palpably feel the anger of the people who were now stuck behind us. The horns were starting up.

The guy straightened up. "It looks okay," he said, wiping his palms against each other as if to clean them, even though he hadn't touched anything. He looked at me for the first time, shook his head. "You got lucky."

"I know," I said. I must have been more thrown than I realized, because then I said, "Hey—do you know who David Foster Wallace was?"

"What?"

"He's a writer. He was a writer. He spoke at my brother's college graduation three years ago."

Before I could say anything else, the guy stepped closer to me. Too close. The tremble in my chest became a buzz. A horn blared behind us. "Listen," he said, like he had something urgent to tell me. "I don't know what you're talking about, but you need to get back in your car. And when you drive the damned thing, pay attention." And then he turned and walked off, got back into his Jeep.

Burning, I glanced at my own bumper—all the bumps and scrapes looked familiar enough—and then got back in my car, sighed, and put the car in drive. By this point, the radio had already moved on from the story. Ahead of me, the Jeep rolled forward, and I did, too. It was very strange to still be right behind him.

Here's the reason I say it made sense to get the news while I was in a traffic jam: Traffic is what David Foster Wallace talked about when I saw him at that commencement. This was Kenyon College, that little woodsy outpost of New York City that's somehow in Central Ohio and is also the place where my little brother spent five very difficult years of his life—difficult years for him and for everyone else—and then finally managed to graduate. I can still see him shambling across the stage toward his diploma, all bone and uncertainty.

Anyway, I didn't know then how famous Wallace was—I'd been a sociology major at Ohio State—but I listened to what he had to say. It turned out to be worth it. He talked about being stuck in line and stuck in traffic and maybe generally stuck, and he said that when you're in a crappy situation like that, you have a choice, a choice as to whether you just go on autopilot and see yourself as the put-upon center of the universe or whether you see things with more perspective. That has really stayed with me, the idea that you have a more generous option, even if I don't always make that choice. And the other thing he said—he said it a couple of times—was that it might save your life, basically. He said that if you made the wrong choice you might end up blowing your brains out. That's what he said, the guy who had just now, according to the radio, killed himself.

I was wondering now, sort of feverishly, about my brother. He had been an English major, and was in fact a big Wallace fan, if I remembered right. I was wondering if he had heard the news. The littlest things—and this might not be so little, for him—could send him careening off in a bad direction. Sometimes very, very bad.

When I got the chance, I pulled into a different lane so I could at least be behind someone besides the obnoxious Jeep guy. Sometimes that's all you can do.

• • •

Finally I got to Union Station. I parked in front of the Postal Museum, where there were always spots, and walked the block to the station, texting my brother on the way. *Coming. Almost there. Where are you?*

Center Café, he wrote back. *Right inside.*

Okay.

You couldn't tell how a person was doing from a text, of course. Anyway, I looked for an opening and then jogged across First Street toward the broad, white palace of an edifice that is DC's train station. Everything about this town shouting, *I'm significant!*

Like I say, I didn't know David Foster Wallace when he spoke, and I'd barely gotten to know his work since—I got like fifty pages into *Infinite Jest* and only managed to read three of the stories in *Brief Interviews with Hideous Men*, and everything I read seemed more or less to be on the subject of how smart David Foster Wallace is—or was, I guess. But his commencement speech came during a very complicated moment in the life of my family. I was sort of flailing, two years out of school myself, but more important, my brother was only a few months out of a brief but intense hospitalization. A psych ward hospitalization. And so he was graduating, and it was a moment of calm and possibility, but all of us were still on edge, that same edge we'd been on for a long time with him.

Inside the train station, everything was as dramatic as you'd expect from seeing the outside—grand arched ceilings and a vast shining marble floor ready for a royal family's ballroom dance. And right at the center, a two-story café with chairs and tables arrayed around it, mostly empty in the lull before lunch. After a moment of swiveling my head around, I spotted him waving at me with energy from one of the little tables, his light hair flopping unbecomingly. One of the reasons I didn't see him right away, I realized, was because I had been expecting him to be alone, when actually there was someone else at the table with him. I waved and headed over there.

My brother—Jon was his name—jumped up grinning as I approached him, bony as ever, and gave me a big, almost dramatic hug. *Okay*, I thought to myself. *Upswing.* There was a smell of martinis coming up off the table.

"Aaron," he said. "This is Niklas."

He said it in that kind of way, so as I turned to shake Niklas's hand, I knew that I was, for the first time ever, meeting a boyfriend. Wow. I had heard about other boyfriends over the years, but they were more ideas than people; they came and went and none of them had ever materialized in person. Until now. I almost actually said "Wow" but luckily didn't. Niklas stood up for the occasion, very tall, and gave my hand a good shake—"Nice to meet you," we both said—before taking his hand back and running it through his schoolboy haircut, thin and straight and blond, and then tucking it into the pocket of his trench coat, a trench coat over jeans and a T-shirt that read *Magers & Quinn Booksellers.* And then I realized that I was scanning him like a police detective and I stopped.

"Welcome to DC," I said, looking from him to Jon and back.

"This is homecoming for Niklas," Jon said.

"Really?"

Niklas nodded, almost bashfully. "My parents were connected with the Finnish embassy when I was a small child," he said, and I heard a slight accent there, the words a little springy.

"The Finnish embassy? Wow. It's beautiful." I had seen it a bunch of times, because some mornings I took my run down Massachusetts Avenue, despite all the cars. The building was modern and sleek, a lot of glass, but with ivy, too, climbing up on either side of the front door.

Niklas nodded again, though he said, "It was in a different facility. Not on Massachusetts but New Mexico Avenue."

"Ah," I said. I had put my hands in my pockets. "The new one is beautiful. You should see it."

"Yes," he said.

"Wait," Jon said, with that focused look in his eye. I knew this look well. "Completely," he said. "We should go see it. We should go see it today."

Niklas appeared taken aback. "You mean we should just go to the embassy?"

"Sure," Jon said. His voice echoed a little under the big ceiling. "Why not? It'll be great."

"I think there's a photography exhibit there," I said. It was easier to just go with Jon's impulses a lot of the time. "I'm pretty sure I heard about a photography exhibit. They're always doing art shows."

"That's fun, right?" Jon said, half-standing, as if set to lead us off at that very moment.

"Well, I guess we could," Niklas said. His face was hard to read.

I checked my watch. "Do you want to eat some lunch first?"

Jon looked over at Niklas. "Maybe we could just get an appetizer to go? You don't have a thing about eating in your car, do you? Because then we could just get moving."

"It would probably improve the car," I said.

. . .

At Jon's awkward insistence, Niklas sat up front with me, but Jon ignored the seatbelt in back, hovering in the space between the two front seats, nudging and prodding our conversation along. His mood was very bright. And so, on the way to the embassy, as the car took on the smell of the melted cheese in the small quesadilla we were all splitting, I talked about my job at the Institute for Poverty Research, and Niklas shared memories of Washington, DC. I discovered that he was my age and a web designer and had been living in New York for three years. Also he was a nice guy, if maybe a little somber. Meanwhile I kept the radio off; I didn't know if they were going to cycle back through the David Foster Wallace story or not.

And I was tired.

My brother had been in town for a half-hour and I was already tired.

Finally we got to the embassy and parked around the corner, and Jon led the way up to the front door. Niklas was close behind. He had never been there before, but still—it must have been like home, in a way.

A slender woman with steel-gray hair greeted us at the door. She was dressed something like a real estate agent, in a black pantsuit. "Welcome," she said, smiling briskly. When Jon elbowed him, Niklas said something complicated and not-English in return, and her smile opened up into almost a grin. She said something complicated herself, and Niklas said something back, waving his hand in our direction, after which she said something to him and then, to us, said, "You're all quite welcome." She stepped back from the door, hesitated, bowed us in. It was the first time in my life that knowing a Finnish person had made me a VIP.

We went through a metal detector and then inside to a room where we would be hanging up our coats if we had any. "Did you tell her about your parents?" Jon whispered to Niklas.

"Just that I'm Finnish," he murmured.

"She's going to be really into your parents," Jon said.

Niklas smiled a kind of smile.

The woman spoke to us in English, but mainly she was speaking to Niklas, who told her we were there to see the photographs. "Oh, it's quite an impressive exhibit. I'll take you downstairs and tell you more about it. So, you've been here before?" she asked, and then was astonished and excited that we hadn't.

"I've been to the old embassy on New Mexico Avenue," Niklas said.

"Oh, that little place," she said. "This is much nicer."

At that point she took us down the curving wooden stairs—everything was wood, buttery finished wood—into the main space, which was huge and open and lined along the back with glass so that you could see out into the forest behind the building, and so that the room was full of light. All through the space were what looked like portable walls, and there were large framed photos on them—photos of, apparently, girls wearing beautiful dresses against backdrops of woods and snow. The whole effect was pretty arresting. It was only the three of us—four, with the woman—there to absorb it all.

Standing at the foot of the stairs, she began an obviously practiced introduction to the photography. "This exhibit is quite a famous one in Finland," she said, "and has toured some of Europe as well. The photographer is Miina Savolainen, and the subjects are girls from a children's home in Finland." She put a finger up in the air—key point coming. "But don't think about poor, sad orphans. The title is *The Loveliest Girl in the World* for a reason. Savolainen put the girls in beautiful clothing, with almost a fairy-tale setting in many of the cases. The effect is lovely. Of course—" here she smiled particularly at Niklas—"all of the locations are in Finland."

We all smiled back.

No one was saying anything, so I said, "Thank you."

"I will let you enjoy the exhibit," she said, clasping her hands together and taking a step backward.

We wandered through the space then, our attention divided between the countless green leaves behind the glass and the photographs on the walls. And my attention was further divided as I trailed behind Jon and Niklas and their murmurings. They were an interesting pair; you could see intimacy in the way they held hands and leaned in to each other, but Niklas had a calm about it, his voice steady, his face serene, while Jon was bouncing on the balls of his feet. Definite upswing.

The photos, meanwhile, were worth attention themselves. They *were* like fairy tales, in fact, though a little like Grimm fairy tales in that the tone of the photos was dark, the greens of the forests in them very deep, and the dresses, though like something a Cinderella would wear, weren't pristine, either. And the girls didn't have the polish of American girls. In one picture, a girl was in a satiny golden dress while sitting on the lip of a very small waterfall, sitting in the shallow water, and her face, which was round but still a little hard, said, *Get me out of this waterfall.*

But mostly I watched Jon and Niklas as they bent toward

one photograph after another. First Niklas bent, and then Jon. Jon reached out and almost touched several of the pictures.

A few minutes in, the woman returned, this time bearing tote bags that said *FINLAND*. "There's a book about the exhibit, and another about the embassy building," she said, handing out the bags, "and a booklet explaining some interesting facts about Finland. Also a schedule of events here, in case you might come back."

"Swag," Jon said.

She smiled. "Yes, exactly." She was, I was glad to see, very comfortable with Jon and Niklas holding hands, reminding me that the Scandinavian countries were more enlightened.

Then she swooped in on Niklas, to ask him some questions in Finnish. Jon and I let them hang back, and went on together.

"Well?" he said. "What do you think?"

"He seems great," I said.

He grinned. "I meant the exhibit."

"Ah—" I started.

"Oh, I'll take compliments on Niklas, too. I can tell you that he's fantastic, basically a dream guy. *Very* stabilizing."

We both looked back at Niklas; he was explaining something to the woman, who was listening intently. He straightened his posture, apparently nervous for the first time since I'd met him.

"Is he telling you about his parents?" Jon called over to her.

"It's okay," Niklas said a little brusquely, waving the question away.

Jon *hmmph*ed. I turned and looked at another photograph. In this one, there was a whole, broad, snowy landscape, no trees, mountains off in the distance, just snow everywhere except this small dark space at the center of the photograph, an opening of dark water. And, standing in the water, a girl in a dark ballroom gown.

"You should tell her about your parents—she'll be excited," I heard Jon insist. "Seriously." And, before Niklas had much of a chance to be forthcoming: "They were part of the ambassadorial staff here. Well, the other place."

There was a burst of excited Finnish from the woman, and then, after a moment, some words back from Niklas. I looked closely at the girl in the photograph, at her dark hair, at the little bit of her face that you could see as she looked down into the water. It must have been freezing.

Then I turned around, because everything had gone quiet behind me. I saw the woman frowning at Niklas. I saw Niklas's red face.

"I will leave you to the exhibit," she said curtly, and then she turned and went back up the stairs.

"What happened?" I said.

"Yeah," Jon said. "What was that?"

"I would be ready to go, if you are," Niklas said quietly.

"I don't understand," Jon said, his face reddening. "What happened?"

"I would rather not talk about it," Niklas said.

"Not talk about it? What do you mean, 'rather not talk about it'?"

I could hear Niklas breathe out through his nose. "My parents didn't leave the embassy under the best of circumstances."

"The best of circumstances? What circumstances?" Jon's voice was too loud for the space, and it was bouncing off everything.

"I would rather not talk about it," Niklas said again.

"Are you seriously going to do that?" Jon said. "I can't stand that."

I stepped forward. "Let's go," I said. "We can just go."

Jon laughed a sharp laugh. "I literally don't understand what's going on."

"Come on," I said. I touched Jon on the back and ushered everyone toward the stairs, which we climbed slowly, Jon repeating his questions and only getting silence for an answer.

"This is *lovely*," Jon said. At the top, he seemed to suddenly notice the tote bag on his shoulder. He took it in his hand and held it at arm's length, a sour look on his face. And then he yelled, "*Finnish warmth*," and flung the bag over the railing.

I think I gasped. The bag tumbled down through the air and smacked into an exhibit wall, very close to a photograph, which shook as the bag fell to the floor, spilling its books and pamphlets out on the floor.

Niklas grabbed my brother by his arm. "*Jon. Are you insane?*" Niklas was a lot taller than Jon, and the picture was slightly menacing.

But I also knew that my brother could be unpredictable, and that he might not be done being unpredictable yet. At the moment, he was visibly astonished. "*You're* angry at *me?*"

"Let's go," I said. I put my hands on both their backs and steered them forcefully toward the coatroom. I couldn't tell you how much of my life I had spent trying to steer Jon in some direction or other.

The woman was there, looking alarmed. "What happened?" she asked.

"Nothing," I said. "Nothing. A bag fell. I'm sorry."

That seemed to trigger Niklas, because he let his tote bag

slump to the floor near the exit. Only then did I get us all through the door and out into the day. I noticed that I was still wearing my own tote bag. "Jesus," I said. "Come on."

Nobody said anything else until we got back in the car, and then it was me again. "Okay. What are we doing now?"

"I just don't understand what happened," Jon said. He was sitting shotgun now. "What circumstances? Did they *do* something?"

I waited a second, but Niklas didn't respond.

"I'm trying to *help*," Jon said to him.

"Okay, then," I said. "Maybe it would be good if we ate something. We're probably all hungry for lunch."

"Fine," Jon said, his arms crossed. "Fine."

"I just—" I started.

"Ethiopian food," he said.

I was so startled by his terseness that I immediately started driving, and only started to think it through a block later—where we were going, how to get there. We'd want to go back east toward Adams Morgan. Fine. Whatever.

Jon turned on the radio as I figured out the route. First take 34th to Garfield, then I figured Cleveland. Somebody on the radio was talking about natural resources. "What is this, the news?" Jon said. "Is this what you listen to all day?"

I was so discombobulated that I didn't even think about the radio for a second, and then it occurred to me: David Foster Wallace. They could mention David Foster Wallace.

"Oh, hey," I said, "why don't you change that?" I said it a little more urgently than I meant to, my hand already reaching for the knob.

He smacked it away. "I want to hear this."

"Jon, no—I just—" I reached for the knob again.

He smacked my hand away again. "You don't want me to hear about natural gas?"

"It's not that," I said. "I just think, you know, what else is on?"

This time he didn't smack my hand; this time he wrapped his own hand around it and held on.

"Wait," he said.

I looked over at him. I could see his mind going, and I returned my eyes quickly to the traffic in front of us.

"What don't you want me hearing about?" he said, but not really to me. He was thinking it through, still holding onto my hand. And when I looked back at him again, I saw him get it. "Oh," he said, staring at me closely. "*Really*? Yes. Oh."

"What?" I said.

"Big brother," he said. "I already know."

"What do you know?"

"You don't need to protect me," he said, giving my hand a squeeze.

"What do you know?"

From the backseat, Niklas said, almost in a groan, "Can we just go get something to eat?"

Jon gazed ahead, nodded, and let go of my hand. I put it back on the wheel and kept driving.

· · ·

It only took us a few minutes to get to Adams Morgan, and the radio station didn't mention David Foster Wallace on the way. I was relieved; I still wasn't sure whether Jon actually knew or whether he was just pretending to know in order to trick me into revealing it. I wasn't sure about anything. I found

us a spot on 18th Street and parked the car, the radio cutting
off into to silence.

Jon turned to me, his eyes intent. "I'm starving," he said.

"Okay," I said.

The restaurant was a kind of run-down place, like an old
house that had barely been turned into a restaurant, but I'd
been there before several times and the food was great. We got
seated at a rectangular table near the window, almost the only
people in there. If it had been a house, it felt like the empty
nest kind, its remaining inhabitants scattered.

We were still in this strangely quiet, almost funereal mode.
It felt like a lot of that was emanating from Niklas, who wasn't
calm and assured at all anymore and was instead giving off
heavy gloom in some seemingly irretrievable way. But we ordered a vegetarian combination platter for three and made our
quiet comments about the surroundings as we waited. "Do
you think the family that owns this place lives here?" Jon
asked, looking up at the ceiling as though he might see them
there. "Like, is this their house?"

One by one, we each went off to wash our hands; we were
going to be eating with our hands and we wanted them clean.
It was strange, though, that we did it one at a time.

Then, after a little while, the food came, one big platter
covered in injera, with circles of food spotted all over it. Each
food was there three times, so that we each had our own. Len-
tils, chickpea puree, cabbage and carrots—all kinds of good
stuff. I hadn't realized just how hungry I was until I saw it.

"Wow. This is great," I said, and the woman smiled a warm
smile before leaving us with a basket of more injera for us to
use in scooping everything up.

"Exactly," Jon said. "This is exactly what I need."

Niklas leaned forward, and I glanced at him. Shyly, he said, "I'm pretty hungry, too."

I caught Jon's eye then. He glanced over at Niklas and back at me. On my brother's face was, *Hey—what are you going to do? Nobody's perfect.* And then his face changed, just a little, and I saw what he was really saying: he did know. He didn't have to say the name David Foster Wallace; he knew David Foster Wallace was dead, and that it had been suicide. I saw it. And I saw that it wasn't, in fact, such a huge deal, this one particular piece of news.

This was not the last time I would see my brother. Not even close. That year would end up being a decent one overall, though Niklas wouldn't stay in the picture for too much longer. Jon and I were in touch a lot for the rest of the year. He visited me and I visited him. And then there was a bad year, and even then I saw him several times, though each time he was skinnier and more agitated. And even after all that, there were a couple Skype calls, the picture and sound breaking up the whole time, but I did see him. And a phone call. There was a phone call after that. Just one, and what he said on that call meant that there was no way I could get to him before it was too late. *I just wanted to let you know,* he said on the phone, his voice stony. He knew there was nothing I could do; that was, of course, his plan. Even the police, I discovered that night, would be too late to stop him.

But this day—this was well before that. And so it's strange, maybe, that I remember it so well. That I come back to it so often. Which I do—I come back to it very often. When I run, sometimes, though I don't go down Massachusetts Avenue anymore because I don't live in the same neighborhood anymore. Or when I'm eating, or just unexpectedly when I'm in the hallway of my apartment or outside, or certainly whenever I'm in traffic.

Maybe I remember that day because it was a moment of shared perspective. My brother and I looked into each other's eyes and knew that we were both thinking the same thing. It wasn't happy, exactly, both thinking about what David Foster Wallace had done—but for the moment I didn't feel burdened. And, more important, I didn't feel that Jon was burdened. I thought that, despite everything, here we were in this restaurant, and incredible smells were rolling up off the table—rich, dark, intense smells—and they were holding us in a cloud together.

"Should we eat?" I asked him, and Niklas nodded in the periphery of my version, and Jon smiled and breathed out and said, "Hell, yes."

HABITAT

SUSAN TACENT

An hour or more into weeding, Margaret caught sight of a pokeweed plant that had grown over three feet tall. It was handsome, obviously happy, and, from what she'd read, poisonous. She wrapped her hands around the thick stem and yanked. Its green top, heavy with leaf, broke away. If she left the root the whole thing would be back in a week, so she dug hard with her fingers until she freed the root, thick too and pale as a parsnip. She was halfway to the compost pile when something caused her to cry out and pain sent her down to her knees. The gardening claw's longest tine, curved past the others like a nasty middle finger, had gone through her flip-flop, pinning it to her foot. A half inch of its rounded tip had disappeared into the fleshy part beneath the ball of that foot. She tilted the claw until it came away. It was made of tempered steel and the steel was rusty. Moss grows thicker on the north side of trees. If you're lost in the woods this is knowledge that should help you.

The rickety black pickup was all she had because earlier and for no apparent reason she'd been so cranky that Jack had taken the car, fleeing to the park with their daughter. It was low on gas but started right away and she pressed the gas pedal with her toes only and eased the truck out of the driveway.

She could stop and slam on the horn if she felt paralysis setting in. A woman frozen to her steering wheel, horn blaring, drivers peering inside as they tried to get around her.

She passed the drugstore, the gas station, three traffic lights. She wasn't in shock, she didn't think. She was just hurt and they would help her. The claw was in the passenger seat, in a brown paper bag. She couldn't exactly remember putting it there. She'd brought it along, she figured, in the hope that they'd look at it and say, oh that old thing, don't worry about it. Kiss the boo-boo, chide the claw, send her home.

Over a building in the middle of a row of stores, large cut-out letters spelled *Urgent Medical Care*. Red. Appropriate. And a fat purple caduceus. If you're in the woods and need food, skunk cabbage can be eaten but should be boiled five or six times first.

Then she was inside, the paper bag cradled in her arm, and she wondered at the receptionist who was briefing her, if somehow this young woman with very red skin and a blondish-green tinge to her hastily upswept hair, thought, *Isn't your life great enough, you indecently ungrateful thing? You have a husband and a child and a house and a garden and almost enough time to do what you want once in a while—why do you need to be coddled by us?*—and was deliberately taking her time, typing her responses slowly into the computer rather than rushing Margaret in to see the medics or doctors or whatever they have at 8 a.m.-to-7 p.m. seven days a week fast-food health places. McFix. Hey! Margaret suddenly wanted to scream. Where's the *urgent*?

There were questions whose answers went on the forms. 09/14/77. Rhode Island. Married. Healthmate. Gardening. No (allergies). No (medications). No (haven't been here before, can't really believe I'm here now). Margaret could see herself reflected back in the mirrored disk to the left and above the receptionist's cubicle. Even distorted, she looked like herself, she thought, like if you met her for the first time, she'd make sense to you. Margaret Flood. Around for a while. The lines and folds to prove it. A quiet face. Darkish frizzy shoulder-length hair she trimmed herself (poorly, but not poorly enough to matter). College graduate. A few long-term relationships before her husband, a few long-term jobs before Lucy was born. A decent sense of humor, and—

"Do you smoke?"

"No."

"Drink?"

Margaret shook her head, then said wryly, "I garden." She felt the irony thin and disappear.

"Garden," she said again, and she took the gardening tool from the bag slowly, menacingly, hoping the woman heard scary movie music, ominous and shrill, when she beheld: the claw. The woman, whose name tag said Patti, did blanch. What would Patti do if faced with the pokeweed instead? Margaret, brandishing a healthy specimen of poke, the plant throbbing with its noxious secret message. *This*, I ingested some of *this*, okay? Now what are you going to do? Patti?

"That must have hurt," Patti said.

"It's frustrating and stupid. I shouldn't have left it face up under a pile of, you know, weeds." Her own voice sounded as matter-of-fact as Patti's. As if they were at a touristy island resort, everything very bright and not so expensive as to be tasteful because, frankly, that was all they could afford. They were considering a swim but not moving. Hoping to meet single men? The sun very strong but the sunblock stronger.

After all the rain they'd been having this summer, it was exciting to think of the sun.

"A doctor will see you shortly," Patti said. She swiveled to retrieve a page from the printer on the desk behind her. "Please have a seat over there."

. . .

The record rainfalls all that year had to do with the relationship between the air temperature and the surface temperature of the ocean. As it varies, the climates worldwide respond accordingly. In the northeast, basements flood, engine wiring fails, shingles swell and doors warp, decks rot and exotic gorgeous green and black molds appear on the undersides of everything stored outside. Insects proliferate. Frogs rejoice and earthworms grow more patient still. Rivers rise and reservoirs bloat. And what isn't washed out in gardens and farms small and large insinuates, curls, and thrives with a vengeance. Margaret was only vaguely aware of the current weather pattern. Jack read her excerpts from an article about El Niño, the boy child, he translated pointedly, and another about the southern fish found in northern waters because of the warmer water temperatures. But she hadn't paid attention. What she privately believed was that the heavy, relentless rains had to do mainly with her state of mind.

. . .

In the brightly lighted examining room, a very nervous intern—"I am an intern," she said, challenge and apology in her presentation—looked suspiciously like the receptionist except for the lab coat and shoes with thick soles that suggested denture gel yet would probably absorb a gardening claw without so much as a burp. This intern's face was beet-red, her hair that same funny shade of pea-green as Patti's. Was it the lights, or a warning—an arcane indicator of lockjaw: All women looked like they had greenish-blond hair, and then the afflicted one succumbed. No one knew about this because no one had lived to tell. If you're ever in a confined place, a phone booth for example, and feel like you're going to faint, get out immediately. Don't faint anywhere you can't fall down. The intern took Margaret's temperature, then her blood pressure. Her own hand pressed against the intern's warm, slightly moist side, held there by the intern's arm. Against her will, Margaret could feel the elastic of a bra biting at flesh, and she felt invaded and invasive simultaneously and then her hand was returned and the intern, who wore no name tag, disappeared.

Margaret was a fairly new gardener, and gardening had turned out to be the only place where she felt at peace, not just freed from the day-to-day worries, but safe. Turning the soil was like winning an argument: hard and satisfying. Pushing fat bean seeds into the little holes and patting a bit of the earth over them was better than crossing your heart for a promise. Watching while day after day small green shoots made it into the fresh air was more like breathing than anything she could recall in her recent past. She told no one but even liked weeding. Did it boldly, perhaps foolishly, with her bare hands. She didn't feel the marketed pesticides or the smothering black plastic were fair. The more she traded sweat with the gritty, teeming life in the ground, the better she felt.

And this was important because her life had soured more than she would care to admit. Jack was working hard but not getting anywhere, and seemed to look for blame everywhere but himself. For a stretch of months they'd fought, and then, even with all the rain, they'd stopped talking things through. If you fall into water with your clothes on, immediately try to remove at least some of them or you'll likely drown. A strong point for them at the start of their life together, talking, had become painful and begun to feel futile.

Lucy, already half grown, was busy with school and after-school activities, and with an only child's unique ability to attach to other families, seemed to have managed for so long that, when she did ask for something, it felt like an imposition and Margaret found herself more and more just saying no.

What was left? Out of the blue Jack had said he wanted another child. He'd seemed to think this was the solution for everything they faced now, the silence, the unease.

"I'm almost forty-three years old," she'd groaned, lying in bed, still, feeling the slightest bit of interest.

"So what?" he'd answered.

"But what about Luce?"

"What about her? Besides, we'd have free childcare." She'd let herself be talked away from the diaphragm and into more sex, which, now that it had a purpose, seemed intriguing again. Lucy, who of late had been working on honing her sarcastic side, looked at her suspiciously and said, "What's wrong, Mom? You look happy." At least Margaret thought it was sarcasm driving the remark.

· · ·

The door opened and the doctor came in. She was about the same age as Margaret, smiling, shaking Margaret's hand as though they were both guests at a required cocktail party and having sighted each other from across the room, wordlessly agreed to survive the thing together.

The doctor perched on the examining table. Margaret was sweated in the black swivel chair she supposed was the wrong place. Lucy had a papier-mâché bird she called Perchie. The name annoyed Margaret, and that disturbed her.

"Gardening," the doctor said.

Margaret pulled the claw from the paper bag.

The doctor grimaced. "That must have hurt."

Margaret started to say it hadn't, then stopped. How could she explain the piercing flash and then the dull absence of feeling?

"Okay, let's see. Let's put that thing away"—the tone here was a chiding mother's. Or father's. Luce was around three. She'd been poking about in a box with old sheets of wallpaper and other supplies. She'd come into the living room with her hand outstretched, palm up. "Look what I found, Daddy." Jack had looked, then maintained the remarkable presence of mind to say, "Let's see, honey" so calmly and so was able to take away the shiny single-edge razor blade before anything else could happen. Margaret had walked into the room moments after, finding her husband on his knees hugging Lucy, and she saw his face go whiter than she'd known flesh could, drained, she suddenly realized, of all the blood that must have been pumping into some other place by his terrified heart.

The doctor was still patting the examining table. Margaret climbed up. The doctor removed the Winnie-the-Pooh Band-Aid. Pooh was smiling at a large purple flower he held in front of him with both paws, and then he was in the trash can.

"I started to clean it, then figured I should just get over

here." Margaret wanted to hear she'd done the right thing. And again wanted to believe the word *urgent*, but the doctor just grunted.

She winced a little when the doctor squeezed the flesh around the wound.

The doctor looked up.

"It doesn't hurt that much," Margaret said at last, a deep sigh following the words because it felt good to admit this.

"Mmm. It's pretty swollen right now."

Margaret waited in vain for more information.

"Let's soak it for five minutes, see what we get." The doctor filled a salmon-colored basin with water and peroxide. She put the basin on the stool and Margaret slowly lowered her foot, expecting it to sting, but the water felt warm and good. The doctor left the room. Margaret swished her foot back and forth gently.

Two wires had—long ago—come loose in her parents' car and, touching, started a small fire inside the middle of the dashboard. Her father yelled for Margaret and her brother to jump out. Her mother opened the door and Margaret, sitting behind her, did jump. Her mother grabbed her arms and Margaret was dragged several feet before the car stopped. She hadn't felt anything until they were inside a gas station and her father applied a mechanic's iodine to her knees. The scabs that came were thick and deeply contoured. It was over a week before she could straighten her legs. Even now she could trace leftover bumps along both knees.

"How does it feel?" the doctor asked when she came back.

Margaret shrugged, swirled her foot again. The doctor lifted away the basin and peered into it. Whatever she was looking for did not seem to be there. She cradled Margaret's foot and dried it gently with a soft white towel. "Soak it in a water-peroxide solution on and off for the next twenty-four hours, then we'll let it start healing," she said. She had the foot back up on the table and was bending at the waist, staring at it but not touching it. "What did you say you were wearing on your feet when it happened?"

"Flip-flops. Those rubber ones, blue and black, very comfortable. Cheap. They sell them everywhere. You know—"

"Too bad."

"Why?"

"There's a chance there's rubber in there. I can't irrigate, though. Too swollen. It'd just make it worse."

Margaret looked speculatively at her foot. She closed her eyes, saw briefly the thick embracing walls of inner flesh.

". . . antibiotics."

Margaret opened her eyes. "Why?"

"Infection. Rubber is risky. A bad infection, if untreated, could become systemic. You don't want to end up in the hospital."

"No, but can't I wait and see? You don't know for sure if it will get infected, do you?" She flexed her foot. "Or if there's anything in there?"

"No," the doctor admitted. Her face twitched ever so slightly.

There was a woman, a mother of another kid in the art class Lucy attended at the museum in Providence. The woman resembled Margaret physically but had a look in her eyes that seemed crazed and maybe even murderous, and she hovered around her child as though she sensed an impending earthquake. The resemblance was slight yet the teacher sometimes confused Margaret with this woman.

". . . safest course. I'll write you a prescription."

"I'm not going to take them."

All her friends were against antibiotics unless absolutely necessary. Besides, when she was pregnant with Lucy she never took anything, not even Tylenol for a headache. The doctor was obviously annoyed. The pokeweed floated into Margaret's mind and she imagined slamming it down on the table.

"It would've been better if you'd been barefoot. Then we wouldn't worry about infection."

Margaret considered this. "But then the claw would've gone through. I'd be in an operating room now or something, wouldn't I?"

The doctor shrugged. "Well . . . you have to watch it closely. If there's any sign of hardness, or white streaks radiating from the wounded area, you'll have to go on antibiotics at once. And you'll have to be on them for a longer time than if you'd just taken them preventatively."

A person struggling hard in the water is not a good rescue choice; they won't mean to but will pull you down with them. "Fine."

"Now. Tetanus. When was your last shot?"

Margaret calculated. More than ten years ago. Tetanus shots, last she'd heard, were good for ten years. "Over ten years ago."

"Well, you'll need one. I'll go—"

"Oh," Margaret began loudly, her voice cracking, surprising them both. The doctor paused just inside the room. "There's a slight chance I might be pregnant. Isn't that a problem, with the tetanus shot, I mean? Isn't that bad when you're pregnant?"

The doctor pulled the door closed behind her. Before she answered, she breathed audibly, and the pin she wore, an enameled sun and moon, rose and fell. Up and down, like a small boat on a large lake. "Well, no. That used to be the thinking. But not now. Turns out the tetanus vaccine is good for pregnancy."

"Says who?"

"Says the people who study the vaccine carefully."

Margaret's own breathing quickened. If she had a pin on her chest it would rise and fall like the doctor's. Two boats. Two lakes. "I don't know. I don't have a good feeling about this."

"But if you have tetanus, the fetus will die. And you'll be ill. Very ill."

"Shit," Margaret whispered. The word came out soft as a caress. The pokeweed floated before her again and grew a mouth and deep, laughing eyes. She focused past it at a rendering of a person's sinus cavities, a list of reasons to have the flu shot if you were over sixty-five or had a compromised immune system, a poster of a field of irises. There was a calendar, the numerals 2019 looking like a child's scribble. The doctor's hair was dark. Not that weird greeny-yellow. "What are the chances?" The question felt baggy, like an ill-fitting jacket.

"The chances of you having tetanus are relatively high, especially if we think in terms of risk-reward," the doctor said. "A vaccine is safe for the fetus." She pulled the claw from the bag. It looked large in her hand. She held it as though trying to estimate its weight. "But you know, if you're concerned about pregnancy nonetheless, we could . . . we can do a blood test that's accurate as early as six days after conception."

Margaret counted with her eyes closed. "It would be more

than six days. It's a long shot, but if it happened, it would be more than six days."

The doctor stood up with a sudden burst of energy that seemed to say, have faith in the medical, we shall prevail and besides, urgent or not, we're all you've got. Margaret's mother had been furious at her for jumping out of the car. But she had opened the door.

"Okay. The test will take around ten minutes. I'll send the nurse, Irene, and we'll draw some blood."

The voices out there were audible to Margaret because the doctor had left the door open.

"I can't. It's, no, I can't. I can't."

"I'm sure she has good veins."

"If she can't, I'd rather she didn't," Margaret called emphatically to the doctor when she returned, her face flushed. "I've been poked ineptly one time too many as it is today."

The doctor nearly laughed but seemed to remember she was annoyed at having to do this herself, and quickly drew a sample. She reached back and squeezed Margaret's hand, then disappeared with the little vial.

The blood had been a deep red, like the clayey part of soil. Broken down and analyzed, would it confirm that she'd been good, good at school, good at keeping house, had an easy pregnancy and natural delivery, with no drugs, no epidural, an instant mother who seemed to have a lot of patience, not quick to anger, someone who found creative ways to pass time with her child, had friends, kept in shape with yoga and a NordicTrack she actually used now and then, someone who didn't watch that much television or fall headfirst into the computer? Yet Margaret felt she didn't *inhabit*. For over a year before actually fingering soil, she read and reread gardening books, catalogues from flower farms and fruit farms with names like *Seeds of Hope, Blossom and Grow, Flourish*, losing herself in a papery, odorless world. She gave a resounding no to Lucy's requests to cut out pictures from the catalogues, and Jack's only comment in all that time was that he hadn't known you could buy a $35 iris.

She could hear the clock on the wall. Her hand closed tightly over her wrist where her watch was, the watch face with a smear of brown dirt on it, a flat little smudge like a baby's first fingerprint. If the doctor came in with a positive result, Margaret would need Jack. They would have to make a decision together. He would have to leave Lucy with neighbors or the blondo out front would have to keep her busy in the waiting room. She thought she felt her foot throb but realized it was her wrist; she was pinching her wrist, hard, with the metal of the watch. She stared at her hand before she could will her fingers to let go.

She took the claw out of the bag and, holding it like a wishbone, wished that the test would be negative. Then she would have the tetanus shot and take her wounded self home. When they returned she would tell them, Jack and Lucy, what foolishness she had done today. She would show them the pile of weeds and the cleared bed, the claw and the punctured place where the shot was and the wound itself and the punctured flip-flop and, finally, the white slip for the antibiotics she wouldn't take. They would forgive her earlier bad mood. She wouldn't tell about the pokeweed, and she would not let Jack know there was no baby.

The doorknob turned, and she held her breath and counted. She was counting to ten, a trick she'd made up years ago for Lucy. You hold your breath to ten, then let it out with all the bluster you could manage. The door opened in slow motion, or she perceived it as such. The doctor's hand, her wrist, the while-coated arm, chest, her chin, mouth, nose. Margaret didn't want the eyes, not yet. She felt cold suddenly. Just like that night. It had been an unusually cool evening, but somewhat drier for a change, and they'd gone to visit nearby friends, a family with two kids on either side of Lucy's age, whom they enjoyed and didn't get to see often. They found them in their backyard, where they'd made a fire. Margaret, Jack, and Lucy joined them on wooden benches around the warm fire, feeding it cherry pits and copper sulfate, and the fire was spiky with color, the orange flickering at its upper edges with soft blues and an almost sapphire purple, and the kids grew busy with marshmallows and constellations.

They'd felt so safe. The freedom to joke around and let their children have too much sugar and pointy sticks mothers weren't supposed to be tolerating to poke into the pretty lapping flames, and as they stood up to warm their bottoms and then take off their sweatshirts and put them back on and sat around merely breathing, just being alive, there came the sound of sirens in the distance, probably half a mile away, no more. One, then two, then another. Too many. Far too many. The cool air had secretly slicked the road. And without trying to picture the scene, they glanced at each other and knew, she and Peggy, the other mom, better than they knew their own addresses or license plates or what to dream of making for dinner, that they could as easily be there where the sirens were. Later that night, Margaret and Jack made love, quickly, hungrily, the smell of woodsmoke heavy around them, their fingers tingling with the memory of marshmallow stickiness. Ten nights ago.

"It's negative. I'm sorry."

Sorry, Margaret meant to repeat, but instead the word urgent came out like a question.

The doctor looked confused, but it was Margaret who was confused. Why sorry? Negative solved everything. She could get her tetanus shot. She should have gotten one anyway when she'd started gardening. They ought to make that mandatory, with your first seed order. Because tetanus was alive and harbored—harbored—everywhere. Every deep wound was vulnerable. Relief, not sorrow. Margaret burst into warm, lively tears. She had hurt herself. It had been scary.

The doctor said Margaret and her husband could try again. Then: "So let's go ahead and do the tetanus shot. And it'll be good for ten years."

Margaret coughed as she tried to say, "Sure. Okay."

$\cdot$ $\cdot$ $\cdot$

Any experienced mother knows that, as life goes on, patterns shift. An El Niño can be followed by a girl-child, La Niña. Places that have seen record rains can go dry. Birds can then bathe frantically in garden sprinklers. Reservoirs can dip. Lakes can sink, and warnings against campfires can go up in every state park. Watering bans can be imposed, then enforced, then enforced with harsher penalties. Perennials can see demise. Trees will always conserve themselves best they can, but some will turn brown and inward when they can't. Sinuses can parch and ache, and women as old as Margaret will have their first nose bleed in thirty years. Mother and fathers both—men and women both—can sometimes sense something is changing but ignore the logical explanations at hand. Sunblock and electricity can always sell in great and greater amounts. Elderly can be warned to stay indoors, and they'll tend to heed such warnings more obediently than children will. And on some days, brightly dressed people on the news will recommend that everyone avoid the air outside if they can.

．　．　．

The place where the tetanus shot was administered was supposed to hurt that night, "like I'd punched you in the arm," the doctor had actually said. But it didn't. The foot, however, did. The pain began slowly, as if the flesh figured out what had happened. It throbbed, then ached, and finally a ripping, wild pain gathered and focused itself, and, at last, Margaret felt calm.

She'd showed Jack and Lucy the shoe, the claw, the beautiful flower bed, and they'd fussed over her and chided and hugged her, and she'd let them.

She watched the foot for signs of infection and found none, and, on the third day, threw away the white prescription slip.

She limped for a while and promised to be more careful and called her gynecologist and later picked up the new packet of birth control pills.

Jack watched her push the first pill through the silver foil.

"Are you sure?"

"Pretty sure."

"Just pretty?"

"No. I'm sure. I can't. . . . It's all I can do to give to you and Lucy. . . . I want to want what I have."

He laughed, a short, sharp laugh. He'd told her he'd read the secret to being rich is wanting what you have.

She reached for his hand, squeezed it, let it go slowly, then swallowed the pill quickly before she'd have a chance to be dissuaded because she thought he might still want to try.

"Jack?"

"Yes?"

"When you boil skunk cabbage five or six times, is it because it will taste bad or because if you don't, it'll kill you?"

"Did I tell you about skunk cabbage? I did, didn't I?"

"You tell me lots of things."

"I didn't think you'd been listening," he said, examining his hands.

"Will it kill you, Jack? The skunk cabbage?"

"You mean, in the culinary sense?"

"In any sense."

"Why do you want to know?"

Margaret found it nice the way he was smiling at her now. "It's important."

"I think it's so you don't spit it out after the first bite. You know, to make it more palatable." He stopped smiling. "Are you planning on heading out for the wilderness?"

"I think I finally realized we're already there."

She looked carefully into his eyes, and he did not turn away.

• • •

The rains continued that summer. Margaret lost five of six scabiosa, one lovely magenta columbine and a caryopteris whose picture in the catalogue promised an indescribable

blue. The rest—daisies, baptisia, poppies, calendula, arteme-
sia, Jacob's ladder, achillea, liatris—outdid itself, along with
the slugs and the mold and the weeds.

The gardening claw wound up on a dusty shelf in the basement. Her foot healed like an onion: concentric lines around
the original puncture, thinning out into an oval. Every three
or four days the lines would appear, then disappear, then appear again. She and Lucy spent time examining the foot, Lucy
playing doctor with a magnifying glass until one day she said,
"Mom. I mean, Patient. I think there's something in here."

Margaret wasn't surprised. For some time, when she'd
walked, it had felt like there might be. She'd been picking a
little at the skin as though she could unearth whatever it was.
She called the "urgent" doctor, who seemed annoyed to learn
that Margaret hadn't taken the antibiotics and said without a
trace of irony, "Well, what do you expect?" before suggesting
Margaret come in.

Margaret was on her way there when she stopped at the
drugstore instead.

After about twenty minutes in an Epsom salts solution,
there seemed to be a very small amount of movement deep
inside.

Lucy was watching her closely. "Mom, are you okay?"

Margaret nodded. She pulled her foot out and patted it
dry. "Tell Daddy I need a tweezers, please. Hurry."

Lucy ran for her father.

Margaret gently prodded the flesh on either side of the
onion. She had been thinking about the shape of the claw, and
it occurred to her that, because it was curved, there might be
a different place to squeeze, not directly above the wound but
over to one side. Now she pushed that place and felt some-

thing come to a head, and her breath quickened and she glanced up and saw the looks of anticipation on her husband's and daughter's faces. The three of them bent their heads over her upturned foot and, lo and behold, a small something, dark and definitely not of her flesh, began to poke out of the place where the wound had been. The onion parted slightly, like lips, and she took up the tweezers and pulled, and after only a little resistance, a bit of the shoe emerged, tiny and wrinkled, blue and black, and Margaret felt that which had been open close, even while other things, of love and endurance, flared on.

BLUE MARTINI

BARBARA DEMARCO-BARRETT

I wanted to be alone. I wanted to be far away. Because every night and every day, Gunther and I fought about stupid things. He always had to have the last word. So did I. Not a good combination. A couple like us couldn't last. The fight we most often had was over the bills. Since he paid all the bills, he'd say, I needed to help him with his new business. Like hell, I'd say. I wasn't going to get involved with crystal no matter what. It rots your brain, I'd tell him. It makes you dull inside. He didn't like that and the last time I said it he squeezed my arms so hard he polka-dotted my pale skin red and made me yelp.

After that, we kept our distance more than usual, which was fine with me. He'd stay out in the RV creating his *Breaking Bad* Concoction, as he liked to call it. If Walter White could get rich manufacturing crystal meth, he'd say to no end, so could he. "You idiot," I finally said, "it's a TV show," and this set off some major league arguing. Gunther had a degree in chemistry, and, like Walter, he thought he might use his education to make real money. He deserved to have a good life, he'd claimed more than once. You call this good? I wanted to shout this time, but now, as our voices were rising yet again, I tried to fight fair by merely saying, "Walter White was a fictional antihero."

To which he said he wanted me to explain "antihero." See, that's what I was dealing with. He was a brilliant chemist but an idiot about everything else.

The bigger idiot for sticking around so long—almost a year—was me. I'd had a front-row seat watching a boyfriend transform from one handsome dude into a pasty-faced, crank-addled asshole. Don't let anybody tell you different—speed turns you ugly, makes you sell out your mother, your grand-mother, your best friend. So I decided, after I told him an antihero was what he'd see if he looked in a mirror and he stormed off to his ugly-ass RV, that this was it.

I wiped my sweaty forehead with a paper towel. No telling if he would be out in that thing for thirty minutes or three hours, so I hurried. I packed the car my mother left me when she died last year, my thirty-third birthday gift, a rusted white '78 Cadillac Eldorado with red leather seats, red carpeting, a red steering wheel, and a plastic hula girl on the dashboard. I loved that car but would have rather had my mother back.

Also from my mother was a set of pink Samsonite suitcases. One I stuffed with clothes. In the other went my baking tools—rolling pin, hand mixer, pie plate. I was all set to go when I jogged back to the house and grabbed the half-full bottle of tequila from the liquor cabinet and one of Gunther's many guns, a .32-caliber pocket pistol, one he jokingly said he'd won from a woman in a game of strip poker. It was a tiny thing with an ivory grip and silver plating, a fancy toy he'd said was suitable for me because it would fit in my pocketbook.

"It's a purse," I'd told him back then. "No one calls it a pocketbook anymore." To which he'd scoffed and mocked me.

I also couldn't forget Tomasina, a jar of sour dough starter named for my mother who gave it to me before I left Costa

Mesa to be with Gunther. I was intent on returning to the beach city where my mother had had me. My cousin had a two-bedroom apartment in a little '50s-style converted motel, she was always saying I could have one of the rooms. I scribbled "Have a good life. Fuck you—" on an envelope and left it under Gunther's stained coffee cup. Outside, the heat felt like somebody forgot to turn off the oven, and let's not forget the smell—good riddance to the rotten egg fumes from the Salton Sea a few miles south.

Before I took off, I checked out my reflection in the rearview. "You are one sad fuck," I said to the gray eyes that looked back. "Get it together."

. . .

My white-and-red land yacht lurched onto the rutted macadam. West of me, the sun was making a break for the San Jacinto Mountains, which carved a jagged line in the empty blue sky. Out here on the edge of the Coachella Valley, an hour-and-a-half from Palm Springs, secondary road care wasn't on the city's list of priorities. I pulled onto the shoulder beside a family of prickly pear cacti and turned off the GPS on my cell. The land yacht had been handling the bumps in the road okay, but something sounded off. Every so often the engine emitted the tiniest of hiccups. I refused to worry. Freedom was at hand. I forged ahead, turned onto the 111, and headed west. If the traffic was with me, I'd be at my cousin's in three hours tops. On the car radio, I tuned in a desert station and landed on Sam Cooke's "You Send Me."

My mother, sister, and I had loved Sam Cooke. When this song would come on with the three of us in this car, we'd sing along, a regular trio girl band. I turned up the radio and sang backup. Cooke sang about someone he loved so much. I couldn't remember anyone other than my mother loving me that much. But as she used to say, it ain't over till the fat lady sings. Whoever the heck the fat lady is was one of the things she never did tell me.

Instead of getting on the 10 west with a clear shot to the ocean, I stayed on the 111 and made a stop in Palm Springs for a late lunch: veggie sandwich and an Arnold Palmer at Sherman's Deli. Sugar cookies. Lining the back wall were signed black-and-white headshots of stars who used to hang out in Palm Springs—Sinatra, Dean Martin, Rita Hayworth. Old Hollywood. When Gunther and I were first together, before his current business took off and while he still consumed food, we would drive into Palm Springs for dinner. It was different being here alone, but I didn't mind. I liked my own company. At an outside table on the patio, misters spritzed fine spokes of water that moistened my arms and made the heat bearable.

I eavesdropped on the conversation around me.

Let's do the Thursday night art walk.

Where can we find Drag Queen Bingo?

Does that Desert Oracle podcast dude still do a show at the Ace?

Let's go to Mr. G's for a puzzle. Thousand piecer.

Yeah, people were planning their todays, looking forward to their tomorrows. I envied the lot of them. I wanted a to-morrow to look forward to. I had a hundred bucks to my name and a credit card that Gunther would soon shut down. I charged my lunch and left a 50-percent tip. Why not? Gunther's parting gift to me.

Back in the Caddy, I set the bag of sugar cookies for my

cousin on the red leather seat, stuck my key in the ignition, and turned. Clickety-click.

Shit. Shit. Shit.

When I first met Gunther, he repaired fancy cars. With that brain of his, he could figure out any engine. He once offered to teach me what was what under the hood, but I was too worried about my fucking manicure.

The engine could be flooded. That much I knew about. I waited a moment and tried again. A click no louder than a lizard's toenail against stone.

Dammit.

I wrangled open the hood, leaned over the engine, and peered in as if I knew what to look for. Dirt from the Caddy's monstrous grille frosted the front of my white jeans and top with an outline of what looked like a giant charcoal mouth laughing at me. Great. Just great.

An older dude ambled over, hands in blue jeans, loose white short-sleeve shirt, blue-billed cap that said SINGLETON LANDSCAPES in yellow, his faded blond hair curling out from it. Eyes swimming-pool green. A Robert Redford look-alike. Grizzled, and still hot.

"What's the problem?" he said. Southern twang. White teeth.

"Won't start," I said.

He grimaced in shared pain. "Let me have a look."

I moved aside and he fiddled.

"Try firing her up," he said.

I turned the key. Zilch.

He played around with the battery connections. "Got Triple A?"

I shook my head. Gunther had never wanted to pay for that, always said he could fix whatever needed fixing.

"I have cables," he said. "Hang on."

He jogged over to a pickup truck with Singleton Landscapes on its side doors and pulled it alongside the land yacht. Dug around in the truck bed, found a wreath of yellow and red cables, connected his battery to mine.

"Fire it up."

This time the engine turned over. My chest expanded with relief. I'd be able to get out of the Coachella Valley today and far away from Gunther and my old, parched life.

He unhooked the cables and tossed them back in his truck. "That battery looks a mite old," he said. "You need a new one. If I was you, I'd get a battery before you get back on the road."

I thanked him, and as he remained watching, I slid behind the steering wheel, revved the motor, and the engine died again. He squinted down the street as if he was looking for something.

"There's a shop just down a ways where a buddy works on vintage cars. My guess is your problem is more than the battery. Let's try jumping it again."

We did, and it stayed running. "Follow me," he said.

At first I hesitated, but I didn't get weird vibes from him and serial killers tended to be younger, so I followed him a few blocks down Tahquitz to the shop. He introduced me to a guy in blue overalls with a white-and-blue embroidered name tag that said Jeb. Chewing a toothpick, Jeb connected the Caddy to a shiny red machine with lots of knobs, outlets, and wires.

"Your alternator's shot," Jeb said, wiping his hands on a

blue rag. "It'll take a day or two to get the part. Alternators for these old cars are hard to find. Come by in the morning. I'll know more then."

"How much will it cost?" I asked.

He withdrew the toothpick, looked at it, then at my car. "Seven hundred at least with labor."

Shit. By the time it would be ready, Gunther would likely have cut off my credit card.

Still, I told Jeb, "Okay."

Outside the shop, my rescuer held out his hand and said, "Billy Singleton. And you are?"

"Pepper Shannon."

"Glad to make your acquaintance, Pepper Shannon. You got a place to stay in town?"

"My cousin has friends not too far from here. I'll give her a call."

With his chin he pointed at the adjacent motel. "I know the owner. I can try to get you a deal."

I must have had doubt written all over my face, because he added, "Don't worry. No strings."

"I dunno," I said. "Maybe I should just try to keep on going, make it to my cousin's in Orange County."

He made a face that said, *Seriously?*

So I said, "All right. I'd greatly appreciate a deal."

"This way," he said, and I followed him across the dusty gravel lot to a one-story pink-clapboard motel with six units, seven if you counted the manager's quarters, and a little connected bar that looked closed. An unlit neon sign that reached into the sky said BLUE MARTINI and was accompanied by a giant martini glass with an olive.

At the front desk Billy introduced me to the owner, Tanya,

who had a turquoise brush cut and a tiny earring piercing her left nostril. Then he helped me with my suitcases. We strolled past the pool to the door of my room. He set the suitcase just inside the door and went to leave.

"Wait," I said. "Shot of tequila as a token of thanks?" I pulled the bottle from my tote bag.

"The holy cactus. Don't mind if I do." His face lit up with a bashful smile.

"Think there's an ice machine?"

He pointed inside the room at the Styrofoam bucket beneath the TV. "Wherever there's an ice bucket, there's gotta be ice." He took the bucket and disappeared into the twilight.

I looked at my phone. Three texts from Gunther. Previously when I left him, he always talked me into coming back. Not this time. I turned up the swamp cooler that rattled and spewed tepid air. I found two plastic cups in the bathroom wrapped in sanitized paper coverings.

Billy returned with a bucket full of ice and filled our cups to the brim. I poured tequila, enjoying the crackle of the ice as the alcohol hit it. We toasted and drank. The tequila warmed me from my head down to my pinkie toes. My future took on a cheerful gleam. Maybe I'd been worrying for nothing. But I was sweating like a pig. I was used to air conditioning at Gunther's. Billy took an ice shard and ran it down the side of my face and neck, stopping at my clavicle.

"How's that feel?" he said, his voice low and raspy.

He could tame scorpions with that voice.

"Very nice," I heard myself saying.

"C'mon." He took my hand and tugged me outside. "The magical hour betwixt darkness and light."

"A poet," I said.

"Just need to open our eyes. Beauty all 'round."

The violet sky did feel magical. The only times Gunther went outside anymore was when he had to go from the house to the RV, or to the store. I'd become like a housebound binge-watching little housewife, me. How had it happened that I'd become immune to boring days on end?

Sinatra played through outdoor speakers. We wandered over to the swimming pool. Billy pulled me to him, and we slow danced. Then we sat on the bullnose edge of the pool and drank some more. He had such perfect arms, like those of a much younger man. Toned most likely from his work. Arms had never been such a turn-on. I wanted like anything to see what was under his shirt, but it was too soon.

I jumped up, fetched the tequila, and drained the bottle into our cups. We toasted, lay back on the cement, watched the night sky. Specks of stars poked through a blanket of indigo. We had the place to ourselves. By the time we finished drinking, the time was not only right, it was perfect. He switched off the pool light and we peeled off our clothes, then jumped into the water where we mated like seals who'd been beached one season too long.

I invited him to stay the night. We watched the motel TV and laughed at Jimmy Kimmel's monologue. It was like we'd known each other forever.

In the morning, the sun through the skimpy curtains woke us up. Eight more texts from Gunther. We drank coffee-maker coffee in bed.

"What the fuck," Billy said, holding one of my arms Gunther had squeezed too hard. The splotches had turned purple. I pulled away.

"How'd you get those?"

"Ran into a wall."

He shook his head and scowled. "That wall had some hands, did it?"

"I don't want to talk about Gunther."

"Gunther," he repeated, looking like he'd just tasted rancid food.

He stayed on simmer for a while, deliberating before he spoke. "That's one thing I can't tolerate, dudes who hurt women. My brother-in-law put my sister in the hospital. And when they released her, she went back to him like nothing ever happened."

"Maybe she needed him to survive financially."

"She was a principal of a high school. Made far more money than that bastard."

"My mom had similar troubles, but she wasn't educated. Needed my dad for money."

"Money or no money," he said, "why don't women want to leave? They just stay and stay, as if saying 'more, more.'"

"It's not that they don't want to," I said. "Maybe they don't know how to leave, or they're scared."

He ran his fingers across my bruises. Leaned over and kissed them. "I'd never do that to you. I'd shoot myself first. Does Gunther know where you are?"

"I can't see how he would."

"GPS on your phone?"

"Turned it off."

"Smart lady."

In the tiny shower stall, we soaped each other's torsos and backs, took turns under the showerhead to rinse, and toweled off. After we dressed, I said, "Want to go with me, see if Jeb found the part?"

"Whatever you want to do," Billy said.

. . .

The service bay smelled of oil and gasoline. On the radio, an angry talk show host blathered words: *socialist agenda, family values.* If I never heard the words *family values* again, it wouldn't be too soon.

"I found you an alternator," Jeb said while chewing on a toothpick. "But it's going to take a few days, and, like I thought, it ain't gonna be cheap. Those old vintage parts . . ." His voice trailed off, but I did hear the words *alternator, fuel pump,* and *a thousand-plus dollars.*

"Can I think a minute?" I asked.

Jeb swiped a red licorice whip from a big plastic jar and replaced the toothpick with it. "Take all the time you need." Probably used to be a cigarette smoker and had that oral thing going on.

I considered asking my cousin for a loan. I stared at fan belts on the wall.

Billy said to Jeb, "What's happening with the bar? Looked closed last night."

"Tanya fired the bunch of 'em. They were stealing from her. She's hiring now. Just put an ad on Craigslist."

"I could use a job," I interrupted. "Pay my repair bill, get me to Orange County. I could give you payments."

Billy and Jeb looked at me.

"That's a shittin' good idea," Billy said. "Let's talk to Tanya."

. . .

That night I started work behind the bar. I'd get to my cousin's in Costa Mesa when I got there. Making money was my number one priority. The Blue Martini was small. Knotty pine, six stools, three booths—that was it. Little neon beer signs, a large jar holding dill pickles in a filmy broth. Old time jukebox. Two vending machines, one with M&Ms, the other with peanuts. Basic liquors, well drinks, beer. Nothing too exotic except for the signature drink, a blue martini made with vodka, blue Curaçao, and triple sec.

The place would fill up. As well as a salary, customers left tips. It was exciting, making money of my own again.

A litany of texts from Gunther kicked into high gear. I responded only once to say, *Leave me alone. Never coming home.*

At the end of my first week, with my paycheck and tips, I had almost half of what I needed to pay Jeb.

Into my second week, Billy stopped by just before closing, as he did every night. He took a stool at the end of the bar. Ordered a Corona. He looked as happy to see me as I was to see him. It hadn't grown old yet and I hoped it never would. Some things were just meant to be.

"Listen, your ex visited Jeb," he said with a slug from the bottle.

"What?" My heart raced. "How'd he know my car was there?"

"That Caddy's pretty unique. Maybe a buddy saw it in the garage's parking lot. The Coachella Valley is actually a small town."

"Would Jeb tell him I was working at the bar?"

Billy shook his head. "Doubt it."

I was rattled. A glass slipped from my grasp and shattered on the stone floor just beyond the bar floor mat. I spaced out on drink orders. Made a lemon drop martini when a cosmo was ordered, a margarita instead of a mojito. Billy stayed until the bar closed. I finished wiping down the counter and put away all the glasses.

"I'll walk you home," he said. "Make you feel better."

And as we walked we both knew he knew how to make me feel good, forget about Gunther, and believe in new possibilities. A slight breeze swept over the San Jacinto, bringing with it cool mountain air. Billy set a brown paper bag on the little table. I got us cups with ice. He poured the tequila and we drank. The moon was a big friendly face. The hissing of sprinklers watering lawns in the subdivision over the concrete brick wall serenaded us. A far cry from my life with Gunther.

"Why do they waste all that water on the desert?" I asked, more to the air than to Billy.

"Ah, you know," he said, "people fancy green lawns."

"I don't get it."

We soaked up the moon's rays and discussed driving up to Joshua Tree where, Billy said, there were trees that looked like someone praying. This was the life. I had a job, a dream of a man. Sure, he was older—much older—and I'd eventually be accused of having a daddy complex. Or he'd be called a cradle robber. I didn't care. Age was just a number.

Gunther was dissolving into the past, a nightmare I needed to forget. Billy and I sat out there for the longest time, and as had become our habit when it seemed no one would be leaving their rooms, we dropped our clothes and went for a swim.

The next morning we went to Sherman's Deli for breakfast. I had a beignet that snowed powdered sugar all over me. We strolled Palm Canyon Drive like we were a honeymooning couple, stopping in at Just Fabulous where Billy bought me a pink flamingo pool floatie.

It was around ten o'clock that night at the Blue Martini

when an RV with bullhorns painted on the front pulled into the lot. There couldn't be two of those ugly-ass RVs around. Gunther.

Everyone in the bar was joshing it up. Amy Winehouse on the jukebox belted "Back to Black." The lights of the RV went off. Every so often I went to the windows for a better view. The tiny spark of orange from his cigarette grew bright and faded, grew bright and faded. He was watching the bar, watching me. I wanted to get out of there, but I couldn't flake on Tanya. I was the only one on, and anyway, where would I go?

Around midnight Billy came in and took a seat at the bar. I placed a Corona before him.

"Sexy outfit," he said. "You were wearing that when we met."

"Took forever to get out the dirt from the car's grille."

"You look good enough to eat."

I leaned over and said, "Gunther found me."

Billy's face became a map of worry. "Where?"

"Don't look now, but that RV in the lot on your way in is his."

Billy pursed his lips and rubbed at a spot on the lacquered knotty pine as I slid my room key across the bar.

"I have his gun in the room," I said. "In the nightstand."

"Is it loaded?"

"I would assume."

"You don't know?"

"I didn't check. Maybe that's why he's here. Probably missed it after all."

"I doubt that's all he missed." Billy shut his eyes, gave a vague shake of his head, and got to his feet. "I'll unload it. You can give it back to the fucker so he leaves you alone. I brought my own gun, just in case." He reached down and tapped his ankle under his jeans.

"I didn't know you had a gun," I said.

"Who doesn't?" he said.

He made a kissy face on his way toward the kitchen, and I made one too. Then I heard the screen door slap shut.

I carried on with the customers as if nothing was going on, as if it was a normal night. But there was nothing normal about Gunther.

Billy hadn't returned when Gunther came slinking in sloth-like.

"You shouldn't be here," I said.

"What time does this dive close? You're coming home with me. We'll fetch the Caddy tomorrow. Get me a beer."

"That's not my home," I said, and did not get him a beer.

"You know you love me." He cracked his knuckles. "What the fuck is wrong with you?"

A couple of remaining diehards watched us from across the room.

"You're in love with your business," I said, "not me."

"My business is why you get to sit on your ass all day and watch TV."

"I'm sick of TV. I need something to do. I'm doing it now."

"Tending bar? That's what you call doing something?"

I waved goodbye to the last customers, regulars who must've sensed trouble and didn't want to stick around for it. Gunther went to use the rest room. I poured the remains of a blue martini from a silver beaker into a cocktail glass and set it on the bar.

Billy was back. He lifted his T-shirt to show me the ivory-and-silver pistol in the waistline of his jeans.

"I left it loaded," he said.

I reached for it. "He's in the rest room." I wiggled my fingers.

"Jesus," he said. "Have you ever used a firearm?"

"Yes," I lied. I took a deep breath. If anything went wrong, I didn't want Billy going to jail. I would be the one.

"Hurry," I said, anxious. "He'll be here any second."

He handed it over reluctantly. I stuck it in the back of my jeans. So much love and concern poured from his eyes, so much warmth. I smiled, but he must have seen sadness or worry because he said, "You're the best woman I've ever known. Please be careful."

"Of course."

"Don't let the bastard get to you." He took a barstool, rested on it on his thighs.

Gunther returned, and, as he approached, Billy rose from the stool, his chest pushed out, trying to look younger, stronger.

Gunther scowled. "You the new boyfriend?"

Billy looked down his beautiful nose at him.

Gunther turned to me and said, "You like old guys now, do you?" He licked his lips and clenched his jaw as he always did when he was high on meth.

I wanted to spew forth a flurry of words, say how at least my old guy knew how to treat a woman. Instead, I folded my arms across my chest and said, "You need to go."

"No. *You* need to come home with me. You've been here long enough."

"Long enough for what? I'm never coming home."

"What the fuck, Pepper."

Billy took a few steps toward Gunther. "Might be best if you left now."

Gunther glanced over at Billy like he was an annoying elderly uncle. They were the same height. Billy was heavier, more filled out, but Gunther was lean and mean and fueled by meth. The pistol was cool against my back.

"Please go," I said. "It'd be better for everyone."

"What's better for everyone is for you to quit playing nursemaid to this old fool." He squeezed my shoulder so hard I felt bruises blossoming right then and there, and I wrenched free. Then he grabbed my chin, forcing me to look at him. "I am not going to keep telling you, Pepper. Time to come with me where you belong."

With a little push, he let go of my chin and my neck cracked, as if I'd just been chiropracted. Something about that crack and his once-handsome–now-gaunt pasty face made me snap. I whipped the gun from my waistband, held it with both hands, and pointed it at him.

He stepped back and raised his hands. "Put that toy away before you hurt yourself." He looked bemused.

"Get out," I said, wagging the gun at him.

"Pepper," Billy said.

"He needs to go," I said. "Now." My voice had a frantic edge to it and it scared me.

"You won't use that on me," Gunther said. "You're too much of a fucking chicken."

That's when I squeezed the trigger, but as I did Gunther knocked my arm and the bullet missed him and hit Billy's shoulder. Billy fell backwards, knocking the blue martini onto the floor, blue droplets splashing onto my white jeans. Billy whipped out his revolver and drilled Gunther in the chest. Gunter's face stayed brave but he went down with an ugly moan. Etta James's "At Last" came on the jukebox.

Billy held his arm as I helped him up and over to a booth, where he said, "Like a nasty hornet sting is all."

"Oh, Billy," I said, and I ran to the bar, grabbed a clean bar towel, and rushed back to him.

I folded the white towel, lay it against his wound, which was bleeding steadily though not profusely. I'd gotten him on the side of the shoulder.

"Press," I said.

Billy nodded and bit down on his lip. I went over to Gunther, who lay there unmoving, and felt for a pulse. Nothing. He looked sweeter than I'd seen him in months. The old Gunther was back, the person he'd been before crystal meth turned him into a monster. Death, the ultimate relaxer, had loosened up the ugly frown muscles of his face. I reached into his front pocket, where he always kept a money clip. The metal felt cool on my fingers. There were at least twenty one-hundred-dollar bills. My severance pay for putting up with him for the last year. I checked his other pockets because sometimes, especially when he knew he'd be out of the house for a while, he'd like to put backup cash in them. In these pockets found thirty more C-notes easily.

I took Billy's gun, wiped it clean of prints.

"What are you doing?" he mumbled.

"I'm not letting you take the fall for this," I said. "Is it in your name?"

"No, ma'am."

"Good," I said.

I wrapped Gunther's fingers around the handle of Billy's

gun so his prints would be on it. Then Billy took over, and I watched as he pointed Gunther's hand with the gun toward the opposite wall and fired. He shook Gunther's hand to make the gun fall. He did it calmly, carefully, as if this wasn't the first time.

Afterward, I called 9-1-1 and said, "There's been a shooting. One hurt, another maybe dead." The dispatcher asked for my name and the Blue Martini's address. When we hung up, I called Tanya, who said she'd be right over.

"You okay?" I called over to Billy, who gave me a dreary thumbs up sign. "They're going to question us," I continued. "Whatever you do, say Gunther threatened me."

"He did," Billy said.

The faint sound of sirens grew louder, and then they were here, whirly lights from the tops of police cars throwing reds and blues on the walls and the ceiling of the Blue Martini. The cop cars fishtailed into the gravelly lot. Firetrucks and paramedics followed. There were so many cruisers and emergency vehicles piling in you'd think a carnival was taking place.

An EMT wheeled in a stretcher for Billy. I tilted the trash can for his blood-soaked bar towel. They loaded Gunther into another van.

Good riddance, I thought. Jackass.

· · ·

I spent the night and most of the next day at the police station detailing what had happened. I claimed self-defense and gave the cops my history with Gunther. I told them about how I'd recently left him because he'd been going loco. I gave them the names of those last regulars who'd witnessed Gunther's aggression before they'd escaped into the night.

In the morning the police sent a car out to Gunther's house and another to the RV in the Blue Martini's lot.

One concerned cop whose name was Glen seemed to have it in for the meth dealers in the Valley, of which there were many. "They're turning this paradise into a sinkhole," he said, scowling as if he smelled something bad.

My story about Gunther must have checked out, because it wasn't too long before this cop said I could go. A cruiser dropped me off at the Blue Martini. The RV was still there, wrapped in black and yellow caution tape.

I walked to my room and was there not even ten minutes when a cab pulled up and dropped off Billy. I ran out to meet him. His arm was in a sling and his shoulder looked bandaged.

"You're a sight for sore eyes," he said as I gave him a gentle side hug.

"Did they question you a lot?" I asked.

He lay back on the bed with a groan. "A fair amount."

"I'm worried. If they get forensics involved, I'm afraid our stories aren't going to check out."

"You watch too many cop shows," he said.

"Maybe."

I poured us tumblers full of tequila with a squeeze of lime and showed him the money. $7,200. The twit obviously carried so much cash because it made him feel more like a man. Some man.

We sacked out the rest of the day. In the morning Billy left to take care of business and I picked up the Caddy, paying Jeb in full. On my way back I saw an unmarked cruiser in front of the Blue Martini, which was closed until further notice. I parked by my room and wandered over. Tanya swept outside and watered cacti while inside a couple of detectives moseyed about.

"What's going on?" I asked her.

She looked over her shoulder, gave a nod, and pointed toward the subdivision.

"They questioned people who live over there. A few heard the shots, and now these cops are back here sniffing around. Who knows when I can open."

"I thought cop shops don't want to waste their energy on loser speed freaks."

"Apparently not every officer shares that sentiment."

Shit.

Tanya must have noticed my concern because she stopped watering and peered at me. "You doing okay? Must've been awful."

"I'm fine," I said, though I didn't sound fine. I wasn't fine.

"Hang tight. This'll all be over soon."

"Right," I said, and I headed back to my room, where I threw back a shot or two of tequila and fretted over what would come next.

When Billy showed up with take-out—guacamole, enchiladas, and chips from Felipe's—he took one look at me and said, "What now?"

We ate in the room, its swamp cooler working overtime so we could talk privately.

I told him about the neighbors hearing shots.

Then I said, "What if someone says they heard the shots far apart?"

"Fuck," Billy said.

"Maybe it's time to leave," I said.

Billy stopped midbite. "You're going to Orange County?"

I shook my head and swabbed a chip in the guac. "I'm not going anywhere without you. Let's go to Mexico. While we can."

"I have my business, Pepper."

"You won't have it if you get thrown in jail. We could go down there and do something good, help women leave bad men. Open a shelter."

"Pepper, it's going to be fine."

"Ever the optimist," I said. I poured more hot sauce on my enchilada. Maybe it would burn away the worry that was festering.

• • •

In the morning I woke up to a voicemail from that detective named Glen saying if it wasn't too much trouble, could I come in. They had a few more questions.

I stroked Billy's cheek to wake him and told him about the call.

"What'll I do?" I asked.

He pulled me to him. His body was warm against mine. "Just go in and be your charming self," he said. Then he began kissing me all over. I soon forgot my worries and succumbed. I had never had a more generous lover. Those women who think young dudes are better should wake up and smell the coffee.

Afterward I said, "Really, Billy. I'm afraid."

He rubbed my back. "Shh," he said. "Go in and play dumb.

If they try to get you to say why the shots were far apart, say the night was a jumble. There wasn't an insurance policy, right? Nothing you want from the asshole's estate?"

"What estate?" I said, calming down.

"There's no motive. What're they going to do? Nothing. They'll lose interest. I'm telling you, I know how these cops work."

"What if it doesn't go that way? What if they arrest me?"

"That ain't gonna happen."

I wasn't so sure, but I nodded. Damn, did that man ever have an honest face. Handsome, sure, but who cared about handsome? I showered while he brushed his teeth and went off to take care of rich people's yards. I put on my nicest sundress that showed my meager cleavage and rubbed honeysuckle oil behind my ears and across my wrists.

On my way to the cop shop, the Caddy hummed along, the hula girl on the dashboard shimmying to the vibration from the engine.

Both Glen, the detective who hated meth dealers, and the other one who didn't so much care led me into an interrogation room the size of a confessional that was all tans and whites. Glen offered me a soda or coffee. I said water would be fine.

They did what Billy thought. Asked me about the shots and the timing of the shots fired. And I did play dumb. That night I was so frazzled, so freaked out, I explained, and bunched my arms tighter to my body so they'd notice my boobs more than my replies. I asked, "You get in a habit, you know?"

And it sort of worked. With Glen, anyway. Though I still had a bad feeling. Especially as Glen alone walked me to the door and thanked me for coming in. He suggested I get some therapy, that this had been a trauma that would likely haunt me. I almost said, *Not more than Gunther alive haunted me.* He explained that they had all they needed and that it looked like they could close the case. But behind him, the other cop lingered and looked troubled as he watched me go.

Glen accompanied me all the way to the Caddy. I was glad to be away from the obviously scheming cop. The sun swiped a silver brushstroke on the topside of Glen's hair. He gave me his card. On it he'd written his cell-phone number.

"In case you think of something, or need to reach me," he said. "Or if you want to have a drink sometime."

I smiled, tried to keep the charm revved up. I told him I appreciated his softer dealings with me.

But as I accelerated down the road that could take me back to the Blue Martini, I knew my days in Palm Springs were numbered. It would be a matter of time before the other cop figured it out and came after me.

I also knew Billy hadn't been lying when he'd said, I have my business, Pepper. And what he'd meant when he'd insisted I keep all of the seventy-two hundred for myself.

I'd be far away from him if I kept on driving and went to Mexico. But I'd also be alone in Mexico rather than being stuck with some stranger in some cell. I squeezed my red steering wheel, sat up a little straighter, then took a quick moment to adjust my rearview mirror. My other mirrors were fine. I pressed on.

THERAPUNITIVE INTERVENTION

MATTHEW GOLDBERG

We are on a death march. There's no other way to put it. What else would you call a series of footsteps ordered by a tyrannical Monk? We're deprived of everything at MonkCare. It's all rituals and being forced to wear orange Reflection Robes, which are baggy and unflattering. Worst of all is the no phones rule. No phones under any circumstance.

I glare at Tadpole, Head Monk, who doesn't have any teeth. He's leading us Forced-Monks down the Sacred Temple steps, carved into the cliff-face in a zigzag pattern, like a switchback canyon trail. Even though we're high up, I can barely tell because of how foggy it is. It's like staring out into the void, or the abyss, or whatever you want to call it. Real mystical vibes. But the fog is just from the weather machines and all that, so the illusion is only so-so.

The main thing to know about Tadpole is he never talks. He isn't allowed. And neither are we. It's so quiet I can hear the sparrows crap overhead. The craps fall like little pats of butter onto the narrow stone steps. Plop. Plop. Plop. All I hear is silence and the plopping. If one of the craps hit Tadpole on the head, he'd just keep serenely shuffling like nothing happened. Like he didn't have crap on the hood of his Reflection Robe. He's the embodiment of calm.

I'm not. Not in the slightest. I would do just about anything for my phone right now. I'd even leave my rabbit, @Bilbobunny, outside in the rain for the whole night. And I adore that rabbit. Back when I was training to be a pharmacist, I rescued Bilbo from an animal testing lab. Bilbo's got a third ear growing out of his rump. Sure, I knew I'd get a lot of Hearts if I rescued him, but that's not why I did it. I did it because he was adorable and I thought maybe he'd be a good listener. I wish I could see how my latest sponsored post went over—the one with Bilbo wearing the golden Burger King crown for the #WhopperHopper campaign.

But MonkCare is a lot worse than not being able to use a phone. All Forced-Monks, including me, must perform a Specific Task until we reach the bottom of the snaking temple steps. Mine is to bang a small gong every fifteenth step. Having to count each and every step makes my toes curl in the sandals we all have to wear, makes me grind and clench my teeth so hard that I'm worried they'll become tooth stumps. How would that look in photos? Not good is how. I shudder to think about a photo of myself smiling with a mouth full of stump teeth. That would get no Hearts at all. Maybe some pity Tears, but no Hearts.

When I reach the fifteenth step, I bang my little gong. The sound of the gong echoes across the canyon, breaking the silence. Earl, the Forced-Monk directly in front of me, glances back when Tadpole isn't looking and makes a forlorn face like, "This is hell."

I agree, but I can't be distracted. I need to count the steps again. Every step-count is like a hammer to the noggin. Step one: whack. Step two: whack. I have a horrible headache from all the noggin hammering. I hate this. I hate it more than anything. Not the Specific Task itself. That's easy enough. I can gong as well as the next guy.

The hard, hateful part is having to focus. That's my punishment. It's also my therapy. The Monks call it Therapunitive Intervention. They think they're so clever.

But, honestly, how is this supposed to reduce my Attention Slippage? If anything I'm feeling more nervy, less relaxed. My hero, Lily Lewis, aka @realQueenLil, always says how Monk-Care is a total time-waste. She was sentenced to MonkCare just like me. But unlike me, she's got millions of followers. She gets to do the coolest things, like sit in the back of limousines while sipping neon-colored cocktails with sparklers in them, and lounge around on mega-yachts in the South Pacific, and swim in huge infinity pools overlooking the Rio skyline. A few months ago, Lily Hearted a @Bilbobunny post. That was the best day of my entire life.

Before getting bused out to the Sacred Temple, I prayed @realQueenLil would end up in my Support Group—the group that goes down the steps together. But she isn't. It's just me and four other nobodies. Each Support Group is always made up of five. I think the Monks split us up into units of five so we're more manageable. They'd split us up into smaller, more solitary units if they had enough personnel. But nobody wants to be a Monk despite the health benefits and the 401 (k) match. Being a Monk is bad for your image. And image is everything.

My Support Group is lined up behind Tadpole in order of Attention Slippage. First there's Earl, who's holding a sack of water made from the stomach of a yak. His Specific Task is to sprinkle droplets from the yak sack every ten steps. I really wish I had Earl's task. He gets to do something five steps sooner than me. I keep wondering what Earl did that got him here. Must not have been as bad as me. Everyone says what I did was bad. Sure, I was the pharmacist on duty at the time, but it wasn't my fault. Is it your fault when a suicidal patient kills himself after you mislabeled his depression meds because you were distracted playing Smack-A-Roos on your phone? Not entirely. It's not my fault that I'm so good at Smacking those Roos!

Of course, Tonya, the Forced-Monk directly behind me, has it even worse. Her Specific Task is to shake a maraca every twenty steps. With so little to occupy her mind, she's at risk of going through Stimuli Withdrawal. I see her neck tremble as she manages, just barely, to keep quiet. Though I guess Tonya's not doing as bad as Kyle and Lucius, the Forced-Monks lined up behind her. Those guys have it worst of all. They're holding these big brooms and only get to sweep once every sixty steps. That's torture. For fifty-nine steps they're alone with their thoughts. Their Attention Slippage must've made them screw up something important. Maybe they crashed a school bus. Maybe they mislabeled *two* depression pill bottles and two suicidal patients kicked the bucket. That's a lot to have on your conscience.

I'd crack if I were them. I'd scream: "Please give me something to do, anything, anything!" But I know I need to keep my lips zipped.

If Tadpole catches any of us with our lips unzipped, he can make us stop and do impromptu Focus Poses. Like Crane, where we'd have to stand perfectly still on one foot while concentrating on the rhythm of our hearts. No way can I concentrate enough to do it. My brain would burst and what then? How would I perform my Specific Task?

Which, oh man, that reminds me: I've been negligent vis-à-vis step counting. Did I remember to gong? Shoot, shoot, shoot. If I missed my gong, Tadpole will fail me. Then our group will be forced to start over at the top. That's a nightmare scenario.

I feel my throat constrict, my Adam's apple bulbous and foreign to my body, like I swallowed a ginormous peach pit. I wait. I wait and wait. Tadpole stops.

Then he soundlessly mouths: "Lunchtime."

I brace myself. According to the message boards that I consulted beforehand, MonkCare lunch is supposed to be gross. Tadpole passes out the Monk Focaccia, the Monk Jam, and a store-brand water bottle. I prefer Fiji Water, just like @realQueenLil, because of its ideal pH balance. But I don't have a choice. I take a cautious first bite. The focaccia is way too chewy. I prefer a softer bread, a nice brioche. And the jam isn't sweet enough. It's grainy with little raspberry seeds that get stuck in my teeth. This place is pure agony. It will be the end of me.

. . .

After lunch, and another three hundred sixteen steps, I hear a muffled series of thumps coming from below. A thump is almost never a good sound in my experience, like when Grandma fell in the tub and broke her hip. Perhaps someone tripped? It wouldn't surprise me. For authenticity's sake, the Sacred Temple steps are uneven. They're also tastefully covered in moss. But don't let that fool you. It doesn't mean they're forgiving.

I notice some frantic movement a long way down—at least

five zigzags down—but can't make out any details. All I see is little orange specks hustling around. It must be another group of Forced-Monks. Typically, there are three or four Support Groups going down the steps at any given time for max Therapunitive efficiency.

We move a bit farther down the steps, and I hear one of the orange specks below cry out, confirming my theory that these were bad thumps.

I keep my eyes on Tadpole, waiting for him to react. Slowly, ever so slowly, he raises his walking staff indicating that our group ought to stop. We stop. Then Tadpole, with his hood still on, heads down the path, sandals slapping with each step. He's left us without any supervision, completely breaking MonkCare protocol. I can't believe it.

Once Tadpole is himself an orange speck and out of earshot, I whisper to Earl, "What do we do? What do you think's happening down there?"

Earl runs his face through his hands. "My God, it feels good to talk," he says, ignoring my question. "It feels *so good* to talk. So, so good."

Earl is clearly losing it.

I turn to Tonya. "This is crazy, huh?"

Tonya stares at me with wide, owl-like eyes. "I might be going berserk," she says. "All this contemplation—it's making me wacko. Am I a wacko? You'd tell me, right?"

"Sure," I say, inching away from her. "I'd tell you."

Meanwhile, Kyle and Lucius slump down on a step and hold each other, babbling incoherently as if possessed by some demonic infants. Poor Kyle and Lucius. Glad I'm not them. I turn my attention back to the orange specks below. They're finally moving on, continuing their downward sojourn. Except for two specks. One is stationary. The other is hustling back up the steps toward us.

It's Tadpole. Upon reaching us, he takes a few toothless gulps of breath, evidently having tired himself out. I open my palms like, "Well, what the heck was that about?"

Tadpole regards me. His weathered face takes on the expression of glass—flat, unreadable. He closes both of his eyes, as if too weary for the world, and bows his orange-hooded head. I have no clue what this means. I think he's being enigmatic just to screw with me.

Then Tadpole lifts his staff and starts walking. I realize he means that we should follow him. I'm becoming an expert at nonverbal communication.

When we reach the spot where I saw all the commotion before, it becomes clear what happened. Somebody really did trip down the steps. There's a Forced-Monk holding her ankle. She looks at us with tears in her eyes. I read her lips: "It's a sprain. I'll be okay."

Tadpole doesn't stop his stride. He doesn't let us commiserate with our fellow Forced-Monk. As we pass, I mouth the words: "Good luck."

"Just make it through," she mouths back. "You've got this."

I sense a spark between us. It's hard to meet people these days. Oh, how I wish I could get her contact details! I imagine the witty text messages we would exchange. I picture the salacious emojis. Of course, now I'll never even know her name.

Our caravan moves on. Step by torturous step. I wonder what'll happen to this mystery woman. Will she get down the rest of the way with her bum ankle? Will she be punished for slipping? Will her ankle injury become chronic? My fingers get antsy as I wait to bang my little gong again. My eyelid starts twitching. The time between each step seems to be taking longer and longer. Finally, it's the fifteenth step. I gong.

It feels so good. I'm renewed somewhat for the intervening fourteen steps where it's just me and my thoughts. Why do we have to do this?

But I know. I can't not know. We do this to repair our Attention Spans: the key to a functioning society. Without a properly functioning Attention Span our minds go to mush. We mislabel antidepressants and some poor depressed person doesn't get the meds they need and then his death is on my hands. It hurts to think about, like being punched several times in the chest, each time harder and more vicious until I beg for the punches to stop but they keep going until I'm numb to it. A day of MonkCare is penance. It's the price we pay.

The worst thing I ever did before the mislabeled pills was accidentally give a few people the flu shot when they actually wanted a hepatitis B shot. That didn't hurt anybody at least. But now things are different—I can barely focus on any single task before another task seems like the most important task ever and the first task is totally forgotten. It's like my conscious brain no longer has control. I just do things. I still take the Attention Slippage medication they give us but that's like shooting a horse with ant tranquilizer. As much as I hate it, MonkCare is the only thing that even slightly works against deep-rooted Attention Slippage like mine. I just need to keep reminding myself that this is temporary. I'm not just Felix Miller, the boring pharmacist. I'm @Fenixrising, lover of travel and sexy-looking food. And I've got @Bilbobunny, the eighth most famous bunny on social media. He's providing joy to countless followers. To be exact: sixteen thousand, three hundred and five followers.

That's a lot of joy! That more than makes up for the pill incident. The thought of my followers' joy gives me the strength I need to focus. Soon, I'll get so popular that I can quit my pharmacy job. I just have to make it through Monk-Care.

I continue focusing and gonging as we all follow behind wrinkled old Tadpole with his mushy-looking mouth. Focus, focus, focus. Gong, gong, gong.

Finally, after one thousand five hundred steps, we reach the bottom—a dusty gorge with a number of porta johns set up for us to relieve ourselves. But the biggest relief is just being done with this nightmare. Tadpole indicates that we should discard our Specific Task Relics. He does this by placing his staff at his feet and making a hand motion like "Now you."

Tonya and I lay our Relics down. Earl does the same. The water in his yak sack spills out, wetting the dirt. Lucius and Kyle hold their brooms a while longer, eyes vacant. Tadpole gently grabs each of the broom handles and lets them fall to the ground.

I could cry, I'm so happy. I open my mouth to speak, but Tadpole jolts his finger up to stop me. Somehow, we're not done. It's already been a whole two hours of counting steps. How much longer can this possibly take?

Tadpole, as usual, has no answers for me. He points at a dirt path cutting through a murky-looking patch of trees. I hate nature. For some reason it feels so unnatural to me. What is there to do in nature? Look around at some dreary old trees? Maybe if I had my phone I could learn how to identify each tree by its unique leaf shape. That way, I could become a tree influencer. I could take photos of various trees, classifying them for my potential followers, showing my followers that the first step to *caring* about nature is *knowing* about nature.

Meanwhile, Tadpole marches us down the path through the nondescript trees. It would be cool to see spooky eyes popping out of the underbrush like in cartoons, but it's daytime and the trees aren't all that thick. If anything, they're a bit sickly. Before long, we enter a clearing cut from the trees. At one end of the clearing is a small waterfall flowing into a lagoon. Near the edge of the lagoon, I see bamboo mats arranged in a tidy little circle. My heart sinks further. It's the Tea Ceremony—the very worst part of MonkCare according to the message boards. Every aspect of the Ceremony is achingly deliberate, impossibly methodical.

With his staff, Tadpole indicates for us Forced-Monks to take our seats on the bamboo mats. I twist my legs into the pretzel position, which is difficult for me due to my tight hip flexors. Even though sitting in pretzel position is extremely uncomfortable, I don't dare groan or squirm. If you interrupt Tea Ceremony, you get punished with Mindfulness Meditation. People can go crazy from that much introspection. So I sit still. I hear a few birds tittering in the trees. I hear the small waterfall trickle over the slick rocks and gurgle into the lagoon. I hear crickets somewhere doing whatever crickets do with their legs. I know it's supposed to be relaxing, but it's not. The noises fuse together, ceaseless, incessant.

Tadpole takes his place in the center of the circle, then rifles around a burlap sack for the Tea Ritual Implements. I thought making tea was simple, but apparently not. There are so many implements: a teawhisk made of bamboo, a teascoo-

per also made of bamboo, a tealadle, which is different from
the scooper and is made of bamboo, a rest for the ladle (made
from bamboo), a teacaddy (surprise: bamboo), then an iron
teapot full of boiling water, and, finally, a tea bowl forged from
humble glazed ceramic. Tadpole wipes each of them down
with a silk cloth.

It's so monotonous. My jaw thumps painfully due to all the
clenching. I glance over at Earl, Tonya, Kyle, and Lucius and
see their eyelids are involuntarily twitching just like mine. My
vision blinks in and out. My legs ache from having to sit in
pretzel. It feels like I'm going to faint and fall flat on my face
into the bamboo.

Instead, Earl, seated to the right of me, collapses backward
onto his own bamboo mat. His limbs start jerking all around
and he makes a blubbery noise and saliva comes out of his
mouth, foaming out onto his chin. He's gone into full-blown
Stimuli Withdrawal! The rest of us put our hands to our own
mouths so we don't gasp audibly.

Tadpole, for his part, remains calm. He continues wiping
down Tea Ritual Implements as Earl convulses on his mat like
a fish left to asphyxiate in a trawler's net.

I can't just stand by and do nothing. I have to record what's
happening, to show the world the kind of depravity that goes
on during MonkCare. Once the world sees firsthand, Monk-
Care will have to be abolished. Attention Spans be damned!
Even Attention Spans aren't worth poor Earl having a break-
down and nobody helping.

I rise from my mat and poke Tadpole on the shoulder.
Then I realize I don't have a plan.

"Can I . . . have . . . my phone?" I whisper.

Tadpole shakes his head.

"Please?"

Tadpole opens his mouth, revealing his conspicuous lack of teeth, the cavernous nothing where his voice resides. "Attention is time," he says. "And time is finite."

He folds his hands and stares at me. It's quiet. Weird noises spurt out of Earl's mouth. Time I'll never get back. I can feel my hands hardening into fists. Though I'm not much of a fighter, I'll have to subdue Tadpole and make him give me my phone back.

I'm about to do it, actually really do it, when Earl stops convulsing.

He straightens up suddenly and goes back into pretzel position, peaceful as can be. Doesn't say a word. His eyes close. Not tightly like he's in pain, but like he's concentrating on something. It's as if the whole episode never happened. It's as if he hadn't been stroking out near moments ago. I stare at him, trying to ask without words if everything is okay.

Then it dawns on me what I've done. I've interrupted the Tea Ceremony, that holiest of holies. This is bad. Very bad. I'm screwed.

Tadpole knows that I know I'm screwed. He indicates that I should remove myself to the Spot of Repose, a stone platform at the other end of the lagoon.

Once I understand my punishment, hot tears fill my eyes. At the Spot of Repose, I'll have to do Mindfulness Meditation. It'll be the end of me. And with me gone, who will take care of @Bilbobunny? Who will cultivate his following? But I don't have a choice. If I refuse, I undo everyone's progress. Doom them. No, I can't do that.

Without meeting Tadpole's hard gaze, I un-pretzel and sulk my way over to the Spot of Repose. I go back into pretzel

position. The stone platform is cold on my bottom, protected
only by the thin fabric of the Robe. It's deathly silent. Needles
of sweat prick my skin.

My mind is supposed to be blank, but it's not. It's filled
with the terror of having to sit still, to think about my choices,
to come to terms with my actions. I could be sitting here for
ten minutes, or ten hours, or the rest of my life. The future
unfolds before me: I'll be sitting here forever. There is no escape. My body will rot away, my bones will turn to dust, I'll
decay into dirt and nobody will remember me. I'll be gone. It
will be like I never lived.

Calm down. I need to calm down. What is it the Monks
say to do if you're having a panic attack due to Stimuli Withdrawal? Take a deep breath?

So, I take a deep breath. I take another, and another. My
eyes are closed and the breathing takes over. I focus on the
sound of lagoon water lapping at the side of the stone platform. I think of nothing. My mind is blank, hollow, and light-
less.

Then something appears before me: a red blob in the darkness. It comes rushing forward, gelatinous and quivering. The
blob expands, swelling as if to envelop me in its blood-colored
goop. But, strangely, I'm not afraid. I stare at this juddering
blob, examining its curves, its messy incongruities. I face the
truth. What happened with the depression meds was my fault.
I can admit it now. And if it's my fault, that means I can prevent it from happening again.

I am in control.

I say this mantra to myself: *I am in control, I am in control,*
and the red blob shrivels like a slug in salt. I push the blob

away. There it goes, hurtling from me until it is a minuscule red dot, a molecule invisible to the naked eye. It is such a small thing. A thing of no consequence.

Then, in the formless space of my mind, I sense a change in perspective. I see myself as if in a mirror. The reflection of me is levitating, rising higher and higher until it vanishes, released from a physical form. I am soaring through the nothingness, untethered from my past, my future, even my body. Tension spills out of me, a screeching teakettle taken off the burner. I know what I need to do to reform my life. I resolve to cast aside vanity and superficiality, to unsubscribe from pointless pursuits, to delete my accounts.

I open my eyes to a strange sensation—the absence of anxiety. I feel no need to occupy myself with trivialities or avoid my thoughts. I am okay with doing nothing. With *being* nothing. I am radiant, calm. The first time in a long time. The Spot of Repose is no longer daunting. I see that now. It's an opportunity to reflect, to sit still and be present. I'm in pretzel. It's not so bad. I meditate there, silent and unencumbered. I don't know for how long.

And then, suddenly, a sound causes me to wince. It's a shrill screech coming from Tadpole. I turn my gaze. He's blowing a thick plastic orange whistle. I see Earl, Tonya, Kyle, and Lucius squirming, hands over their respective ears. I take their lead, trying to keep my head clear and preserve this newfound calm.

But it's in vain. The noise breaks through, and my eardrums ring.

Next thing I know, Tadpole rises from his bamboo mat and gathers up all the Tea Ritual Implements in a burlap sack.

From a different, smaller burlap sack, I see him hand black rectangles to the other Forced-Monks. Their eyes shimmer with glee.

I stand up from the Spot of Repose as Tadpole shuffles toward me. He digs into the burlap sack and hands me my phone in a plastic baggie.

"Time to go," he says.

"It's over?" I ask.

"Yes, Felix," Tadpole says. "Nothing is forever."

Before I can ask anything else or thank Tadpole for my newfound clarity, he crouches back down into pretzel position and closes his eyes.

I look down at him and then at my phone in the baggie. I place it into my pocket. An Assistant Monk I've never seen before emerges from between two skinny trees. She gestures for us Forced-Monks to follow her back to the Sacred Temple parking lot, where we got dropped off. She appears to have a full set of teeth. Soon enough, we're seated on a bus that'll take us and another five Forced-Monks back to the city. The woman with the injured ankle is nowhere to be found. The engine starts and we pull away from the Sacred Temple grounds. Staring out the window, I glimpse Tadpole's orange shape by the lagoon and watch it fade away in the distance. I smile. MonkCare worked this time. What a relief. No more mixing up medication labels, no more screwing up lives. It'll just be me and Bilbo from now on. Everyone will be so thrilled to know about my breakthrough. I should probably share it, if only to dispel the fear about this place. Just one last post before I sign off forever. I mean, people should know how enlightening MonkCare can be. My post could definitely be an example for others. I might even get a few Hearts in the process, maybe a lot of Hearts. Not that it matters. But I do wonder how many Hearts I can get. What would be a good hashtag? Can I say I saved Earl's life? That's not totally inaccurate. I helped at least. He's got a lot of followers. If I tag him, that'll probably up my Heart count. That would be nice. That would be a win. How funny would it be if my Monk-Care post got me a new Heart record? Ha! It's silly, I know, but I really want to make this last one something special.

HAPPY BIRTHDAY,
HONEY VANLANDINGHAM

LEE MARTIN

The invitation came in the mail on Monday. A postcard with Shuman's name on it asking him to please join The Patio Club at 7 p.m. on Saturday, September 5, at the home of Lynn and Ernie Fontaine to celebrate Honey Vanlandingham's fiftieth birthday. He'd felt close to the Fontaines since the evening he sat with them on the anniversary of their son's death and did them the favor of listening to them talk about their grief.

"Please come," Lynn had written on the invitation, and she'd drawn a smiley face followed by two exclamation points. How could he refuse?

His first thought was he'd have to ask his wife what sort of gift he should get a woman like Honey, but of course he couldn't do that because Elsa had moved out a few weeks ago, unable to tolerate his incompetence any longer, and was now living in an apartment in Marble Cliff just west of the Scioto River at a place called The Quarry. It was only twelve miles up I-71 from Grove City, but to Shuman it might as well have been twelve hundred.

Although he knew he no longer loved Elsa, he couldn't imagine never seeing her again.

"Can't we, please?" he'd said when he'd last talked to her on the phone. "Really, Elsa, I just need to know you're there."

"I don't think that's a good idea," she'd said before ending the call.

He'd driven through The Quarry a few nights after that. The complex had been built around a lake. The buildings were two stories high, each of them with gingerbread shingle siding on their fronts painted ocean blue as if The Quarry were a New England seaside village. Fountains sprayed in the lake. Mute swans floated. It was dusk and the water reflected the light fixtures outside the apartments. A skein of geese flew in and nested on the shore.

It felt strange to see Elsa's red Mini Cooper in the parking lot. Shuman knew which apartment was hers. He'd been able to get that much information from her, 2425 Quarry Lake Drive in the East Bay, but he promised himself he wouldn't disturb her. Maybe time was what they both needed, time to be away from each other, time to be alone. He didn't think it would make any difference—what was done was done—but he told himself to be open to the possibility that they'd right themselves and go on. "Keep your heart open," his mother had always told him, and he found, the older he got, how wise her advice was. No matter what happened with him and Elsa, he didn't want to become a bitter old man.

Her apartment was on the second floor. Her small balcony that overlooked the parking lot looked cozy with hanging baskets of ferns and twinkle lights and a hibachi grill. Shuman heard a dog barking, and when he looked through the sliding glass door that opened onto the balcony, he was surprised to see Elsa—her blinds were open—stooping over to pet a cocker spaniel. He'd never known her to like dogs. He supposed there was so much he'd never know about her, like precisely why she'd chosen this time to leave him. Of course, he had a history of disappointing her (there was the fire he'd caused in their old neighborhood, the one that had spread to neighbors' yards and decks, and after they'd moved to The Cove, he'd accidentally run into Lynn Fontaine's SUV), but he thought Elsa had accepted his mistakes and blunders long ago. He imagined she'd just been looking for an excuse to make a move, and for some reason she chose the accident in The Cove to be the final straw.

She was talking to someone on the phone. She straightened and left the cocker spaniel to paw at her feet. She brushed her hair out of her face and laughed, and for just that instant she was all alive to Shuman. He found himself drawn to her capacity for joy, something he supposed his presence had threatened to take from her. Now, she was reclaiming it. In this apartment on the lake at The Quarry she was returning to the girl she'd been, the one who'd first caught his eye. She had this apartment with its balcony. She had her dog. She had someone to talk to on the phone—someone who could make her laugh.

Despite his lingering sense of how he drove away from The Quarry that night, telling himself he'd leave Elsa to her new life, this invitation to Honey Vanlandingham's birthday party now threw him into a state. He so very much wanted to be a part of this group of neighbors who, after he'd run into Lynn Fontaine's SUV, had kept him at a distance. What to do? Decline or accept the invitation? He picked up his phone and called Elsa. He knew, even as he waited for her to answer, that he was calling so she'd know the neighbors now thought his company was something they thought they'd like to have, but he also really had no idea what sort of gift to bring.

"Oh, honestly, Sam," Elsa said after he'd explained his predicament. "You really have to make up your own mind about such things."

"I'm stumped, Elsa," he said. "You know I've never been good when it comes to things like this."

"Get her something pretty," Elsa said. "Women always like pretty things. They make us feel young and beautiful."

Which is how Shuman found himself later that day at Kay Jewelers, explaining to a clerk with lavender nail polish and flecks of red lipstick on her front teeth that he was shopping for a gift, a birthday present for an acquaintance.

"It's her fiftieth," he said.

"How nice." The clerk had a key on a yellow stretchy cord that she wore like a bracelet around her left wrist. Her name tag read BETTS. "And is this a special friend of yours?" Shuman swore he saw her wink at him. "Are we talking diamonds?"

"Gosh, no," he said. "I hardly know her. I just thought . . . well, you know what they say, women like pretty things."

"Indeed we do." Betts used the key on her yellow stretchy cord to unlock the display case where she was standing. "How about this?" she asked holding a pendant necklace to the hollow of her throat. "I can give you a good price here at the end of summer. It's a mini seashell pendant in sterling silver. What do you think?"

The days were still warm, but mornings the dew was heavy on the grass, and Shuman had seen spiderwebs in the yew bushes. The sun set a bit earlier each day and the night air had a bit of a chill to it and was filled with the chirps of crickets. He feared that winter days were just around the corner, those days of short light and the cold and the snow, and him all by himself, so for that reason alone he found the idea of the seashell pendant appealing. It carried with it an insistence on sunny days and ocean breezes and daylight that promised they would never leave.

The jewel lay on Betts's bosom at a point where her cleavage began. Shuman could see a shadow of powder there. He could smell its lilac scent.

"Only eighty-five dollars," she said. "Is this an eighty-five-dollar sort of acquaintance we're talking about?"

Shuman could remember hearing Honey telling Lynn Fontaine about her and Peter's trip to Sanibel Island in Florida. "It's my favorite place in the world," Honey had said. "White sand, and *all* that ocean."

Eighty-five dollars might be a bit much for a gift—might it seem like Shuman was trying too hard to make the neighbors like him?—but he couldn't stop imagining how much Honey would like the pendant, and he found himself saying, "I think it's perfect."

"Shall I gift wrap it?"

"Please," Shuman said.

He stood on the other side of the counter and watched Betts's lavender fingernails while she cut and folded and taped the silver wrapping paper. She cut a length of white ribbon and asked Shuman to put his finger "right there" while she tied a knot.

"Lucky girl," she said as she curled the ribbon. She slipped the gift-wrapped box into a Kay bag and handed it over. Again, he swore he saw her wink. "You come back and see me," she said.

. . .

On the appointed evening, Shuman showered and shaved and put on a new pair of khaki slacks and a cabana shirt he'd purchased at Kohl's. The shirt was an electric blue and covered with oranges. Tiny white script curved around each one of them. The words were so small Shuman had to squint to read them—*Eat me and stay young!* He wondered if it was an old advertising slogan or just something a designer had made up. Whatever it was, it spoke to him. No more gloom and doom, it seemed to be saying. Taste the juice of life. He thought the saying was bold and witty and the shirt festive with its bright colors, just the sort of thing for The Patio Club, but once he was at the Fontaines and in the company of the other men—Ernie Fontaine, Gunther Mikkler, Mitchell Stitt, and Peter Vanlandingham—each of them wearing a pastel-colored polo shirt, he felt out of place, and the slogan on his shirt now seemed vulgar.

"What's that say?" Ernie put his hands on his knees and bent down to get a good luck at the white script. He had a cigar clamped between his teeth, and the ash brushed Shuman's shirt. "Eat me and stay young?" Ernie straightened. "Hey, everybody, check out Shuman's shirt. It's the darnedest thing."

Mitchell Stitt angled over and took a look. He was a tall, slender man who wore horn-rimmed glasses. He peered over the top of them. "Excellent advice," he said. "One must lap up the juice. Isn't that what you say, Gunther?"

Gunther Mikkler was a broad-shouldered man who went to spin classes at the local YMCA. Shuman had seen him mowing his lawn in biking shorts and always shirtless. Similarly attired, he spent afternoons reading on his patio and turning darker as each day of the summer went on. Now at the end of the season, he was deeply tanned. He wore a pair of pale blue linen shorts, and his calf muscles bulged as he strode across the patio to where Ernie and Mitchell were standing with Shuman.

"I bet your wife got this shirt for you, yes?" Gunther lifted his eyebrows and gave Shuman a knowing grin. "Yes, of course she did. And where is she now? Don't tell me she's letting you go stag tonight."

Shuman had assumed everyone in the neighborhood knew about Elsa by now, but apparently he was wrong.

"Ixnay," Ernie said in a hushed voice. "That's a topic that's off limits."

He leaned toward Gunther and whispered something Shuman couldn't hear.

"My apologies," Gunther said with a curt nod of his head. "I don't always know what I should know. Let me get you a drink. A margarita, yes? Or would you prefer a glass of wine?"

Shuman was not ordinarily a drinker, but he didn't want to be a snob. Besides, Gunther had been so genuine with his apology. How would it look if Shuman were to decline his offer?

"Whatever everyone else is having will be fine," Shuman said.

"A margarita it is, then," Gunther said.

Suddenly Honey Vanlandingham was at Shuman's side.

"You wore that just for me, didn't you?" She was drinking a margarita in a glass the size of a small fishbowl. A curly lime-green straw stuck up above the rim, and she sipped at it. Then she said, "You're trying to make an old dame feel better, aren't you?" She laid her hand on his forearm and leaned in to whisper to him. "Did you know I'm fifty years old today? A half a century. Imagine that."

Honey was a pale woman with gray eyes, a small woman Shuman had previously considered icy and fierce, but as she stood beside him now, her fingers trembling slightly against his arm, he sensed that her birthday had knocked her flat. A half a century indeed. Shuman resisted the urge to take her hand in his. He knew he should say something comforting or at the very least make a joke that would make light of the fact that they were all moving closer, day by day, to the end of things, but he couldn't quite manage it. Instead, he looked into her eyes, and she looked into his, and for a moment it was as if they were the only two people in the world, and Shuman was filled with light because he had the sense that they understood each other. They were looking into each other's eyes, and what they weren't saying was how much they loved being alive, loved it so much because they knew how fragile it all was—this living.

"I saw an ad for burial plots." Ernie was trying out his latest quip. "And I said to myself, 'Hey, this is the *last* thing I need.'"

Shuman heard Peter Vanlandingham's braying laugh rise up above the others. Then Lynn said, "Ernie, you're a stitch. Isn't he just a stitch?"

"He really is," said Fiona Stitt. She was a short, stocky woman who always seemed to be smiling. "He always cracks me up."

Honey leaned even closer. She ducked her head and her hair brushed Shuman's shoulder. "Sometimes I get so scared," she said. "You know what I mean?"

"I do," said Shuman. Then Gunther was bringing him the promised margarita, and music came from somewhere, Jimmy Buffett's "Come Monday," and Peter swept Honey up in his arms and danced with her across the patio, leaving Shuman alone.

The gift-wrapped jewelry box was in the pocket of Shuman's slacks. He glanced around the patio, hoping to find the gifts the others had brought, but all he saw were envelopes with Honey's name on them tossed onto the patio table. He wondered whether he'd miscalculated, and for a moment he was tempted to keep the gift to himself, but what would he do with a pendant necklace? He'd bought it for Honey, and she should have it. He walked over to the table and added the gift-wrapped box to the envelopes, which he knew were full of birthday cards. He berated himself for neglecting to have a card to go along with his gift. He took in the sight of the couples. Honey and Peter were still dancing; Nan and Gunther were talking with Fiona and Mitchell; Lynn was coming from inside the house with a platter of hamburger patties for Ernie to put on the grill. She handed him the platter and then turned in Shuman's direction.

"Oh, good." She moved across the patio to him. "Someone got you a drink."

Shuman hoisted his glass to her and then took a sip of his margarita. "Thank you," he said. "Thank you for having me."

"Oh, pish." She waved her hand in the air as if to dismiss any thought of having done a charitable deed by inviting him. "You're our neighbor."

Shuman remembered the night—in fact, the last night Elsa had spent in their house—when he'd found himself on the Fontaines' patio, listening to the story of how their son had died. "It was a car crash," Lynn had said, "on West Broad Street. It was years and years ago, but sometimes it seems like it happened yesterday."

Then she swallowed hard and couldn't go on.

Ernie had picked up the story. "He was driving too fast, and a tire clipped a mound of dirt at a construction site and sent him flying. He wrapped his truck around a tree."

"His new truck," Lynn had added, barely audible.

Ernie had then looked at Shuman and said, "I was the one who bought him that truck. A high school graduation present. If I'd only known . . . "

It was then that Shuman had realized nothing was required of him but to sit there and let the Fontaines talk. Which he'd then done, long into the night, a night that endeared him to them and led to the invitation to Honey's birthday party.

"The birthday girl wants to keep dancing," Honey said now, as the Jimmy Buffett song stopped playing.

Peter begged off by saying his feet were aching and he was tired. "I mean it, Honey. I'm tapped."

So when the music started again, more Jimmy Buffett, this time "Cheeseburger in Paradise," Honey danced in a small circle that included Fiona and Nan. They weren't particularly good dancers, but they were enthusiastic, and Shuman, watching them, envied their abandon. How he wished he could be so at ease and so at home with himself. He remembered the first years of his marriage, when he and Elsa had been silly together. They'd danced to music, shared jokes, even thought up elaborate pranks. Somehow over the years that had all gone away, but now, watching the women dance brought it all back to him, and for a brief moment he wished he and Elsa could be those people again.

He also now realized that Lynn and Ernie had stayed together despite all the grief they carried with them about their
son's death. Couples split up all the time, but to lose a child?
Shuman couldn't imagine.

And still here they were, Ernie tending to the burgers on
the grill, and Lynn, noticing the gift-wrapped box on the
table, turning to consider her guests.

"Someone was naughty and broke our rule about gifts,"
she said. She swung her arm in an arc, pointing her finger at
whomever as she said, "Eeny, meeny, miny, mo."

"It must have been Peter," Nan said. Her close-cropped
white hair was spiky, and she wore red-rimmed glasses. She
nudged the gift-wrapped box with her finger. "Ja, what did
you get her, Peter?"

"In the tradition of honor common to all Englishmen,"
Peter said. "I cannot lie. No, dear Nan. I'm afraid I'm not the
culprit. I've already given Honey my gift."

"An Instant Pot," Honey said with a frown.

"You said it was what you wanted." Peter's voice shrank.
"Really, you did."

Shuman suddenly realized everyone was looking at him.

"I didn't know," he said.

"Oh, I should have told you," Lynn said. "Well. It can't be
helped. Honey, you might as well open it."

The margarita had gone to Shuman's head. He felt a little
fuzzy around the edges, just enough of a lift to loosen his
tongue a bit.

"Yeah, Honey," he said. "Open it. Happy Birthday."

He set his margarita glass on the low stone wall that curled
around the patio, then watched Honey walk, just a tad un-
steadily, to the table, where she picked up his gift. Her finger

caught a curl of the ribbon, and she pulled it out to its full length before letting it go. It curled back up, which delighted her.

"It's so nicely wrapped," she said, suddenly shy. "It seems such a shame to unwrap it."

Nan scrunched up her nose to lift her glasses higher. "But you must." She squinted. "We all want to see what Shuman got you."

"Yes, indeed," Peter said in a voice that was too bright, one that tried to compensate for what Shuman sensed was an anger rising in him. "We all want to see." He stretched his arms out in front of him and lifted them to the sky. "Every one of us wants to see."

This was Shuman's first inkling that he'd made a mistake. He'd spent too much on a gift that was too personal, one that would insult a husband who had given a wife a kitchen appliance.

"Go on," Fiona said. "I'm dying to know what's in that box."

It was too late now. Nothing Shuman could do could rescue the situation. So he stood on the periphery while the others gathered around the table where Honey was slipping the ribbon from the box.

"A seashell." Honey held up the pendant so everyone could see. "Isn't it the most beautiful thing?"

Lynn came up behind Honey and took the ends of the pendant's chain so she could fasten them around her neck. "There," Lynn said. "How's that?"

"Thank you," Honey said.

The silver seashell sparkled in the last of the sunlight. Shuman thought of sandy beaches and ocean waves.

"Geez," Ernie said. "I could have sworn it was a gag gift. Like a tube of denture adhesive, maybe. Or Preparation H."

"Oh, cripes, Ernie," Lynn said. "Give it a rest, will ya?"

"How did you know?" Honey asked Shuman. Her voice was full of wonder, and he thought it the most delightful thing he'd heard in quite some time. "How did you know I love the ocean?"

"I heard you tell Lynn about your trip to Sanibel Island." The truth, of course, was that it had all been serendipitous— the clerk at Kay Jewelers had merely picked it out of the case—but he decided not to tell Honey that, to instead make her believe he'd gone shopping for precisely this item because he'd remembered how much she said she loved the ocean. "What can I say?" He shrugged. "I pay attention."

Honey had to turn away. She put her hand to her mouth, and Shuman saw her shoulders wobble. He knew the gift had touched something in her, something raw, and for a few moments, no one knew what to do.

"Well, for heaven's sake, Honey," Peter finally said.

He tried to take her by her shoulders, but she shook him off. It was the slightest motion—no one would have noticed had they not had their senses heightened by the undeniable fact that Honey was near tears—but it was there all the same, that lifting of her shoulders that rejected Peter's offer of comfort.

"It's just so sweet," Honey said. "It's the sweetest gift anyone has ever given me."

Shuman would hold on to what Honey Vanlandingham had said to him all through the rest of that night. And when he woke the next morning, it would be the first thing he remembered—the way she'd looked at him with watery eyes and the way she came up on her toes and kissed him on the cheek.

"Who wants another margarita?" Gunther asked now, and, just like that, the party was back in full swing.

Only now, Shuman felt he was very much on its edge. From time to time, he caught one of the other guests staring at him, trying to figure out, perhaps, why someone like him—someone they barely knew—would make such a gift to Honey, who seemed to be embarrassed now. She went out of her way to avoid Shuman the rest of the evening. At one point, he observed her and Peter in the shadows of the patio, their heads close together and bent in conversation. Shuman took his opportunity to thank Lynn for the invitation and to make his way home to bed.

He woke for good the next morning, after his dreamy memory of Honey's kiss on his cheek, to the sound of his cell phone ringing. It was Elsa calling to see how things had gone at the party.

"I got to thinking," she said. "Well, I hope I didn't give you a bum steer with my advice to bring something pretty."

He told her, then, everything that had happened. He told her about the seashell pendant and the way Honey had been overcome with emotion. He also told her how odd he'd felt once the gift was opened and the pendant was on display.

"Like I'd gone too far," he said. "Like I had no right."

"Oh, Sam," Elsa said with a sigh. "You've done it again." Such was their history. Who knew how many times Elsa had been embarrassed by Shuman's inability to read people and situations, thereby leading to all sorts of missteps and bumbles. Once he'd told a co-worker of hers that her cat, with a black smudge of fur beneath its nose, looked like Hitler, and Elsa had been mortified. "Who wants to be told her cat resembles a monster like that?" she'd said in the car on their drive home. "I mean, really, Sam." Then there was the little matter of the day he accidentally caused a grass fire to move through their old neighborhood because he'd been burning leaves and had no regard for the wind. In other marriages, blunders like these might have made for the sorts of stories the husband and wife would tell over and over—*Remember when?*—inviting their listeners to laugh along with them, but in their case these mishaps became shameful secrets to carry around with them, their burden growing heavier over the years.

"I'm tired," Elsa had said when she left him. "I'm just so tired."

Now she said, "The gift was too expensive and too personal."

"I realize that now," he said. "I don't think Peter was very happy about it."

"No, I imagine not," Elsa said.

"But she loved it. She really did love it."

"You may have thought she loved it, and maybe she thought so, too. But really all it did was remind her of everything she doesn't have." Elsa paused, and Shuman heard her take in a long breath and let it out. "People are unhappy in all sorts of ways they don't realize until something comes along to remind them."

"Is that what I did? Remind her?"

"I'd say there's a very good chance that's exactly what happened."

Now, as he tried to decide whether to ask his next question, it was Shuman's turn to inhale. "So what was it that brought you to realize your own unhappiness with me?"

"It wasn't just one thing," she said. "It was everything. I felt like I was carrying our marriage on my back."

"Because of my . . . being a dope?"

"You should know something, Sam. I'm going to file for divorce."

After all their years together, it was finally coming to this. Shuman couldn't say he was surprised. In some ways, it came as a relief. No longer would he fear that something he might say or do would upset her. He was on his own now. He had no one else to answer to. Still, there was the prospect of all that time alone.

"You're certain that's what you want?"

"Yes, Sam. I'm certain."

Neither of them raised their voice. Neither of them cried.

"I'm sorry again about the gift," Elsa said.

"You tried to help," Shuman said. "You said buy something pretty. I should have known what to buy. I've never been good when it comes to people. Now what do I do? About Honey, I mean, and that pendant?"

"When you're in a hole," Elsa said, "it's best to stop digging. Don't do anything, Sam. Don't do anything at all."

• • •

That afternoon, Shuman was startled when his doorbell rang. He'd been nodding off in his chair, when he heard the chime. Peter Vanlandingham was standing on his front step.

"I say, do you shoot?" he asked when Shuman opened the door.

"Shoot?" Shuman's head was muzzy with sleep, and he was having trouble understanding. "Shoot?" he said again.

"Skeet," Peter said.

"Shoot skeet?"

"That's right. Do you shoot skeet?"

"I never have," Shuman said.

"Would you like to?"

"I don't have a gun."

"You can use one of mine." Peter pointed his finger at Shuman. "Eight o'clock tomorrow morning. I'll pick you up."

Which is how Shuman found himself at the Black Wing Shooting Center with a Benelli SuperSport 12-gauge to his shoulder, waiting to call "Pull!" so a machine in the skeet house could fling a clay target out ahead of him and he could try to shoot it. He'd already seen Peter take twenty-five shots and break twenty-four targets. In that time, Shuman realized that the reason Peter had invited him was he knew he would be lousy at shooting. Peter wanted to embarrass him the way Shuman had done when he'd given Honey that pendant.

Still, Peter had kindly and patiently shown Shuman how to mount the gun, raising it to his shoulder as he gently swung the barrel to track the flight of the target. Peter had shown him how to lay his face to the stock, to keep both eyes open, to see only the bead on the barrel, to hold his face still after the shot.

Shuman had watched Peter's perfect form. Now he was ready to try to duplicate it even though he knew there was little hope.

"Lean forward to absorb the recoil," Peter told him.

Shuman could hear him even though he was wearing earplugs. "Right," he answered. Peter had lent him a pair of safety glasses. Shuman nodded. "Pull," he said.

Then the clay targets were flying at all angles—from the

high house and the low house, sometimes singles, sometimes doubles, sometimes incoming and sometimes outgoing. Shuman had no time to think, only to react, and because of that, he'd reason later, something miraculous happened. His vision narrowed and all he saw were the bead and the targets, and each kick of the gun seemed the natural result of his having pulled the trigger. He'd never been good at much of anything in his life, but for some reason he was good at this. He moved from station to station, maintaining his focus, and when all was done, he'd hit all twenty-five of the targets.

"I thought you said you'd never shot," Peter said.

"Never in my life." Shuman was still quite dazed by the experience he'd just had. Never had he been so good at something. It was like he'd been shooting skeet for years. "I really can't explain it," he said.

He wanted to revel in the memory of the targets shattering as he fired. He could feel the soreness in his shoulder from the shotgun's kick, and he would be sad in the days to come when the ache would fade and then completely disappear. He liked carrying it with him as a reminder of that glorious morning in September—the bright sun, the cornstalks in the fields beginning to turn from green to brown, the sounds of the crows overhead—the morning when, for a brief time, he'd been perfect.

But Peter was now demanding an apology. "I don't know who you think you are," he said, "to give my wife a gift like that, but it's caused a row between us." He broke his gun, a double-barrel 12-gauge, open at the breech and cradled it over his left arm. "A royal row," he said.

Then he waited, one eyebrow lifted, for the apology Shuman found himself unwilling to give. Whatever trouble his gift had stirred up had been there long before he knew the Vanlandinghams, so he saw no good reason that he should say he was sorry.

"I don't know anything about what's between you and Honey," he said, "but I'm not sorry I gave her something she liked. The clerk at the jewelry store suggested it, and when I saw it I thought immediately, why, that's just the thing." He took the plugs from his ears and shook them in his fist like they were dice. Then he said the thing he'd never be able to take back or make right. "I know a thing or two about misery," he said, "and I can tell you your wife is unhappy, the kind of unhappy that doesn't go away easily, the kind someone carries deep inside, the kind that's hard to fix."

"What do you know about what Honey feels?"

"I know." Shuman knew because he'd seen the way she was close to tears after she'd opened the gift box and seen the pendant. That and the way she'd shrugged off Peter's grip on her shoulders when he tried to comfort her. He knew because when he saw Honey do that, he understood how Elsa had felt in their marriage, as if she couldn't get away from Shuman's incompetence. Oh, if she'd only been able to see him shooting those clay targets. Who knew what that might have meant to the two of them? "I didn't cause it," he said now. "I just brought out what was already there. If it hadn't been that pendant, it would have been something else. You might say I did you a favor. Now you know where you stand."

Peter suddenly snapped his gun together at the breech. He shouldered the gun and put his finger on the trigger. "Who are you to say these things to me?"

"Me?" Shuman winked. He stared at the gun's muzzle, only inches from his face. "I'm a straight shooter," he said.

And what happened next became the sort of story told in whispers, when it was spoken of at all, at the Patio Club's future gatherings. The story of the day Peter Vanlandingham, angry over the gift of that pendant and what Shuman had said to him at the Black Wing Shooting Center, trained his 12-gauge on Shuman and pulled the trigger.

What happened was the hammer came down on an empty barrel, but the sound of it caught Shuman by the heart, and his breath quickened the way it did sometimes when he was coming down the stairs and missed a step and, for an instant, before he regained his footing, thought he was going to fall.

"Bang!" Peter said. Then he got in his car and drove away, leaving Shuman to find his own way back to The Cove.

. . .

So it was that Shuman thought himself a lucky man. How else to explain what had happened at the Black Wing Shooting Center? Lucky he hadn't made a fool of himself. Lucky he'd been darned good shooting those clay targets. Lucky Peter Vanlandingham had only been bluffing when he pointed his gun at Shuman and pulled the trigger. Lucky to be alive. He had his cell phone. He knew how to arrange an Uber pickup. He was about to become the stuff of legend among the members of the Patio Club, the man who'd gone toe-to-toe with Peter shooting those targets and had come out on top.

"What did you do when he pulled that trigger?" someone in the club—Ernie or Mitchell Stitt or Gunther Mikkler—would ask from time to time whenever the story got told.

Shuman would tell the truth. "I laughed."

What else was he to do? Then he called for the Uber and

went home, and walked into his house, feeling as if he were on the verge of a new and exciting life.

A few days later, he walked into Kay Jewelers and asked the clerk with the lavender fingernails, Betts, if she'd care to have a cup of coffee with him sometime.

"Seashell pendant." She pointed a finger at him. "I hope your friend liked her gift."

It was hard to say whether Honey Vanlandingham had approved of the pendant, or quickly disliked it because it was something that would always remind her of how unhappy she was, but Shuman felt confident of one thing.

"She found it painfully beautiful," he said, and Betts gave him a quizzical look.

"I never quite heard it put that way," she said. "Painful and beautiful."

"I think it made quite an impression," he said. "What time do you get off work?"

Betts glanced at her wristwatch. "Another hour," she said.

"I'll be back," Shuman told her.

Which he was. Promptly at five o'clock, he opened the door and found Betts reaching under the counter for her purse.

"I thought maybe you'd change your mind," she said.

"Am I late?"

She laid her hand on his arm. "Only by about thirty years. What the heck took you so long?"

They laughed about that as they had coffee at the Giant Eagle market on Stringtown Road. Betts told him her story—widowed young nearly thirty years ago and never remarried—and he told her his.

"Two broken people," she said with a laugh.

And Shuman surprised himself by answering with something perhaps too forward for a first date. "Two pieces can fit together. All it takes is a little glue."

That's when she reached her hand across the table, and he knew she was offering it to him. He was about to take it. Right there in the coffee cafe with customers waiting for their lattes and their espressos and folks browsing the wine aisles and lining up at the sushi counter. It was near the dinner hour and people were stopping to pick up this or that before hurrying home to their families. Shuman dreaded the empty house. That was the worst part of having Elsa gone, all the hours alone, and he wasn't quite used to the silence and the feeling that anything might happen to him—he could drop dead, for Pete's sake—and there'd be no one there to stand witness. Now here was this woman who'd taken a fancy to him, and who was he to resist? He lifted his hand from his coffee cup, knowing it would be warm when he took her hand, which he was just about to do—he was so close his fingertips brushed hers—when Honey Vanlandingham suddenly appeared at his side, her arms open to him.

"Stand up, you," she said, "so I can give you a big hug."

She was wearing a white tennis dress, the seashell pendant resting just above its scooped neck. Her voice was too loud, too bright. Shuman saw a number of the other coffee drinkers look up from their tables to see what was happening. Most of all, he saw the hurt look on Betts's face as she drew her hand back and let it drop to her lap.

"Honey," he said, and he knew right away this had been the wrong thing to say. How would he ever be able to explain to Betts that he was merely calling Honey by her name and not using a term of endearment?

To his surprise, he was rising. Something in Honey's eyes—some pleading—was calling him to her. Then her arms were around his neck, and she was pulling him against her, and he felt her desperation, which he knew was his own, and what could he do but slip his arms around her waist and hug her back?

"Oh, you sweet man," she said. "You sweet, sweet man."

Over her shoulder, he saw Betts, her head bowed, picking at the lavender polish on her nails. He wanted to tell her the truth, but then she lifted her head and looked at him with such a sad longing, as if she truly believed he was the sort of man a woman like Honey Vanlandingham might love. He wasn't sure if any woman had ever looked at him like that, not even Elsa when they were first starting out, and he let himself revel in the thought that he was indeed that kind of man, unwilling to let the illusion go even as Betts stood and walked away from him.

Honey smelled of some sweet perfume mixed with perspiration. He could feel the knots of her spine beneath her tennis dress. A damp strand of hair had come loose from her scrunchie and stuck to her cheek. She settled into their hug, and Shuman allowed it even though he knew what it was costing him. He knew he'd probably never go back to Kay Jewelers. He'd be too ashamed. And so he and Betts would go on with their separate lives, and he'd wonder from time to time about what might have been. But so much was on the horizon, so much that was uncertain—what twists and turns might await him with Elsa and the divorce, not to mention Peter Vanlandingham and whatever was going on with him and Honey—but this hug right now was the realest thing Shuman knew, and he gave himself to it, unwilling to let it go.

"You know me," Honey whispered to him. "You really, really know me."

The two of them clung to each other, and Shuman found himself asking her what he'd been wondering on and off since Peter pointed his gun at him and pulled the trigger. "Are you happy? Truly happy?"

Honey didn't answer. She kept holding him, and he kept holding her. He knew there was no good answer to his question—what would he have said had she asked him the same?—so finally, just to fill the silence between them, he said, "Me, too."

That's when she slipped out of his arms. He watched her walk away, out through the sliding glass doors, out into the last of the sunlight, knowing for days and days to come he'd recall the feel of her body against his, and the pain on Betts's face, and the way Betts looked at him like he was someone special she'd almost had but not quite. Someone worth mourning.

THE TALLEST MOUNTAIN IN THE WORLD

MICHAEL HOPKINS

Dr. Merton gave Shelby Aronowitz bad news. The pain in her knee was osteosarcoma. They would have to amputate the leg.

"Can't they replace it?" Shelby's mother asked. "I mean, just the knee?"

"No," Dr. Merton said. "We need to remove bone too far above and below the joint." He brought up an image from Shelby's MRI. On the large screen in the small room, he pointed at the dark spots. He cleared his throat. "But the good news is you can be fitted with a prosthetic leg. The technology is evolving quickly. There's no reason you can't have a full life."

Shelby's mother wrapped her arms around Shelby's broad shoulders and began to cry. It wasn't her strongest embrace. Shelby pictured her mother in bed at noon, propped up with pillows, a box of Kleenex on her lap, whining on the phone to Aunt Arella about this or that.

Dr. Merton continued, "Ride a bike, dance, even run. You have a very strong physique."

Shelby pulled away from her mother and stretched out her leg. "I want to keep it," she said.

No one answered her, so she glanced up at Dr. Merton's face. It reminded her of the fudge cheese her Aunt Arella made and sometimes gave her: Chew it all you want but you could taste neither fudge nor cheese.

He finally spoke up to say, "Not recommended. It's localized now, but probably, very likely, it will spread into some of your other systems."

"No," Shelby said. "What I'm saying is—all I'm saying is, I want to keep the leg."

"Shelby," her mother said. "For god's sake, listen to the man. He knows what he's talking about."

"You don't know what *I'm* talking about," Shelby said. "I want to keep what they cut off." She stood and remained standing despite the pain shooting from her knee up into her groin.

"Impossible," her mother said. "Right, Doctor? Tell her."

Dr. Merton looked at his watch and stood. Obviously he had other patients to see, some with cancer, some without.

He turned to Shelby's mother. "Believe it or not Mrs. . . . believe it or not, there *is* a protocol for Shelby's request." He allowed himself to take in a deep breath. "As a minor, she'd need your approval, and there'd be plenty of papers for you to sign and a few additional costs, but, to be honest with you, it's not impossible."

"No way," Shelby's mother said. "No way are we spending money to be reminded of how you had cancer."

"Says who?" Shelby asked.

"Says me," her mother said. "Who else?"

• • •

The phone rang and Shelby's mother answered it and put it on speaker and set it beside her on her bed, as she was wont to do. Shelby, in her own room, wasn't listening closely at first, even though she recognized the voice as belonging to her uncle Jacob. Then, after she heard her name mentioned, she tiptoed over to the slightly open door to her room, opened it wider, and gave their conversation her full attention.

"No, listen to me," Uncle Jacob was saying. "You should know something. I talked to her. She wants me to sue you."

"Sue me? Did you say sue me?"

"Yes."

"But I'm her mother."

"She also told me the cancer has changed her. No more aspiring to be an actress; she wants to go into law."

Shelby's mother went silent.

"Can't you imagine," Uncle Jacob said, "Shelby and my little Zeke, seeing to it that the family business lives on? Benjamin and I discussed this many times when he was alive. And Shelby would be a great attorney, by the way. My brother—I mean, your husband—is now doubtless smiling down on how well this could all turn out."

Shelby's mother was still at a loss for words.

Then: "You are *not* seriously considering this."

"*Aronowitz and Aronowitz.* I thought it would end when Benjamin passed, but now it could live forever. There's that psalm Benji loved so much: 'One generation shall commend your works to another, and shall declare your mighty acts.'"

"You're saying this psalm was written for Shelby's ears?"

"I'm saying it was written and her father read it and said it out loud many times. And I'm sure she heard it—because, well, even though he's gone now, here we are."

"Well, if the point of her practicing law is so she can sue her mother, I'm not sure the psalm ended up doing what it was supposed to."

"That's not the point of her wanting to practice. They're two separate things, her wanting to practice and her wanting to sue you by having me file a complaint."

"So you're telling me you're going to let her do it."

"Do what?"

"Sue her own mother."

"Of course we're not going to let her sue you," he said. "Because she has a case, which means you *really* don't want her to sue you. This is why I called you. I agreed to work with her, and she's my deceased brother's daughter, so now I'm letting you know you should stop trying to control what she and I and for that matter god will succeed in doing anyway."

"What do you mean, work with her?"

"I've researched it. There's no law here against keeping the leg, or any body part. In some states—Louisiana, Georgia, Missouri, it's against the law—but even there, if you're part of certain religious groups that believe the body is physically resurrected, as when the Christ supposedly returns, you can keep these parts to be buried with you."

Shelby smiled. Her uncle, she realized, was as full of subtle wit as he was smart.

"Jacob, do you hear yourself?" her mother asked.

"Even in states where there is no law against this . . . I have it right here. The Native American Graves Protection and Reparation Act makes it illegal to own or trade in Native American remains. It's unclear to me if this still applies to Native American individuals and their own body parts. But, see, that's not our problem here."

"Can we quit discussing this?" Shelby's mother asked, and Shelby, holding on to the doorframe because her knee was throbbing, rolled her eyes.

"Sure, but you should probably know a reporter's already been here," Jacob said. "From *The Sentinel.*"

"About Shelby?"

"Not at first," Jacob said. "He wanted to interview me about the Brazilian acquisition of Madison Dynamics. This reporter was a young man, but nice. I couldn't answer most of his questions for legal reasons, but then Shelby called—right then, right when he was sitting across my desk. And I was so happy about her decision to go into law, I told this young man everything she told me."

Jacob paused long enough that Shelby was sure her mother would go off. But all Shelby heard was the sound of herself breathing.

"I thought the leg thing might have been a joke," Jacob continued, "since Benjamin was always a practical joker. I never knew when to believe him and figured maybe it had rubbed off on her. Anyway this reporter plans to talk to her. I guess her leg is news."

"My god, Jacob."

"I may have made an error in judgment," Jacob said. "That's basically why I called you."

"My god."

"You've got Benjamin's ashes on the mantle in your living room. I don't see harm in letting Shelby hang her leg on the wall of her bedroom. Seriously, what would be the harm?"

The call ended, apparently because Shelby's mother hung up. For the first time, Shelby imagined her bad leg mounted on the wall above her bed. It would be visible from the street at night if she had the light on and the shades up, she realized.

And she thought, No.

Not there.

Someplace else.

· · ·

Despite having very little factual information, the reporter's article ran the following Sunday, in the community section of *The Sentinel*.

Upon reading it, Shelby's mother said, "I want you to sue *them*."

"There's nothing slanderous or fallacious in the article," Uncle Jacob said. He was visiting, drinking coffee with Shelby and her mother that morning. "We have no legal grounds."

"But the thing is, she's being taunted at school."

"I'll be fine, Mother," Shelby said, sipping coffee.

But Shelby's mother pressed on, facing Jacob: "At dinner she tells me a boy, a hunter, offered to mount her leg. And now we're getting calls from other reporters. And the TV wants her to come in and be interviewed *live and on the air.* I'm losing my mind!"

"Why?" Jacob asked her. "So they ask a few questions? She answers them and—"

"You were going to sue me," Shelby's mother said. "All I'm saying is I want you to sue *them*—to get them to stop."

"That might backfire," Jacob said. "I mean, they might write articles about *that.* I say just sign the consent form. She needs the surgery and wants the leg. You're holding her back."

Shelby's mother fretted, then frowned. She batted her eyes angrily.

"This is an abomination," she said.

. . .

Shelby sat on the edge of her bed and straightened out both legs. She thought the right one, the cancer leg, was a little shorter than the left. Certainly that knee hurt more than it had the day before. Her phone rang, caller unidentified. She answered it with a flat "Hello."

"Am I speaking with Shelby Aronowitz?" The caller had one of those low-toned voices, a late-night radio voice.

"Yes," Shelby said. "Who's this?" She settled back and shut her eyes, and her shoulders dropped, a puppet with the strings cut.

"Glen Smith," the caller said. "I work for—actually, I own—Casselton Skulls. We specialize in the preservation and sale of bones: mostly skulls, animal skulls, and some full skeletons, mostly animal skeletons."

Shelby sat up. "Is this a joke?" She tried to place the voice. "Who is this? How did you get my number?"

"Please, Miss Aronowitz, this is not a crank call. We are one of two companies in the States that handle human needs of your type."

Shelby thought he now sounded like the man from the funeral parlor who'd met with her and her mother after her father died. There'd been an attempt at solemnity in that man's tone, and Shelby had known right away back then that this must be part of the job, so with this guy, this Glen Smith guy, she wanted to believe that he was genuine—that he understood and cared, but she had her doubts about that.

"When you say my needs," she managed to say, "what do you mean exactly?"

"I would receive your leg, personally and directly, from the surgeon. In advance I would discuss his methodology with him to ensure the separation from the body is done . . . with respect, I mean with more care than is taken by surgeons who tend to be in a hurry. If you wish, I could even offer to be present at the procedure."

Shelby realized she hadn't thought through the details of what would happen between the surgery and when she'd be handed back her leg.

"You've done this before?" she asked.

"Yes. We don't deal with soft tissue: breasts, ovaries, intestinal lengths, or tumors. Just bones—kneecaps, feet, hands. But we've never had the privilege of such a large portion of a limb. You'd be our first."

"How much does this cost?"

"It might seem insensitive to charge you, but not charging you would set a precedent—everyone would expect the same. Though we *are* prepared to give you a thirty percent discount, meaning our fee of three thousand dollars would be reduced to twenty-one hundred. And, should you want one, we'd provide an extra observer at the procedure for no charge."

"Why so much money?" Shelby wanted to know. "My friend had a deer head mounted for four hundred bucks."

"Here's our process: After removal and transportation, we deflesh the limb with dermestid beetles, a very common practice in this industry, and then, of course, we sterilize and whiten the bones."

"So I'd get only the bones."

"Correct. But they'd be spotless and disinfected."

"May I ask what you do with the beetles when they're done?"

"After skeletonization is complete, we keep half and any associated larvae; the other half we release back into nature."

"Could I choose where the beetles are released?"

"We've never had that request, but I'm sure we could work it out."

Shelby imagined a package arriving by an overnight Federal Express. Inside would be part of herself, solid and clean and permanent.

"Well, I'm interested," she said to Glen Smith.

"You'll also be glad to know we wire the bones together to insure long-term stability. In your case we'd be dealing with quite a few bones: four in the knee, fourteen in the ankle, and thirty-eight in the foot. Labor intensive. I'm assuming you want the leg intact, versus a box of bones, which we could do at a greatly reduced rate."

"Oh, no," Shelby said. "I mean you're right—if I'd do this with you, I'd want the leg in one piece."

"Very good, Miss Aronowitz. We would suggest that."

"The thing is, I need to talk to my mother about the money."

"We've handled that for you. Have you heard of the Mutter Museum, in Philadelphia?"

"No."

"They have a large and varied collection of human artifacts. About three thousand. Wet and dry."

Shelby wondered how they distinguished between wet and

dry. Was it how the piece arrived in their hands, or how it was displayed?

"They have parts of Einstein's brain and John Wilkes Booth's spine."

Glen Smith paused. He seemed to want a "wow" from Shelby, but she remained quiet as she tried to figure out where he was going with all this.

Then he said, "They've offered to pick up the cost if you agree to will them your leg, to be delivered after you . . . pass on, which, naturally, we're all hoping won't be for a long, long time."

"Why would they want to do that?" Shelby asked. "I'm not famous."

"Uh . . . if Twitter is any indication, your fame will be growing for quite a while."

"Really? I'm not a Twitter person—"

"Hashtag *Keeping It*. Everyone's into you, Shelby, and most of them think you're pretty cool. And they seem to enjoy exchanging theories about why you want to do this."

Shelby was taken aback. Twitter? She'd always been more into Instagram, where she'd posted nothing whatsoever about her leg.

Why Twitter? she wondered. Did that reporter tweet something?

"Do you mind," Glen Smith asked, "if I ask you?"

"Ask me what."

"Why you want to keep it?"

"I'm not sure," Shelby said.

"I'm guessing the answer is part of the same mystery we've dealt with again and again. It's a feeling, a calling, a notion that something—some action that's out of the ordinary—is significant."

"Yes," Shelby said. "That's a good way of putting it. What you're talking about right there—that feeling—that's pretty much the feeling I've felt."

. . .

Shelby sat at the table in front of a plate of wild-caught salmon and broccoli florets, googling images of Glen Smith: buzz cut, a plain face pink as a pencil eraser, a fairly honest-looking guy.

Her mother finished her dinner quickly and started washing the dishes. For almost forty minutes, neither she nor Shelby spoke.

Shelby broke the unspoken truce:

"Mom. No charge. A guy named Glen Smith at a place called Cassleton Skulls does this with human bones full-time."

A plate fell from her mother's hand and smashed on the kitchen floor. Pieces shot everywhere. Thankfully this plate wasn't from the good china in the front-room cabinet; this was an everyday plate. Still, there was redness in Shelby's mother's cheeks. The redness of embarrassment, the redness of rancor, the redness of both—Shelby couldn't be sure.

"Fuck all these people!" her mother shouted. "Fuck all these reporters, fuck your uncle, fuck my friends! Who *is* this guy who wants to petrify your leg? You. Are. *Dying*, Shelby! You need *cancer surgery*! First your father, and now I'm also supposed to lose *you*? Fuck your leg—I don't ever want to see it again. Fuck everybody. Fuck you!"

She grabbed a wet glass from the sink and pitched it at the floor, Shelby shielding her eyes from ricocheting shards.

Shelby feared for her life as another glass shattered.

Then another, and another, and another.

. . .

"You'll see a counselor," Shelby's mother said.

She was standing just beyond the open door to Shelby's room.

"You'll see a counselor," she added, "if you want any chance whatsoever at having me sign those papers."

"*I'll* see a counselor?" Shelby asked from her bed, phone in hand.

Her mother nodded.

"*You'll* see a counselor," Shelby said. "That is, if you want any chance at having me have the surgery in the first place."

"Oh, don't going playing insolent."

"I'm not, Mom. All I'm doing is letting you know that you have as many problems as I do."

Shelby's mother raised her before-dinner wine to her lips. Sipped some.

Said, "Okay, but only if you see the guy, too."

"You mean go with you?" Shelby asked.

Her mother sipped again, this time maybe less out of habit.

"No," she said. "I mean we'd go separately. I want us both to be able to tell the truth."

"Okay," Shelby said, the pain in her leg all at once worse, and her mother turned around and walked off without a sound.

And Shelby's mother stayed that way—silent—for the three days that passed before Shelby was off, out of the house, driving their only car herself despite her bad leg, which she'd told her mother felt fine but didn't, to see Dr. Lubitsch.

Dr. Lubitsch's office was large. Dark. Slatted wooden shades covered the windows. Floor to ceiling bookshelves lined the walls, crammed with sets of old hardbacks. Shelby kept her eyes on the books as she walked to the brown leather chair Dr. Lubitsch had motioned her to sit in. She could not recognize a single title. She thought the lights in the room needed brighter bulbs. How could the guy read in here? She sank into the chair. The chair enveloped her, was comfortable.

"Nice to meet you, Shelby," Dr. Lubitsch said. He sat on a straight-backed chair across the room.

Shelby nodded in his direction.

"Are you comfortable?" he asked. "How does your knee feel?"

"It hurts. Like a bad sprain that won't get better."

"Yes," Dr. Lubitsch said. "And I understand it won't."

Shelby winced. It was as if this man was about to recite lines her mother had emailed him.

"Still holding out hope?" he asked. "For a miracle?"

Shelby shrugged.

"That's normal," Dr. Lubitsch said. "I've seen many patients who hope for miracles, but I've never seen a miracle that can't be explained." He shifted in his chair. "There *are* solutions, though, based on science. The mind can work wonders. It can be tuned to work better than it normally does."

Shelby laughed a nervous beat's worth. "So what are you saying? What are you saying my problem is?" She was anxious to talk about her mother. About how she'd had to do everything for her mother the first year after her father's death: the cleaning, the cooking, and always making sure her mother took her meds. About how her mother never let her use the car, going even so far as hiding the keys. About how she'd then always wondered if her mother would be there to pick her up after school activities—about having to hitchhike home more than once. How her mother would then, on those nights, refuse to make eye contact, never listening about how *Shelby* felt about the man who, yes, had been her mother's spouse, but who had also been Shelby's father. How her mother never paid much attention to her until now.

Lubitsch finally composed himself enough to say quietly, "I never said you had a problem." He was a small man, perfectly proportioned but very small. "We're here to talk—that's it."

Shelby rolled her eyes. The deck was clearly stacked against her with this jerk. She tipped back her head and looked at the top of a bookshelf, on which sat skulls. Some were big, one maybe from a massive boar; another obviously from a horse's head. Many with horns both straight and curved. Some tiny ones probably from birds.

Dr. Lubitsch turned in his chair. "Do those bother you?"

"No," Shelby said. "I like them."

"Some of my patients don't," he said. "I usually meet clients in a different room. I was wondering if you'd appreciate them."

"I do," Shelby said. "When did you start collecting them?"

"The first was the horse skull I found in the trash. I trash-pick around the university when the students move out. You can find lots of interesting stuff. I didn't really have a collection until people—friends, clients, so forth—started giving me skulls they'd come across. The coyote is from Colorado, from a woman suffering from a borderline personality disorder. The ram is from Nevada. That particular young man had bipolar tendencies. The large bird was from an elderly couple I treated for hoarding; their collection is vast compared to mine. The deer was from a friend, a hunter who also likes to give me venison every year."

He scanned the collection, his eyes stopping here and there.

"Each has a story."

"I imagine," Shelby said.

"Did you know," Dr. Lubitsch asked, "that some forms of meditation direct you to imagine your flesh dropping away until you're just a skeleton? Then you're supposed to imagine removing your head—as just a skull now, of course—from your body, and inserting it, upside down and reversed, under your ribcage."

He patted his stomach as if maybe Shelby hadn't understood.

"I've heard it's quite effective," he added.

Whatever, Shelby thought, but she said, "I don't see why it wouldn't be."

"Do you know what phantom limb pain is, Shelby?"

Shelby nodded. "I've read about it."

"Sometimes patients go out of their minds with the pain, believing that their lost limb is spasming." He held out his hand and made a fist. "Clenching up."

"Isn't there medication for that?"

"No. Acupuncture, massage, the mirror box. Have you heard of that?"

Shelby shook her head no.

"Let's say you've lost your right arm. Imagine you are sitting to the side of a big mirror, and you insert your stump into a box behind the mirror. You are then instructed to look at the reflection of your other arm and imagine it's the one that's missing." He held both his arms out. "When you stretch out your good arm and wiggle your fingers, you look at the reflection and imagine it's your other arm, the missing one."

Shelby nodded, trying to remain patient until they talked about her mother.

"You don't seem too impressed," Dr. Lubitsch said.

"Sounds like something that could work just fine for some people. For me, I think simply keeping my leg will help me be cool with what's what."

Dr. Lubitsch nodded slowly a few times. His eyes seemed to twinkle just a bit for a few moments on end. Or maybe, Shelby, thought, I'm imagining that. She looked back up, at the top of the bookshelf with the skulls.

She pointed. "Is that from a cat?"

"Yes," Dr. Lubitsch said, looking up as well. "My Smokey. Had him thirteen years, then . . . well, I hate to say this, but cancer got him."

Shelby waited for his gaze to meet hers, then brightened her expression as if to say, *See?*

"Sometimes I hold his skull," Dr. Lubitsch admitted. "I wonder if the seat of the soul isn't in the skull." He smiled. "Once a friend wanted to give me a human skull, but my wife said no. Too creepy." He glanced at Shelby's bad leg.

She pointed again. "What's that one? Where did you get it?"

Dr. Lubitsch looked up at the large damaged skull. "A long story." He leaned in. "It's fragments of an allosaurus."

"How old is it?"

"About 150 million years."

"Immortal," Shelby said. "In a way."

Dr. Lubitsch raised his eyebrows.

Then he nodded.

"Shall we talk about your mother?" he asked.

"Sure."

"Tell me what's your biggest gripe concerning her."

"That she's not talking to me. Hasn't been for days. And that, last we spoke, she made it clear she still doesn't want to sign the papers that would let me keep my leg."

. . .

During the next two weeks, Shelby became nervous about everything. It didn't help that, the day after she met with Dr. Lubitsch, she met with two young doctors, one who would be her surgeon, and they were both very direct, even more so than Dr. Merton had been. About the fact that she would be "knocked out" for the surgery. About the need to "amputate." These were the words they used, *knocked out* and *amputate*, as well as other turns of phrase that assured her and anyone else within earshot that they were, probably because of their training, all business. As she met with them, she felt herself shift into a new level of nervousness, which she tried to convince herself was really only a new depth.

Then, during the nearly two weeks that followed, as she waited for the day of the surgery itself, she found herself feeling this level of nervousness about most everything. It was hitting her, the significance of the changes that were coming to her life. For most of the twelve days before her surgery she sat in her room, where she was waited on by her mother, who told her again and again to remain immobile, a directive one of the young no-nonsense doctors, the one who was not the surgeon, had given her mother over the phone.

Her mother said little else to her, certainly nothing about signing the papers that would let her keep her leg, and at first this reticence disappointed Shelby, but as the twelve days went on, Shelby sensed courage was not her mother's greatest strength, and she felt sorry for her mother and tried to please her by keeping their conversations as short as possible.

It was with six days to go that summer break started, a bad coincidence of timing, since this only reminded Shelby she was not outside running or walking or doing whatever every other person her age was doing now that the weather was nice and school wasn't weighing anyone down. For her it was now only google this, google that, eat, watch a Netflix movie that wasn't as interesting as the movies she used to see when she was a kid, check Instagram, check Facebook, binge a TV series, eat, check Insta, sleep, wake up, check Facebook to allow more possibly interesting posts to build up on Insta for when she'd finally break down to allow herself to click up Insta again.

It was during these last six days that she realized she didn't have any real friends.

At least none that were real enough to stop by and visit.

Uncle Jacob and Aunt Arella had been stopping by sometimes during the last six days, maybe three or four times altogether—but family doesn't count as friends, Shelby thought.

. . .

They were sitting on two leather chairs in Shelby's father's old study. Shelby was glad to be out of her bedroom, finally allowed to move around, and she didn't mind talking to Dr. Lubitsch. Her mother came in and gave them each a glass of coconut-flavored sparkling water. Her mother left and pulled the door shut until the latch clicked.

"Were you always active at school?" Dr. Lubitsch asked.

"After my father died."

Shelby squeezed the thigh of her bad leg and scanned the room. An old dirty coffee mug of her father's sat on his desk, adjacent to the last legal pad he'd used, his cartridge ink pen still lying on top. The blinds were down. It was quiet.

Shelby said, "I did a lot more with my father than I knew until later. Fishing. Hiking. Talking. Once we drove clear around a lake, like a hundred miles on a Sunday afternoon, just to do it."

Dr. Lubitsch, appearing more comfortable here than in his own office, said, "You could be . . . overfunctioning, a lot of activity with no meaningful connections. A behavior not uncommon when filling a void. Never a minute to stop and take a breath. Like an insect, a water strider, zigzagging on the top of life's pond, afraid to stop for fear of sinking. Our technology, all the screens we carry, makes it easy."

Shelby wanted to check her phone, felt guilty, and instead reached into her pocket and just touched it.

Dr. Lubitsch leaned back. "And your mother?"

"What about her?"

"Has she decided whether to sign the papers?"

"I thought that's what you were going to tell me."

Dr. Lubitsch shrugged.

"I guess she's still deciding," he said. "But I guess that's her right. It's a big decision for both of you, you know."

No, it's not, Shelby wanted to say. It's a big decision for me, and it's not right that she's not letting me make it.

"Anyway," Dr. Lubitsch said, "how are you two getting along of late?"

"I'm mean to her. Probably more than I should be."

"Not uncommon for teenagers. Especially if the opposite sex parent with whom you had a good relationship is now gone." Dr. Lubitsch waited to see if this registered with Shelby. "Very common in divorce."

Shelby swirled her drink. Bubbles in it rose to the surface and fizzed. It was a comforting sound for Shelby, and it reminded her of the time when she was maybe three or four, when her father bundled her up to take her on an adventure. They drove through a blizzard to a golf course and hiked to the ninth hole. Looking down, Shelby thought they were on the tallest mountain in the world. Her father positioned the red plastic toboggan with him in the back and Shelby in the front, secured between his legs, then launched them with three strong pushes. The world rushed by. Snow stung her face and she screamed in delight. At the bottom, they turned and tumbled off into a drift. They laughed. For a moment before they got up, her father squeezed her in his wiry but strong arms, kissed the top of her head. He told her to shut her eyes and listen, listen to the sound of the falling snow. And she did. She heard it come at her from all directions.

"Shelby?" Dr. Lubitsch said.

Shelby looked up from her glass. Scanned the room and this time saw the urn.

"Once, when we were hiking," she said, "my dad told me he wanted to be buried in a forest, in a biodegradable coffin that would let his body decompose into the ground. So he could live on as part of the trees."

"I've heard of that method," Dr. Lubitsch said. "Honorable."

"Since then I always imagined walking through the woods, alone, or with my own children someday. Feeling his presence."

"Where is he now, Shelby? Do you ever think about that?"

Shelby bit her thumbnail and pointed with her head. "Right up there." She talked around her thumb. "My mother had that done."

"Did she know about your father's wishes?"

Shelby pursed her lips, then said, "I think so. I mean *yes.*"

. . .

The operating room was nothing like Shelby had imagined: small, a low ceiling, mostly beige and gray, hardly any equipment. Each member of the team was busy with a task. A nurse inspected neatly lined up instruments. A doctor watched a screen; another positioned a camera over her leg. Another nurse swabbed her knee with something cold.

Dr. Merton stood over Shelby. He was there to assist and observe. He had a mask on so she could not see his face below his eyes. One of his eyes was bloodshot.

"We're going to give you something to help you relax," he said, and Shelby watched the nurse put a needle into the IV port burrowed into her arm. She barely felt the sting, then felt nothing until she woke up, when she heard incessant, calm beeps keeping track of something, her heart, she hoped.

She opened her eyes. A nurse probably near retirement was covering her up to her waist with a thin blanket. She didn't remember why she was here until she remembered the cancer and looked down toward her leg.

It was gone, clearly. Gone. But she was still breathing and her heart was still beating, if faster. And the other leg was still there, and her arms were still there. She raised the arm that wasn't hooked up to things to see if it could move, and it could, as could her good leg.

"You're up," the nurse said. "You'll feel groggy for a while. Is there anything I can get you?"

Shelby could think of nothing except her father.

"Maybe some water?" the nurse asked. "Some ice chips?"

"Is my mother here?" Shelby asked.

"I believe so," the nurse said. "At least she was a few minutes ago."

"Could you please get her?"

"Sure. But then that's all you want for now? Maybe a cracker—"

"Yes, please. Just her."

The nurse nodded and walked off as if Shelby had all the power in the world.

The beeps beeped. Shelby waited.

The door to the room swung open, and her mother walked in, followed by Uncle Jacob, followed by Aunt Arella, followed by Glen Smith, who was straining somewhat to carry the long, white plastic bag he was hugging against his chest.

"Mom," Shelby said as her mother stopped beside the bed, even as Glen Smith kept walking all the way in, so he could hand Shelby the white bag, inside which she could feel her leg, which had not yet gone completely cold.

And Shelby's mother said, "*Shelby.*"

FIFTH OF JULY

MARY TAUGHER

They allow Tessa to search the playground for her son Blair's lost identification tag, but she finds only cartridge shells and a prescription bottle packed with weed. She pockets the weed, then picks up Blair and Riley from afterschool care and heads to the Division of School Safety to get Blair new tags, stamped, like the lost ones, with his name, emergency contact, religion, and blood type. A line snakes along the perimeter of the low-slung brick government building, and she assesses the hidden dangers: the teenagers with bulky backpacks, the parents with oversized briefcases, the gaunt man with a long, shrouded object jutting over his shoulder. Dread enervates her like a low-grade fever, prickling her skin, drying up the inside of her mouth.

The line moves slowly. Tessa has to remind Blair and Riley to keep sheltered between her and the building. Their protection, their survival, are always on her mind. She finds little reassurance in the fact that their school was recently rebuilt with serpentine hallways to reduce a shooter's range and classrooms that lock on demand. No school or office or factory, no street corner or park or beach, and certainly not this exposed line of people is truly secure. Gunfire is as omnipresent as guns.

In the past two years alone, Tessa has lost three friends, two in a mass shooting, the third when his toddler found a handgun in a bedside table drawer. At last, she and Blair and Riley pass through the metal detectors and reach the counter, where a glassy-eyed clerk informs Tessa the tags will not process for at least six days. He hands her an electronic clipboard of forms with the expected date of delivery, 05-28-33, requesting four signatures and nine sets of initials. Then he reminds her, "No tags, no school."

It is late afternoon when they get home. Tessa takes off her shoes and Kevlar vest, and lets Charlie out the back door. The golden retriever makes a beeline toward a bed of brown pine needles near the fence, where Tessa finds him sniffing and nudging a featherless baby bird. Before she can collar him, a dozen crows swoop in, cawing with frightening belligerence while Charlie runs in mad circles, barking and growling. She collars him and drags him inside. She pulls on a pair of gardening gloves and drops the baby crow, floppy weak but alive, closer to the pine tree where it nests. It's no bigger than her thumb and she doubts it will live.

After dinner, she and Blair take Charlie for a walk, and a flock of crows descends upon them again, squawking and flying so low she can hear their wings flapping. She and Blair and Charlie run home as Blair blinks wildly.

Later, with the kids tucked safely in bed, she rewards herself with a few hits from the bottled stash. The pot calms her body even as it stimulates her mind. Whatever the blend, it doesn't increase her paranoia, and maybe it will actually help her sleep. She hasn't smoked in years, not since pot was legal in some states and buying it didn't mean risking prison.

How strange that this mellow high was once an ordinary

weekend escape. Her thoughts drift, flit like startled goldfish, back to a night when she was sixteen, near the pond in Bowsher Park where she lay in thick grass beside Bobby Steffen, staring at the stars, talking about infinity and eternity, so young and invincible, so unafraid of life's impermanence.

The mattress sinks when Keith climbs into bed just before midnight. He wraps his hand around her hip, and she feels its warmth spread down her thigh like heated syrup. He whispers in her ear, "Night, when words fade and things come alive."

"Shakespeare?"

"No, more obscure. Come here."

He pulls her toward him, and, buzzed, she feels a tug of lust she has not experienced in months. Their bickering, modified only by periods of strained politeness, has dulled her appetite for sex. Keith is naked and together they peel off her oversized T-shirt, and then they are nose to nose, eyelashes nearly interlocking, kissing roughly and insistently. On top, she clamps her legs around her husband and they rock together with tender aggression, which rapidly ramps up to not-so-tender aggression. She begins to gnaw at his flesh like a dog on a bone, biting him so hard he yelps and shoves her off.

"The fuck you doing, Tessa?" Never has she bitten him.

Rolling from bed, she locks herself in the bathroom, and for a moment, she does not recognize the woman in the mirror, the woman with freckled skin, bloodshot eyes, and shoulder-length auburn hair washing to pale red at the roots. She startles when Keith knocks while asking if she is all right. Without answering, she retreats to the shower, where she listens to the massage-nozzle spraying and whirring with mechanized repetition: *breathe, breathe, breathe.*

She does her best thinking in the shower. After a few minutes, she recognizes the root of her aggression, her instinct to bite her husband. Keith is always so certain, the driver in their marriage. She wants to take over, maybe shove him from the car altogether. Her resentment has morphed to anger.

She was twenty-six when they met and he thirty-nine; he was a top prosecuting attorney for the Cuyahoga County Prosecutor's Office and she a reporter for a legal publication. It was his voice that captured her, never ugly and bullying as many prosecutors' voices were, but urgent and persuasive and steady, a deep baritone that conveyed conviction and justice. When he asked for a life sentence instead of the death penalty after winning a conviction for a murder committed during a liquor store robbery in downtown Cleveland, she'd choked up with relief and admiration. The defendant—she still remembers his name, John Loudermilk—was only seventeen, with severe learning disabilities, and had grown up bouncing from one foster home to another.

When had their marriage started to flounder? Probably sometime after Riley's birth, she thinks, when they both switched jobs, he to a private law firm and she to editing for a psychology journal. She'd get ticked off that he didn't help enough with the kids or the house chores, and she hated how he tapped his fingers on a surface when he wanted to make a point, how he swallowed noisily when he drank. Had she missed those traits or just overlooked them? He'd carp at her for giving money to homeless panhandlers, for sleeping too late on weekends, for devoting so much time to the children that she was too tired at the end of the day to connect with him. Yep, zapped, she'd say. At least they could agree on that.

Of course, Keith has been unhappy in his new job for a while, but unwilling to give up the higher income. They've grown reliant on it. She cannot blame him for turning toward the Resistance. As a prosecutor, he'd witnessed the flood of guns on the streets, the carnage police were helpless to stop, and he was dogged in his certainty that he could help push through gun reform measures. He had moved quickly up the ranks of the Resistance.

Keith is asleep by the time she gets back in bed, and she's relieved. She does not want to start another quarrel, which of late, is always the same quarrel: his commitment to the Resistance opposed to her desperate desire to leave Ohio for safer ground in California. Their arguments often devolve to name-calling. Zealot v. Frightened Do-nothing.

The next morning, Tessa can barely force herself out of bed. She's not sure she slept much. Blair, with his night terrors, woke her up twice. Downstairs, she finds the kids arguing in the kitchen, Riley smirking with her hands on her hips, Blair red-faced, about to go into meltdown mode. A heavy cloud layer presses against the window above the sink like a wall of newly poured cement.

"It was not!" Blair screams.

"Yeah, it was. Rotting like a piece of fruit. Squishy and purple." At ten, Riley is just three years older than her brother, and yet she speaks in a precise, rational voice, as if she were a teacher schooling a child in the ugly realities of the world.

"Stop upsetting him," Tessa says to Riley. "Anyway, what the heck are you talking about?"

"The crow, Mom. He thinks it lived."

"You don't know that it didn't," she says to Riley.

"When I let Charlie out this morning, I saw it. It was gross."

"She's lying, Mom," says Blair, blinking uncontrollably.

There is now no doubt his tic has worsened. The half dozen specialists he's seen can't agree on its cause, but Tessa is fairly certain she knows. Chronic fear does horrible things to the mind and body; she's edited numerous articles on the topic for *Psychology Now and Then.*

"That's enough," she says, and she wraps her arms around Blair, hugging him against her stomach. "Why are you teasing your brother about it?"

"Why do you always take his side?"

Riley has a heart-shaped chin that juts out like she's brooding over a secret grievance. When upset, she pushes it out farther, which she does now as she glares at Tessa and says under her breath, "He's a spazbot."

"Goddamn it, Riley," Tessa yells. "Don't you ever call your brother that. Go upstairs and put on a longer skirt. You'll get sent home. No way that's midknee."

Riley stomps up the stairs, and Tessa tells Blair the baby bird might not have made it, but that was part of nature, the cycle of life, the strong survive, blah, blah, blah. She wonders if this were ever true.

Finally, Blair's blinking resolves. She settles him in front of the holovision with a cup of hot chocolate. He needs more therapy, all sorts of therapy, but so does she. She has put his therapy on temporary hold because two therapists put a strain on their budget, already tight because of tuition for the safer private school and their monthly mortgage with its astronomical interest rate. She rationalizes her decision: It's like grabbing the oxygen for herself first in the event of an inflight emergency.

After Blair's babysitter arrives, Tessa drops Riley at school and heads to work, worrying once again that editing for the psychology journal fuels her anxiety. She wishes she didn't know so much.

Sometimes she wonders if the strange sensations she's experienced the last year or so—instances when her hands turn icy and tremble, when her vision tunnels and blurs, when she loses herself so deeply in thought that she forgets where she is, what she's doing, and begins to question the very reality of her surroundings—are psychosomatic symptoms that spring from her knowledge of all that can go wrong when a person lives with unremitting anxiety.

Like forgetting. Here she was thinking about Blair's lapsed therapy, and she's forgotten her own appointment. This happens every so often now, this foggy struggle to recall information she knows, weekly appointments or lunch dates with colleagues. Once, she found a Target bag of new clothes in her car she had no memory of buying.

Two blocks before she reaches Dr. Timmons's office, she sees a man wearing red-tinted sunglasses, a hospital wristband, and mouse ears standing on the street corner, offering roses to passersby. Pricked by thorns, his hands are covered in blood.

Tessa is not sure he is real. She blinks, but he's still there. You're not well, she thinks. You have not been well for some time.

. . .

"Your dishwasher?" Dr. Timmons asks, peering over her reading glasses. She writes something in her notebook, then looks expectantly at Tessa.

"Yeah," Tessa says. "The dishwasher makes a repetitive swishing sound, and in my head, I hear: *Open carry. Open carry.*

Open carry. But it's not just the dishwasher . . . sometimes the earworms come out of nowhere. If it happens in bed, I'm up half the night."

"And how long has this been going on?"

Tessa looks down at her chipped nails. "A few weeks, I guess." She wonders how many of Dr. Timmons's clients are permanently on the edge of full-blown panic.

Although it's only early May, Dr. Timmons's sleekly furnished office is sweltering hot because it's not her building's day to use the air-conditioning. Spring in Ohio was never this oppressively hot when Tessa was a child. Who could have imagined even a few years ago that intense heat waves nationwide would cause bulls to become sterile and cows and pigs to miscarry their offspring? Tessa's mouth waters at the thought of steak, a luxury item. But what a stupid thing to focus on.

"What did you say?" Dr. Timmons asks.

"What?"

"You said, 'such a stupid thing'?"

"Did I?" Maybe the border between Tessa's private thoughts and words has cracked.

"I was just thinking how hot it is in here, but how it's not really a big deal in the scheme of things. I mean, like I'm always ranting to my mother: My generation got screwed, right? We grew up with 9/11 and terrorism, the wars in Iraq, Afghanistan, and North Korea, the Great Pandemic and civil unrest and insurrection in the early 2020s, a wealth gap that's a fucking abyss, and abortion back underground. And all these spoiled, macho politicians forever screwing us with their alternative facts, raging conspiracy theories, one-party courts, and white nationalist militias given free rein when no one else is? I can't walk down a city street without a Freedom Party member waving a gun like a victory flag. It's a wonder we all aren't agoraphobic by now."

Tessa's tirade hangs momentarily in the air before Dr. Timmons says, "You're worried, rightly, over the upcoming Supreme Court decision. We've all got to be prepared."

Dr. Timmons takes a sip of water from the glass on the side table beside her. Her hand trembles, and she grabs the glass with both hands.

"But at least," she says, and she sips again, "open carry everywhere and anywhere won't be as shocking here as it will be for people in states like California or New York."

"I miss maple trees," Tessa says, staring at the blue sky out the window. When did the clouds clear? "The blight happened so fast . . . I used to climb them when I was a girl . . ."

Dr. Timmons allows the silence to settle before she asks, "How are you and Keith getting along?"

"Better," Tessa says. She does not want to talk about Keith today, about the bite mark on his shoulder, about his stubborn belief that life in America will someday return to normal, whatever normal is. "Did I tell you Blair started pulling out his hair?" she asks. She twists and tugs a lock of her own. She looks at her feet and sees a cockroach crawling across Dr. Timmons's plush beige carpet. Seconds later, she's sure the bug is skittering across the crown of her head.

Dr. Timmons does not seem to see the cockroach. Tessa combs her fingers slowly across the top of her head so as not to alarm Dr. Timmons.

"He's pulling out too many strands," she says. "He has a little bald patch."

Dr. Timmons hesitates. This diversion from Keith—of course she, ever the therapist, recognizes it. "There's a name for hairpulling," she says. "It's a form of obsessive-compulsive disorder called—"

"I know what it's called," Tessa snaps.

Dr. Timmons has told her, but she cannot remember, trick-a-something.

"The blinking isn't much better either," she says. "We had an incident with some crazy crows yesterday. Charlie found a baby crow in our backyard, and later a flock, which, well, you know is actually called a murder, nearly attacked us. We asked Alexa15 about it, and she described such a group of them as flying monkeys, so smart they learn by imitation. She said crows attack to protect fledglings and can recognize specific people and animals. They must have thought Charlie killed the baby bird. Anyway, Blair couldn't stop blinking when the crows came at us, and again this morning when he found out that the baby bird died."

After scribbling in her notebook, Dr. Timmons asks, "Have you checked into the referrals I gave you for him?"

"Yes," Tessa lies. Another bad-mother moment she will not cop to. She looks at her watch and Dr. Timmons looks at her watch.

Time's up, Tessa thinks, and immediately these words begin to loop and swirl like flags snapping in a strong wind, trapped unremittingly in her mind: *time's up, time's up, time's up.*

. . .

In early June, Tessa reviews her calendar for the next few months. Keith sits next to her on the couch, scrolling through a court pleading on his laptop. They've barely spoken since dinner hours ago. The holovision is on mute. Batman, fantastically real, floats above her. The Joker leers in her face. She switches the channel to the local news where the mayor of their small town announces there will be fireworks for the Fourth of July, despite the fact that many cities nationwide have canceled them given the drought in wide swaths of the country.

Celebrating the birth of the nation with fireworks is a matter of civic pride, the mayor says. A beefy man with thick lips and a tattoo on his forearm, *We the People* in Old English font, the mayor is a Freedom Party member, up for reelection in November. He promises the town will take every precaution to avoid a repeat of last year's GV, when twenty-six people were killed. Police and private security guards, equipped with military-grade weapons and tactical tourniquets, will screen for alcohol and prohibit anyone without a flak jacket and helmet from entering the park where the fireworks will be set off.

"You might also consider carrying your ammunition separately," the mayor says, couching his advice with a wink, "or maybe leave your weapons at home."

"Now that's a radical idea coming from you, Mayor," shouts one of the news reporters.

"Only a suggestion," he says, turning away from the microphone.

Keith curses and bats at the mayor's image, but of course, it's only air.

Tessa circles Fourth of July on her calendar. She loves fireworks, misses watching them. Every summer when she was a child, her family went down to the river where the holiday was like a community festival, people dancing to jamboxes blaring country music, water lapping at the shoreline, the sharp scent of mosquito repellent, hissing sparklers, fireflies and firecrackers, the dazzling colors exploding and pinwheeling across the night sky.

Watching the fiery brilliance, she always felt a powerful sense of freedom and possibility, the kind of wonder others might experience listening to wolves howl or seeing the setting sun dye clouds blood-orange, pink, and purple. She would gaze at the stars glimmering through the lingering smoke of the fireworks and wonder what it would be like to ascend into the cosmos, to see the blue marble of earth far below her, like an astronaut on a celestial tour. Fireworks are her madeleine.

"What do you think of taking the kids up on the roof to watch the fireworks this year?" she asks Keith. The children have seen fireworks only in virtual reality.

"Are you crazy? Where's your common sense?" He's using his litigator voice, which infuriates her.

"We're miles from the park, and it's not like we live in an urban area where people will be shooting off," she says.

They moved last year to this suburban neighborhood to get farther away from inner city Cleveland. Tessa had wanted to move into a gated, gun-free neighborhood, but Keith argued that they weren't any safer, and maybe less safe because intruders didn't have to worry about homeowners with guns standing their ground. Plus those homes were overpriced, he claimed, and would plummet in value overnight if the federal open carry law were upheld by the Supreme Court, meaning there'd be no more gun-free zones.

"To be safe," she adds, "we'll wear our double-thick tactical vests and bulletproof headgear. The kids will love the fireworks. . . . It'll give them a bright diversion to focus on."

Keith grips the sides of his laptop and leans toward her. He has lost hair along his forehead and looks more like his father, whom he despises. "How do you think Blair will react? And don't tell me people won't celebrate with guns out here."

Tessa knows he's right, especially about Blair, but she hates caving in so easily. "We could sit in my car and watch them," she says. "That way the noise won't be as loud for Blair, and we'll be protected." Her car has the latest anti-bullet penetration technology.

"Where the hell is this coming from? Maybe you should talk to Dr. Timmons about this. Have you told her how you nearly took a chunk out of my shoulder the other night?"

Charlie appears from the kitchen, ambles into the room toward them, and Tessa reaches out to pet him. "Charlie is in a feud with crows."

"You bit me because—"

"Jesus, I don't know why, Keith." Tessa lets her voice trail off, and she buries her face in the fur on Charlie's neck.

"Maybe if you rejoined the Resistance and—"

"Enough already. It's always back to the same fucking argument. I'm going to bed."

And without another word between them, that's what Tessa does. But once in bed, despite feeling exhausted, she can't sleep. She feels wired, vibrating and humming like a hive, so hyperaware she senses the molecules of the cool air from the open window colliding with the warm air in the bedroom. She nods off only after she promises herself she'll go up on the roof despite Keith's objections. She'll watch the fireworks alone, goddammit.

• • •

The last week of June, after school has let out for the summer, Tessa attends the funeral of Wendy Moretti's fifteen-year-old daughter, Brittany, who babysat Blair and Riley almost daily last summer. She goes alone because Keith is preparing for a big trial, and she doesn't want to take the children. They've been to more funerals than birthday parties, which they think is normal. Maybe it is normal. Tessa is no longer sure.

Back home, she finds Riley at the kitchen table with a pouty look on her face. Maybe she's still upset that Tessa joined a cooperative with other mothers to share babysitting and play dates for the summer instead of sending the children to camps. But Tessa worries enough when her children are in school. She's not going to worry about them at summer camp.

"I don't like Sierra or Natasha," is the first thing Riley says.

"You have other friends."

"Why didn't you take me to say goodbye to Brittany?" Riley smears strawberry jam onto a cracker, clots of it falling to the pine table and pooling like welts on skin.

"We're eating dinner in an hour."

Riley scowls at her and asks, "Why did Brittany kill herself?"

"We don't know for sure that she did, honey," Tessa says, surprised the gossip has already reached her daughter. Neighbors have been speculating whether the gunshot wound to her head was an accident or suicide, but most people guess the latter; as a toddler, Brittany accidently shot and killed an older brother while playing with her mother's handgun.

"Ava said she shot herself in the face, and the bullet went through her bluer eye."

Tessa had forgotten that Brittany had uncanny, mismatched blue eyes, like the Siberian husky a neighbor owned, one flecked with brown, the other a robin's-egg blue. During the funeral at St. James, Tessa sat next to a girl around Brittany's age, with tatted teardrops on her left cheek, who seemed to be in a trance, ripping up the funeral program.

As bits of Brittany's photograph began to fill the girl's lap, Tessa felt an unnerving sense of apprehension. She wanted to flee the church. Instead, she looked up at its vaulted ceiling, inlaid with gold-leafed Byzantine tiles, a sea of midnight blue. Soon the very air around her seemed bathed in a blue luminescence, and she transported herself elsewhere, to Istanbul's Blue Mosque, a place of splendor she once visited in virtual reality, not long after its destruction during Turkey's civil war.

"I'm sorry you had to hear that," she says, kissing her daughter's forehead. "Try not to dwell on it."

Then she lectures Riley, again, about how suicides are often impulsive, and that if Brittany's parents hadn't owned guns or had secured them, Brittany might be alive.

Riley shrugs, pops a jam-covered cracker in her mouth, and asks, "What's for dinner?"

. . .

A few days later, Keith returns from a Resistance meeting with a stack of flyers warning people to shelter in place during fireworks displays in the Cleveland area. It's a Saturday afternoon and Tessa's been waiting for him to get home so she can leave the children and grocery shop. Keith reads from the flyer, then waves it at her face.

"I told you I won't take the kids with me up to the roof," she says. "But I'm watching the fireworks up there. With an abundance of caution, I promise."

"Be my guest," Keith says. "We're already paying unafford-able gun-death insurance, so I might as well get something out of it."

"Thanks for that," Tessa says.

"Jesus, Tess, it was a joke. Come on, we need to be in this together. We've got buses next weekend going to Columbus to push for a new gun reform bill— "

"It's too l-l-late," Tessa stammers, grabbing her car keys and backing away from him. "Too late. Too late."

On the way to the grocery store, down the main boulevard pocked with potholes, she passes the boarded-up shopping mall; the brown field where the movie-theater complex once stood; and a noisy bulldozer plowing down an encampment of tents and cardboard boxes, empty now that the homeless have been moved to an internment camp in a rural part of the state. All the while, she tries to displace the earworm, *too late, too late, too late*, by switching stations on the car radio.

At the entrance of AmazonLand, Tessa slides her hand across her protective vest and scans the store to remind herself of the exits before she grabs a cart and heads toward the veg-etable and fruit aisle. A soft crack of thunder heralds the mist over vegetables. Tessa flinches. She stops to inhale deeply, looks down at the floor. There's an advertisement, a red Campbell's soup can, decaled on one of the large floor tiles, and next to it an ad for a Stop-the-Bleed kit with the latest military combat tourniquet and pressure dressings. Red, gleaming slickly under the fluorescent lights, the ads seem etched in fresh blood. Her heart begins to pound as a sense of foreboding overtakes her.

She again surveils her surroundings. There's an elderly man in a mechanized wheelchair sporting an American and Confederate flag, a young mother with a toddler. The old man looks at Tessa and tips an imaginary hat. Tessa smiles weakly. She wonders if he, if the young mother, if everyone is as acutely conscious of mortality as she is, of how a decision made in a split second—say to run, or hide, or play dead in the midst of the chaos and terror—might mean the difference between a future and oblivion.

She rushes from the aisle, forgetting the broccoli for dinner, and turns into the cereal aisle. Frosted Flakes. Captain Crush. Wheaties. Patriot Puffs. Froot Loops. Lucky Pistols. Rice Christians. Her vision starts to do strange things. Brilliant colors pop out brighter while others recede into gray tones. Sparks of light burst in the corner of her eyes like sunlight flaring off a field of mirrors. A wave of dizziness washes over her. She cannot push her cart.

After some time, and Tessa doesn't know how much, a woman's cart pulls up next to Tessa's. The woman is trailed by a girl around Riley's age, humming "Mary Had a Little Lamb."

It takes Tessa a moment to realize the child has substituted the lyrics: *Mary had a little lamb. Click, click, bam, dead, dead lamb.*

"Excuse me," she says. "Do you know what your daughter is singing?"

"Not my daughter," says the woman, whose eyes are hidden by mirrored sunglasses. "I'm just the sitter." The woman, wearing an ugly orange sweater that matches the Wheaties cereal boxes, has bleached blond hair tufted like cotton candy. Tessa looks for the bulge of a weapon at the woman's waist, for a bulge at her ankles, but the woman is all bulge. The little girl, too young for the lipstick glistening on her lips, wears camouflage sneakers and a smirk.

"She's slaughtering a sweet nursery rhyme," Tessa says.

"So what. Mind your own damn business, lady."

The little girl begins singing again, this time more loudly, looking directly at Tessa.

"You're a little shit," Tessa whisper-growls at her.

Cursing, the woman rams her grocery cart into Tessa's and shoves her hand into her shoulder bag. Tessa runs, zigzagging as she's practiced so often, toward the exit. But there's no sound, nothing but the new refrain looping and sticking, looping and sticking in her mind: *Click, click, bam, dead, dead lamb. Click, click, bam, dead, dead lamb. Click, click, bam, dead, dead lamb.*

. . .

It's the last day of June, the start of a long four-day weekend. Fourth of July falls on a Monday this year. In her cubicle, Tessa's line-editing an article about how brains perceive reality selectively and individually. The author, a neuroscientist, believes reality is a collection of individual hallucinations.

The office begins to hum, and her co-workers move toward the big screen in the center of the office. Tessa gets up from her desk to join them just as Nancy Pierce, whose retirement party is slated for that afternoon, wails. A few people cheer and grab their weapons from their desks or waistbands, jubilantly waving them. One of the younger hires, a blue-haired boy with tatted sleeves, lets loose a stream of invectives and slams his plastic cup against the cream-colored wall. Lurid red-orange liquid splatters and runs down.

The Supreme Court has upheld the federal reciprocity law,

the newscaster announces. Anyone over eighteen can carry a weapon openly or concealed, without a permit, anywhere— in banks, private businesses, churches, schools, colleges, national parks, gated neighborhoods. The few exceptions include the White House and the Supreme Court. The screen begins flashing names and models of weapons on banners that burst holographically like streamers from a gigantic party popper: AR-57, Armscor AK22, Barrett M82, Beretta BM 59, Bushmaster M4-Type Carbine, Colt AR-15, Glock 54, Heckler & Koch HK433, KelTec Sub2000, LaPierre & Trump AK-59, M25 Sniper Weapon System, Mercer Carbine.

A holographic chyron appears before Tessa amid the ghostly weapons: *California will not obey the court decision. Threatens to secede.*

Tessa leaves work, but it seems half of Cleveland has left with her. The streets are crowded with men and woman cheering and waving guns and assault weapons. Three men wearing Freedom Party hats goosestep in formation, holding rocket launchers aloft like torches. Shots are going off amid a throng of truckdrivers parked outside the Rock & Roll Hall of Fame. Sirens blare. Somewhere, maybe everywhere, people are dying to celebrate.

At home, Keith waits in the dining room with a bottle of scotch, two glasses, and a grim look on his face.

"Looks like California is no longer your safe haven," he says. "The federal government won't stand for secession. California could be under siege soon."

"There are other places. We've got to consider leaving here."

Keith rubs his forehead and sighs. "Our *lives* are here. We are not moving to California or emigrating to Australia or Japan or your latest gun-safe nirvana. We can't afford a home in California anyway, and it's too hard to get a visa overseas. Who wants Americans?"

"I can't do this anymore."

"Tessa, please. Listen to me. My work in the Resistance here is too important, and it's not for nothing. We've made progress on gun show loopholes, red flag laws, and bump stocks. Guns aren't going away. We've got to change the laws we can. Besides, California's too dangerous now."

"And it's not dangerous here in the land of Freedom Party fighters armed with long guns and AK-47s? Now we'll be surrounded by more guns, everywhere."

"Calm down. The kids will—"

"You'd rather endanger us than give up the Resistance. That's it, isn't it? Fighting here in Freedom territory. The high you get in battle is what you care about most."

Keith clears his throat and pours a shot of scotch. "Tessa, that's not true."

It is true. She can feel it, like an object wedged in her throat. She knows her husband's subtle tells, and realizes he'll never surrender his devotion to this higher purpose. She'll never convince him to leave. The Resistance is his lifeblood.

. . .

Tessa sits alone on the slanted roof of their two-story home. She wears a bulletproof helmet, her double-thick tactical vest, and her children's strike-plated backpacks strapped on her thighs. Keith claims she has a death wish. Maybe she does have a death wish. She's no longer sure.

Fireworks blaze across the night sky. The explosions nearly cover the sound of celebratory gunfire. Tessa gazes at the showers of candy-colored light, giant white and blue and green chrysanthemums blooming and overlaying one another until they fizzle out. The booms rocket through her and lift her up as if she's on the highest arc of a swing. What a strange contradiction, she thinks. These glorious displays, blasting and exploding and ripping through the dark sky, simulate her greatest fear, and yet her euphoria overpowers her dread.

The finale is brilliant, as moving to Tessa as the finale of a symphony when the full power of the orchestra's string, woodwind, bass, and percussion swell with furious glory.

Afterward, she contemplates the night sky and abrupt silence, until Keith, leaning out from their bedroom window, looks up and yells, "Stupidest thing you've done in months. Please, come down."

Tessa crawls down the slant of slick shingles and climbs through the window to join him. "I needed to see them," she says as she unfastens her helmet. "I was celebrating my life, liberty, and pursuit of happiness."

"You could have been killed," he says. He pulls her close, hugs her tightly.

And that night, for the first time since she bit him, they reach for each other in bed. While they make love, she conjures red starbursts, blue coronas, and gigantic white chrysanthemums blazing through the cosmos. She does not bite him or herself, or lock herself in the bathroom. No earworm stalks her. When she returns to bed after washing up, she tells him, "That was nice."

. . .

The next morning, she and Keith wake to the sound of Riley and Blair screaming in the kitchen. Downstairs, they find both children staring out the sliding glass doors. Blair yanks the door open and scuttles out to the backyard with Charlie, who growls as if ready to attack. Blair blinks frantically as he takes in the scene. Keith snatches Blair into his arms, and Tessa grabs Charlie.

Their backyard and the neighbors' rooftops are littered with the bodies of hundreds of crows, some clumped together in pairs and trios, many with distorted heads, crumpled wings, smashed beaks. It is a scene of bloodless mass carnage, preposterous and grotesque.

Riley begins weeping and screaming, weeping and screaming, "This is the end time, this is the end time."

Unprompted, Alexa15 bellows from the kitchen. The fireworks, she reports, frightened and flushed out a massive murder of crows, the noise so disorienting that the birds, with poor night vision, crashed into buildings, into telephone poles, into cars, into one another. In bigger news, she announces, the federal government has sent troops to California. It has begun: civil war.

Tessa closes her eyes. Charlie yanks her here and there as if she's as small as a chew toy. She releases him. Her hands go numb, her skin tingles. She feels herself splitting off from her body, drifting above her other self, above her family, above the dead crows. From overhead, higher than the treetops, she surveys the carnage. Dead crows in her neighbors' yards, dead crows on the roof of the firehouse two blocks away, dead crows in the YMCA parking lot half a mile off. Time slows and expands, and then, some time later, she has no idea how

much time later, she plummets earthward, back into her petri-
fied body.

Beside her foot, a crow twitches, then squawks faintly. It
looks like a black cross, its oily black wings outstretched, its
violet-black head twisted to the left, its feral brown left eye
wide open. A small line of its blood trickles down its beak.
When it opens its mouth as if to whisper, Tessa gets down on
her hands and knees to listen.

CONTRIBUTORS' NOTES

S. A. COSBY is an award-winning writer from southeastern Virginia. His bestselling novel *Blacktop Wasteland* won the *Los Angeles Times* Book Prize for Best Mystery/Thriller, the Macavity Award for Best Mystery Novel, the ITW Thriller Award for Best Hardcover Novel, and the Anthony Award for Best Hardcover Novel. His short story "The Grass Beneath My Feet" won an Anthony Award. When he isn't writing, he's hiking or sampling a fine whiskey or two.

THE STORY BEHIND THE STORY: So the idea for "Pantera Rex" came from two parallel desires. I wanted to write a humorous story, and I wanted to work my favorite animal into a story. Hopefully I succeeded. I think humor is a kissing cousin of suspense because both depend on timing and atmosphere. I hope people enjoy this little departure from my usual work.

BARBARA DEMARCO-BARRETT is the editor of *Palm Springs Noir* (Akashic, 2021). Her first book, *Pen on Fire*, won the Outstanding Book Award from the American Society of Journalists and Authors. Her fiction, essays, and journalism have appeared in the *Los Angeles Times*, *USA Noir: Best of the*

Akashic Noir Series, Rock and a Hard Place, The Literary Hatchet, Crossing Borders, Shotgun Honey, Authors Guild Bulletin, Poets & Writers, Writer's Digest, and *The Writer* magazine. She hosts the radio show/podcast *Writers on Writing.* She's obsessed with fountain pens, grows weed in her garden, and is married to a musician. More at penonfire.com.

THE STORY BEHIND THE STORY: All of my writing comes from experiences from my life, but not every moment, or even most, in "Blue Martini" are based on truth. I've never pulled a trigger intending to kill a human being—or intending to kill anything alive period. I've never been stuck in the desert with a boyfriend or been on the lam because police had probable cause to arrest me.

However, when I was seventeen, I almost moved in with a meth head. I was so into him we even talked of marrying. At night we'd be out cruising in his vintage '57 aqua Chevy, and one night we were stopped by several policemen who quickly arrested him and told me to drive the Chevy home.

But our problems didn't end there. More than once after that night, I'd go over to his place, and police would be there ransacking it, arresting him again. It was a dark time to be sure. My parents were breaking up then, too, and soon I dove deep into a period of depression that lasted for months. I did finally break free of the meth head when, on my own, I sought out a shrink and, not long after, auditioned for a CBS Philly affiliate special and got the paid acting gig. This set me on a positive path, dissolving my depression. There were possibilities other than life with Mr. Meth.

He must have had a serious effect on me, though, because I've featured him, one way or another, in a handful of short stories. The female protagonists in these stories are all different—different concerns, certainly different from me—but they've all needed to escape his hold.

Then there's the Cadillac that Pepper inherited from her mother. Through my childhood and teen years, my shoe designer father bought a new Caddy every year. God forbid he drive the same car two years in a row. Rumor now has it he belonged to the Western Pennsylvania Jewish mafia. Is that where the money came from? He was a notable shoe designer, but did shoe designers make enough to buy that many new cars, and diamonds and luxurious furs for their wives?

And the desert. It's a setting I return to again and again in my fiction. I should just move there already. The place has a hold on me, and what better way, short of being there, than writing a story that takes me there? No wonder the setting in "Blue Martini" was the easy part. What happened in it was the hard part. Precisely what would the characters *do*, especially when there was a threat? After all, if what we write is fiction, we are not our characters. We might not even want to hang out in real life with people like our characters, but our characters are our characters, right there in front of us, often in the same places where we eat and exercise and sleep, living and doing what they want. Say what we will about them and their decisions, good or bad, mine have always been generous to me. I mean, if nothing else, they've always let me occupy the front seats and watch.

DAVID EBENBACH is the author of eight books of fiction, poetry, and nonfiction, including his most recent novel *How to Mars* (Tachyon Publications), and his most recent story collection *The Guy We Didn't Invite to the Orgy and Other Stories*. His books have won such awards as the Drue Heinz Literature·

Prize and the Juniper Prize, among others. David lives with his family in Washington, DC, where he teaches creative writing at Georgetown University. Every summer he asks himself why he lives in the Capital of Humidity—and every spring, when the lawns and trees and bushes burst into bloom, he remembers.

THE STORY BEHIND THE STORY: In 2005, when David Foster Wallace delivered the speech "This Is Water" at Kenyon College's commencement ceremony, it must have been deeply inspiring. He was a literary giant at that point, having already published *Infinite Jest* and *Brief Interviews with Hideous Men*, among other books, and the speech he made at this commencement was a stunner. Poetic and yet also conversational, simultaneously humble and profound. It's even been turned into a (very short) standalone book, people like it so much. In "This Is Water" he talked compellingly about how to shape one's thinking in order to live a sane life, a task that he called "life or death"; reshaping your mind, he suggested, could save you, whether from a deathlike misery or, as he mentions in passing along the way, from suicide. Like I say, it must have been truly inspiring to hear his words that day.

But I didn't hear Wallace deliver that speech live. I read it—in that little book I mentioned—in 2014. That was six years after David Foster Wallace had taken his own life. And so it read very differently to me than it must have come across to people at Kenyon that spring day in 2005. To me, this speech was a glimpse of a complex tragedy. Here was an author who *did* know something profound, whose ideas might in fact have saved some folks—but who could not save himself. A man who wanted to reshape his mind but couldn't reshape it enough. As a person with depression myself, reading this speech was a sobering experience.

The experience was particularly powerful for me because it happened two years after we lost my sister-in-law, also to suicide. Naomi was a person of extremes, smart as hell and full of energy and exciting ideas at times, but also very susceptible to a deep darkness at other times. She, perhaps like Wallace, was perpetually trying to reshape herself. The final note she left us suggested that she just didn't want to do that anymore.

Among the many other very hard things about this loss, I was strongly affected by the way my wife grieved. I watched her looking back with changed eyes at years and years lived with her sister. Now that Naomi was gone, what did their shared past mean?

This story came from all of these things. It's for David Foster Wallace. It's for Naomi Gartner. It's for Rachel Gartner.

MATTHEW GOLDBERG is an emerging writer who specializes in offbeat fiction. His stories have appeared in a number of literary journals and magazines, including *Bending Genres*, *Pif Magazine*, *Entropy*, *Apiary Magazine*, *The Hoosier Review*, and others. He is also a winner of the *Arcanist's* 2021 Hunger Flash contest. Matt earned his MFA in creative writing from Temple University and lives in Philadelphia with his partner and their two fancy rats. He can be found on Twitter @mattmgoldberg.

THE STORY BEHIND THE STORY: The idea for "Therapunitive Intervention" arose after a friend told me about his experience at a silent retreat. For over a week, he wasn't able to use his phone or talk to anyone. During the first day of the retreat, he described the near-constant impulse to check his phone, as well as his anxiety from the lack of stimuli. However, by the end of the retreat, he had more or less adjusted. He was living in the moment and felt more relaxed overall. He called it a detox. I could definitely see why he'd found the experience restorative, but I wondered what it would be like for someone who was forced to attend this kind of retreat against their will. I imagined a world in which going on a mindfulness or silent retreat was actually a terrible punishment. "Therapunitive Intervention" emerged from that reimagining. I wrote from the perspective of a character with extreme social media addiction and an inability to function in society. I enjoyed channeling the character's voice, especially their exaggerated fears about the retreat (aka MonkCare). At the same time, I wanted to express how looking inward can be a useful process for letting go of past trauma or mistakes. Much like my friend, the protagonist in this story leaves the experience feeling detoxified. And, just like my friend, once they reentered society and its myriad distractions, a relapse was inevitable. I dedicate "Therapunitive Intervention" to my early readers, who provided great advice on how to find balance between the punitive nature of the retreat and its potential benefits. I hope my story will make readers laugh, think, and, perhaps, take a deep breath before they continue on with their day.

MICHAEL HOPKINS was born in Philadelphia, Pennsylvania. He has a degree in electrical engineering from Drexel University. His book and music reviews have appeared in the *Philadelphia Inquirer*, *Philadelphia Weekly*, *Milwaukee Journal Sentinel*, and *Magnet*. His short fiction has been published in *Pleiades*,

Wisconsin People & Ideas, *365 Tomorrows*, *Moss Piglet*, and *Black Petals*. He is the winner of the 2018 Wisconsin Academy of Science, Arts and Letters annual fiction contest and the third place winner in the 2019 contest. He lives on a small farm in Wisconsin, with his wife and their dog, cats, chickens, and bees. He makes and throws knives to satisfy his addiction to hearing the *thunk*!

THE STORY BEHIND THE STORY: One of my writing mentors announced he was having a hip replaced. I asked him if I could keep his old hip. He asked me why, and I explained that I have a skull and bone collection in my office, and if I had his old hip, he would always be there with me. He said it was a gruesome idea, and answered no.

I wondered what it would be like to keep a body part, once integrated to my living system. What about a big body part, such as a leg?

All my short stories start with a fragment stuck in my head: something I hear (or overhear), see, say, read, or an unusual experience. The interesting ones continue to pester me; the strong ones throw a switch in my brain and I decide it could be a good idea for a story. When I am asked where you get your ideas, I always explain about these fragments. The moment I decide to write about a fragment the universe starts opening doors, each one leading to another part of my story: I'm presented with characters, settings, and conflicts. An unseen hand uses magical thread and begins to sew the parts together.

Typically I forget about the skull and bone collection that surrounds me as I sit at my desk. The fragment urged me to notice them. I held a pig skull, a horse skull, the pelvis from a cow, a deer's spine, and I let them speak to me. Each one has an elaborate story about its unique journey from their natural habitat to my shelf.

One night, Shelby materialized: a young, strong woman, whose life was about to change. Faced with an amputation, Shelby wanted to keep her leg. Then her mother entered and refused to allow it.

Shelby's uncle Jacob, Dr. Lubitsch, and others showed up in my head, vowing to help me find out if Shelby would be allowed to keep her leg, and probe the depths of her psyche to understand why she wanted to.

At that moment I had no choice but to write the story: It was the only way I would find the answers to these questions that would not leave me alone.

In his book *The Way of the Writer*, Charles Johnson states, "Real fiction makes the familiar *un*familiar." I hope readers of my story are entertained, and knocked a little off balance, to see some aspect of *their* world from a new perspective.

JOHN JEFFIRE was born in Detroit, a city that, in his words, is "a quaint village of endless charms and bottomless graces." John's first book of poetry, *Stone + Fist + Brick + Bone*, was nominated for a Michigan Notable Book Award in 2009. His *Shoveling Snow in a Snowstorm*, a poetry chapbook, was published by Finishing Line Press in 2016. He has broken many bones, both his own and those of others. For more on him and his work, visit writeondetroit.com.

THE STORY BEHIND THE STORY: A few years ago, my wife and I visited Florida and stayed with one of her friends from her crazy days before we were married. The friend lived in what I as a Detroiter would call the swamp. Her house was a spooky gothic thing buried deep in the woods on a jungle trail off a dirt road, and according to the locals it had been owned by drug smugglers back in the sixties and seventies. The place was a writer's goldmine. Beneath it were escape tunnels, and, inside, a wall panel that hid a kind of panic room—intriguing stuff with so many possibilities. And over-looking the road at the end of their path was the lookout chair nailed to a tree and the pulley described in the story. Each morning I'd take our dogs on a long walk around the property, and the foreignness and unfamiliarity of the setting, all its sights, sounds, odors, and claustrophobic humidity, started to speak to me: I knew I had found a story of some sort, but I didn't know exactly what. After we returned north, my mind kept working. My wife used to be sales manager at an auto dealership and knew all the ins and outs of that world, so I started picking her brain for an understanding of the people and processes involved in that lifestyle; she had also worked in public relations for a TV station, and I did the same regarding that, taking notes as she reminisced about her career. Straight up the story wouldn't have happened if not for her vivid memory. When I got moving on a draft, I combined elements from that house in Florida with her former work experiences and tapped into the folklore of the neighborhood characters I knew in Detroit (as well as specific unpleasant memories of a boss who was like Gary, a vacuous dipshit) and, well, the story took off. May God bless my amazing wife for tolerating all my annoying questions!

LORI D. JOHNSON has an MA in urban anthropology from the University of Memphis. She is the author of two novels, *A Natural Woman* and *After the Dance*. Her short stories and essays have appeared in a variety of publications, including *Novel*

Slices, *SFWP Quarterly*, *Midnight & Indigo*, *The Root*, and *Mississippi Folklife*. Excerpts and links to her published work can be found on her blog *Lori's Old School Mix*. When she's not writing, Lori can usually be found somewhere engrossed in a book, research or watching old episodes of Rod Serling's *The Twilight Zone*.

THE STORY BEHIND THE STORY: The idea for "Shepherd's Hell" first came to me in 2002 and was sparked by a newspaper article about a house fire accidentally set by a woman whose last name, interestingly enough, was "Lamb." I'm not sure why I was so struck by the tragedy, but a number of the details stayed with me, swirling and churning in the darker recesses of my mind until they finally transformed themselves into pliable blocks of material. Over the course of several weeks, the plot basics and most of the dialogue in "Shepherd's Hell" came to me in unexpected and unplanned bursts of creativity and imagination. A great deal of the work was jotted on bits of paper and scribbled in the margins of magazines. But for some reason, I never made time to work on the story in earnest. While I somehow managed (even in 2006 during the tumultuous process of relocating from Ohio to North Carolina) to keep all of the marked up bits of paper, torn pages, and notes together, 2020 was the first time in years I'd felt the urge to pull them out and look at them. In many ways, I have the pandemic to thank for providing me with both the incentive and the degree of angst I needed to finally piece the story together.

LEE MARTIN is the author of six novels, including *The Bright Forever*, a finalist for the 2006 Pulitzer Prize in Fiction. He has also published four memoirs, most recently *Gone the Hard*

Road, and two story collections. His work has appeared in such places as *Harper's*, *Creative Nonfiction*, *The Georgia Review*, *The Best American Mystery Stories*, and *The Best American Essays*. He is the winner of the Mary McCarthy Prize in Short Fiction and fellowships from the National Endowment for the Arts and the Ohio Arts Council. He teaches in the MFA Program at The Ohio State University and is the magic behind Stella the Cat's Facebook page.

THE STORY BEHIND THE STORY: Four years ago, my wife and I moved into a new home, and early the next morning I backed into a neighbor's car parked across the street from our driveway. It was an inauspicious beginning to say the least. The neighbor ended up being very understanding, and the matter was quickly resolved and forgotten, but not by me. My idiocy haunted me and still does from time to time. I often find story material in the things that make me uncomfortable, and that was the case with this event. I found myself writing the opening scene of a story called "The Patio Club," a scene that features a man named Shuman who hits a neighbor's car. I wrote that scene, and then I had no idea where the story wanted to go, so I put it away and didn't return to it until a few years later when Vivian Dorsel, the editor and publisher of *Upstreet*, asked me to send her a story. I picked up "The Patio Club," at a time when my wife and I had become good friends with a group of our neighbors and had sat on patios listening to their stories. We writers are often thieves, stealing this or that from the lives around us. When I lived in my previous home, I wasn't particularly close to many of my neighbors, so I had no qualms about borrowing their lives to make stories. Here, in my new neighborhood, though, my wife and I adore our neighbors and have formed a bit of a family with them. I feel guilty stealing from them, but I guess I don't feel guilty enough. "The Patio Club" put a cast of characters on the page, and I wanted to follow them, so I wrote this story, "Happy Birthday, Honey Vanlandingham." In this story, Shuman gets invited to a birthday party, and in his attempt to fit in with his neighbors he ends up bringing the perfect and the only present. His misunderstanding of what his neighbors expect of him creates a chain of events that brings him to a place where his new life becomes even more complicated. At the end of the story, he's involved with the lives of his neighbors but possibly at a great cost to his future happiness. I'm not done with these characters. I've written five more stories about The Patio Club, the real neighbors behind the stories be damned.

FRANCES PARK is the author or co-author of ten books, including the novel *To Swim Across the World* (Hyperion, 2001) and the memoir *Chocolate Chocolate: The True Story of Two Sisters, Tons of Treats, and the Little Shop That Could* (Thomas Dunne, 2011). A forthcoming memoir-in-essays *That Lonely Spell: Stories of Family, Friends & Love* (Heliotrope Books, 2022) deals with the universal themes of love and loss against the backdrop of her unique Korean American experience. A finalist in both the 2020 Dzanc Diverse Voices Book Prize and the 2019 Dzanc Novella Prize, Frances earned a spot on The Best American Essays 2017 Notable List. She co-owns Chocolate Chocolate in Washington, DC. Walk in and feel the magic.

THE STORY BEHIND THE STORY: Three decades ago, I began to jot down ideas for "Around the Block," a short story about Suzy, a self-perceived ugly duckling teen of Korean descent, and Courtney, her troubled white friend who stands up to the racist bullies in school. Although I'd been writing since fifth grade, creating an Asian character was a first for me, and it felt a bit daring. Taboo, even. Maybe Benetton was a big deal back then, but that colorful optic—diversity—was nowhere to be found in my town or library, not then and certainly not during my childhood. Indeed, from kindergarten through college, I never came across a single Korean American student. Once finished and hoping for the best—should I mention that the two characters in a fit of rage destroy all the neighborhood gardens in the middle of the night, damning everyone to hell?—I printed off copies, dropped them in the mail, and held my breath.

Fortunately, "Around the Block" was accepted, but not before receiving a particularly memorable rejection from a literary magazine in Cape Cod where the editor had circled the following paragraph on my submission:

> Courtney was the first person who ever told me I would grow up to be beautiful, and she told me this all the time, as a given. I would stare into the mirror and pray for the day. Silk dresses and pearls, silk dresses and pearls. Even bullies love beautiful ladies, I told myself, not knowing this was a dangerous way to think. Years later men would love me for all the wrong reasons, and I would do everything in my power to poison their lives for having poisoned mine when I was a homely schoolgirl.

"This should be your story," the editor noted.

With that, a seed was planted, but several years would pass before "The Summer My Sister Was Cleopatra Moon" would take root in my head, later branching out into a novel. Because I love the lawless and rarely edit myself, the story fell out of me: two Korean American sisters grow up confronting and internalizing seventies white suburbia in polar fashion. One sister is plain, obedient and studious, the other is rock 'n' roll gorgeous and acts like she doesn't give a shit; what they share are spiritually deformed identities.

I wrote this short story long ago, about a time even longer ago. And while it almost feels like historical fiction, the Moon sisters are still cruising around in my mind in a yellow Mustang.

MEGAN RITCHIE earned her undergraduate degrees from the University of Southern California. She is currently pursuing her MFA at the University of Miami, where she received the Lester Goran Award for fiction. She is at work on a novel. Also, she owns not a single pair of matching socks, thanks to her mischievous dog.

THE STORY BEHIND THE STORY: For a semester in college, I worked a terrible public relations job on Sunset Boulevard in West Hollywood. The location, while glamorous, was quickly offset by the dullness of the job, which consisted mostly of PR efforts to reshape celebrities' personal narratives—and often included stuffing said clients into closets.

The one redeeming quality of this job was that it was directly across the street from an iconic Hollywood drag bar. During slow days, I spent my time watching tourists and locals alike flit in and out of its doors and witnessed small dramas— fights breaking out, lovers reconciling, and strangers flirting— play out among the widest range of people imaginable. That people watching, and the very strange contradictions of Los Angeles, a queer city in theory but (as I learned on the job) not always in practice, congealed and so "Good Actors" was born.

"Good Actors" is dedicated to the Gay & Lesbian Alliance Against Defamation, to which the proceeds of the story have been donated. GLAAD is devoted to expanding queer narratives in media and aims to tell stories that resist common stereotypes of the LGBTQ+ community.

A William & Mary graduate, **D.Z. STONE** holds a master's from Columbia University, and has reported for the *New York Times* and *Newsday*. She's the author of *No Past Tense: Love and Survival in the Shadow of the Holocaust* (2019) and co-author of *A Fairy Tale Unmasked: The Teacher and the Nazi Slaves* (2021), both published by Vallentine Mitchell. She grew up over her father's bar, falling asleep to the click-click-clack of Eight Ball from the pool table below. During the day, her Polish grandmother would tell her, "Remember you somebody!"

THE STORY BEHIND THE STORY: My short story "Spies" was born in 1994, when I got a call from my older friend Grace, a local politico and Virginia Woolf scholar. Grace lived up the road from me in Grand View-on-Hudson, New York, the same Hudson River village where Betty Friedan wrote *The Feminine Mystique*. Grace would tell me Betty stories, and secrets about the women back in the 1960s stuck in their houses popping Valium. What I liked best were her tales about the "key parties" hosted by a local freethinking church. I never would have thought, from the looks of Grace, that she was into key parties, but, well, there she'd be, giving me the steamy details about them.

Anyhow, when Grace called that day in 1994, she said I was wasting my life by writing for a bank. I didn't know what to say, so I said nothing, just listened to her insist I join a fiction workshop someone was starting up.

Okay, fine, I thought. I didn't believe workshops could help me, but, what the hell, I'd give this one a try.

During the first meeting, the workshop leader, Lynn, talked about how women were often held back as fiction writers. Women, she noted, were often afraid to write about certain things because people might think they actually *did* such a thing. Men, on the other hand, I joked, wrote stuff so people would *think* they did it.

So I created Anna. Anna was my age at the time, forty, and facing all the issues of aging: feeling a bit schlumpy and not quite satisfied with what she'd done with her career—so much lost promise. Next in my mind came Charlie, a composite of qualities I liked and thus to me the perfect man. As I'd write, I'd go to town with them. I would allow them into the same bed, sometimes even throw in a little S&M. The writing group loved it.

I would write about Anna and Charlie in fits and starts in three different writing groups over the next twenty-five years. I would end up with numerous drafts of unfinished novels and screenplays that all never felt quite right.

Then the author Mark Wish and editor Elizabeth Coffey announced they were starting a new short story anthology and looking for submissions. I sat down and, within forty-eight hours, wrote a short story about Anna and Charlie. As I finished drafting it, I thought: This is it—this thing between these two people has been dying to be a short story all along.

Mark read it and asked if I were open to revising if given a few editorial suggestions. "Sure," I told him, and we sent a few drafts back and forth.

No one was more surprised than me when "Spies" was accepted for the first volume of *Coolest American Stories*. After more than a quarter of a century, Anna had a place in the world, proving the power of women, especially if they are given a chance.

Originally from Brooklyn, **SUSAN TACENT** consolidated her love of reading and teaching by earning a PhD in comparative literature from Brown University, where she received an Excellence in Teaching Award. Over the years, she has taught literature as well as creative writing to folks of all ages. She also facilitates a lively assisted-living book club, seven years strong now, where the participants' collective age exceeds 900 years. Her interviews, book reviews, academic, and creative pieces have appeared in *Dostoevsky Studies*, *Blackbird*, *DIAGRAM*, *decomp*, *The Common*, *Tin House Online*, *Michigan Quarterly Review*, *Slice*, and elsewhere.

THE STORY BEHIND THE STORY: Some stories emerge from writing prompts, and some from the work of showing up at the desk every day. "Habitat" was born the morning I stepped on a gardening claw and, because I was alone, had to drive myself to the local urgent care. Pressing gingerly on the accelerator with my throbbing foot, I already sensed a story incubating. "Habitat" first appeared in the Fall/Winter 2003–2004 volume of *Ontario Review* in a slightly different version, under a different title, and a different last name. It's a story I still love for how it weaves the natural world into the familial, and for how it leaves its protagonists in a hopeful place. Like many, I find it hard to write happy endings. "Habitat" also has some humor in it, humor that feels real, and earned. I grew up in a neighborhood in Brooklyn where trees grew out of cement blocks and the tiny grass lawns were bordered by thorny bayberries. Research for "Habitat" included gawking at stunning photos and enticingly unfamiliar vocabulary in flower catalogs. With each draft, questions arose about vulnerability, both personal and in the delicate intimacy of marriage and family. My gardening protagonist believed she was safe in her own backyard, responsibly pulling pokeweed rather than allowing a toxin to thrive. Working to tell her story, I felt the beautiful danger we live with pull at me, demanding my attention, refusing to be ignored. *Ontario Review* folded some years ago, and when *Coolest American Stories* put out a call for previously published or unpublished stories with a certain appeal to the heart, I sent them the gardening claw story, hoping to give it another chance to live in the world. The editors of *Coolest* worked with me on edits that strengthened the piece and taught me so much about the contract between writer and reader. I'm grateful and honored to have "Habitat" appear in the debut volume of this amazingly well-intended anthology.

MARY TAUGHER has published fiction in *Narrative*, *The Gettysburg Review*, *Alfred Hitchcock's Mystery Magazine*, *Santa Monica Review*, and other literary journals. After working in journalism, fundraising, and political consulting, she earned an MFA in creative writing from San Francisco State University. She volunteers for literacy groups and other nonprofits in San Francisco, and currently serves as head of the fiction jury for the Commonwealth Club's California Book Awards. When not writing, you can find her standup paddle-boarding, trekking through the nearby Presidio, and trying to tame Ollie, her daughter's cat who recently moved in and regards ankles and arms as chew toys.

THE STORY BEHIND THE STORY: I'm from the Midwest, and my father and brother hunted every fall. They sometimes took me skeet shooting. I'm not anti-gun; I'm pro–gun safety. And I've long supported groups like Brady, Giffords Law Center, and our local Moms Demand Action, part of Everytown for Gun Safety. I've marched and phone banked for gun reform, so I suppose it's natural that I wanted to write about gun violence, and, hopefully, inspire readers to get involved in gun reform advocacy. Of course, writing about anything political can come off as preachy and polemical. Several earlier attempts failed before I decided to set this story in the near future where guns are omnipresent. My writing group immediately told me that my future had already arrived.

Covid-19 had not yet happened by the time I was working on the last drafts, but what we experienced in this pandemic—the fear and anxiety, relentless death toll, and divisive partisanship—was the atmosphere I wanted to depict in "Fifth of July." I decided not to focus on mass shootings, which get the most publicity, because suicides account for nearly two-thirds of gun deaths and homicides the other third. Gun violence has already reached epidemic proportions. Here I bumped it up to the pandemic level.

I don't live in an open carry state, but when I started researching this story, I was shocked by how many states allow open carry with or *without* a permit, although firearms are still restricted in certain locations. Only five states and the District of Columbia prohibit open carry. I imagined a world where any adult could carry a gun anywhere, openly and without a permit, because that would terrify me.

My subconscious gifted me the idea to set the story around

the Fourth of July. I've always loved fireworks, explosive and dangerous like guns, yet beautiful. The holiday symbolizes American freedom and individualism, which seemed to dovetail with the story. One last element, the crows. I'm fascinated by reports of creatures going rogue, like swarms of grasshoppers invading Las Vegas or Africanized bees attacking people in California. The scene about the birds actually happened; more than 5,000 blackbirds, confused by fireworks, died and rained from the sky in a small town in Arkansas in 2010.

This story is dedicated to victims and survivors of gun violence, in particular my beloved mother-in-law, Gloria Booth, who was shot and killed during a home invasion in 2015.

ABOUT THE EDITORS

Under the name Mark Wisniewski, the surname of which he's changed because it's too difficult to google, **MARK WISH** has seen more than 125 of his short stories published in print venues such as *The Best American Short Stories*, *The Georgia Review*, *TriQuarterly*, *American Short Fiction*, *The Antioch Review*, *Crazyhorse*, *The Gettysburg Review*, *The Southern Review*, *New England Review*, *Virginia Quarterly Review*, *The Yale Review*, *The Sun*, *Paris Transcontinental*, and *Fiction International*. His short stories have also won a Tobias Wolff Award, a Kay Cattarulla Award, an Isherwood Fellowship, and a Pushcart Prize. Mark served as the fiction editor of *California Quarterly*, was the founding fiction editor of *New York Stories* and a contributing editor for *Pushcart*, and has long been known as the freelance editor who has revised the fiction of many once-struggling writers, leading to its publication in dozens of respected venues, including *The Atlantic*, *Tin House*, *The Kenyon Review*, *Michigan Quarterly Review*, *The Antioch Review*, *The Hudson Review*, and *The Best American Short Stories*. His novel *Watch Me Go* was published by Putnam.

ELIZABETH COFFEY is an award-winning art director at Random House, where she has designed book interiors for

Barack Obama's *A Promised Land*, Michelle Obama's *Becoming*, Glennon Doyle's *Untamed*, and numerous other bestselling titles. She dabbled in poetry in the nineties and published in several small magazines. She is working on her first novel, a mystery about estranged sisters. Her pen name is a tribute to her beloved great-grandmother Johanna Coffey. Elizabeth has been Mark's go-to editor for virtually all of his published short stories and *Watch Me Go*.